LEARNING TO

Sarah Hampton

2QT Limited (Publishing)

First edition published 2012
2QT Limited (Publishing)
Burton In Kendal
Cumbria LA6 1NJ
www.2qt.co.uk

Cover design
Hilary Pitt

Images supplied by Shutterstock.com

Learning to Tie A Bow is a work of fiction and any resemblance to any
person living or dead is purely coincidental

Printed in Great Britain by
Lightning Source UK

A CIP catalogue record for this book is available
from the British Library
ISBN 978-1-908098-48-1

For Alex, Issy, Philip and John

ACKNOWLEDGEMENTS

My gratitude to Gwenda and Steve Matthews for introducing me to John Murray; without his encouragement I may never have written this book. My thanks to Lesley Atkinson who has patiently dealt with my IT problems. To the kind helpful team at 2QT, to Zoe Dawes and Karen Holmes for their indispensable editorial guidance.

Most of all, thanks to my husband and family for their unfailing support.

I am not what you see,
a rough-barked tree, roots too deeply buried,
trunk split
life pierced
bent
shaped by a wind in axial time,
gnarled,
pumping still a weary sap through risen purple veins
silver lichen crowned

I am a sapling still,
spring leafed supple
swaying in a gentler breeze
bending to winds that change
yielding to a different rhythm

A whip late planted,
slipped into a·spade's crevice
heeled down by man,
filling the space of one early withered
to sprout again through shell hard husk
shouting faith

CHAPTER ONE

The post was late that day. Julia finished the outdoor chores, feeding and checking the remaining livestock, and sat down at the kitchen table for her guilty mid-morning whisky. However often the children and grandchildren mentioned sheltered accommodation, she was not giving in yet. Initially she did not notice the postcard wedged between the sheets of junk mail which assailed her every morning. How on earth did she get on their lists? Numerous girlie fashion catalogues, nubile models blatantly reminding her of the passage of time. Canvassing blurb for the European elections, the usual avalanche of profligate bureaucratic edicts from English Nature and Defra, which she never read but kept just in case. She still had an agricultural holding number, was still on Defra's hit list.

The postcard was one of those dog-eared relics found in cardboard boxes in bric-a-brac shops. 'The Beach at Sandsend', a communication from her younger brother, kindly sent, meant to evoke happy shared memories of childhood family holidays. Instead it had unleashed a raw shame, long forgotten.

The vintage sepia photo, a Yorkshire coastal resort,

its miles of pristine sand winter empty, captured on film when the river still flowed its original course to the sea, before the storms of 1939 changed its direction and the estuary became a confusion of shallow tributaries. The place where, from the age of six, Julia and her three elder brothers had been taken by their parents in August to join other comfortably-off middle-class families with their minions, entourages of parlourmaids, cooks and nursemaids.

The large red sandstone house was taken for a month, linen not provided, a mini-version of Julia's real home, requiring the same level of maintenance and domestic help. Mother drove the bull-nosed Morris, number plate BRM 777, her passengers father's black Labrador, christened Ponto by his previous owner – an unsuitable name for a gun dog, and Buster, a brindled Staffordshire bull terrier, mother's bitch, plus Nellie the cook and Thelma the housemaid. Marjorie the kitchen maid, who didn't live in, was not included. Nanny had been tearfully dispensed with when Julia reached the age of seven. Mother, born in an era when passing a driving test was considered unnecessary, drove with total disregard for others, rules of the road interpreted by her as: 'You either have common sense or you don't.'

James, her father, drove the follow-up car, a square, dark maroon Rover, with the children. Crossing the North Yorkshire Moors, the plum-purple, early emerging sea of heather stretched as far as the eye could see, fleeting glimpses of the real sea between the trees, the edge of Julia's world. There was the uneasy metallic grind of double declutching, the gnashing of gears reluctant to synchronise with each other at the top of

Lythe Bank in readiness for the one-in-five long steep incline down to the coast.

The challenge for cars and drivers was an adventure in itself. Shuddering reliance was placed on brakes, the descent hazardous, the weight of the huge wicker laundry basket containing four weeks' supply of linen perched precariously on the grid, taking over the steering wheel, making the car unstable and Julia anxious. She always wanted to get out and walk, give the excuse that her bare legs were hot and sweaty and needed a break from the burning heat of the sticky leather seat and the squabbling of her brothers, but that might have been seen as chicken. Julia's mistrust of anything mechanical had tormented her for the past eighty years.

Julia loved Nellie and Thelma 'Live in, all found, 12/6d a week.' They were her equals, surrogate sisters, her confidantes, dependable; they didn't tell tales. In their early teens, they had come into domestic service straight from school, contemporaries of her eldest brother David, worldly-wise, with authority and responsibilities beyond their years. Nellie was short, plain and shy, kirby grips attaching listless straight hair to her cook's hat, a purposely hidden smile which, when allowed expression, lit up her eyes and exposed a mouth of rotten teeth. Mother had insisted upon a visit to the dentist. Thelma, flighty, attractive, happy-go-lucky, full of fun, glancing in mirrors to titivate and preen, her predisposition to underarm perspiration leaving dark stains on her maroon afternoon uniform, taking the eye away from the crisp white apron, collar and cuffs and lacy headdress. Thelma, the purveyor of naughty, not understood songs and jokes. Mother explained the significance of Thelma's version of 'Hark the herald angels sing, Mrs Simpson stole our King' during the abdication crisis of 1936; Julia kept quiet about other songs, mainly about bodily functions.

Mother was known in the neighbourhood as a good employer, a just disciplinarian with a reputation for not expecting anyone to do a job which she was unprepared to do herself. Local fourteen-year-old school leavers and their mothers lined up in the hall to be interviewed for any job going, counting themselves lucky to have seen the advertisement in the newspaper. They were chosen because Mother knew what she would make of them, teaching them how to cook or run a home; her two priorities that they were cheery and had common sense; sullen looks were dismissed. The interviews took place in the large oval dining room with its confusion of doors, a trap for the less observant. Leaving by the wrong door once, Mother put down to nerves; make the same mistake twice and it was goodbye.

To be taken on at the big house was a good apprenticeship and training for life, staying warm and well fed in a happy home. Local farmers' sons, looking for a capable, hard-working wife, kept their eyes open and Mother had to restrict followers to weekends.

Julia and Nellie were pupils together in the kitchen, taught how to skin, joint and cook rabbits, the boys shooting for the pot, excellent marksmen with their 4.10s by the age of ten, bringing a constant supply of warm rabbit seething with fleas to be dealt with in the kitchen by the novice cooks.

Decapitate the rabbit with a cleaver, both having

a go, missing and giggling until confidence overcame squeamishness and the look in the rabbit's eyes less reproachful. Cut off the legs, slit the tough furred belly and undress the smelly reality beneath, pull off the pelt, like taking off a tight-fitting glove inside out, reveal the shot-peppered flesh beneath, only the hind legs and tail still attached, then the final tug. The carcass simmering with home-made stock, nutmeg and an Oxo cube until the tender flesh fell away, leaving a multitude of pellets, hazardous fragmented rapier bones and a delicious smell.

As preparations for that annual pilgrimage to the seaside began to disrupt everyday routine, Julia's excitement did not match that of her brothers. She had no need to exchange the private happiness of her rural childhood for a large expanse of sand amongst strangers and rainy cold days, confined in unfamiliar surroundings. She was content with her own company, happiest alone with her imagination, a blessing which had accompanied her into old age. The only companionship and friendship she sought, other than that of her brothers, was her Exmoor pony, Betty, her warm velvety muzzle against her cheek a substitute for mother's physical aloofness.

As a child Julia hadn't been good at humans, hated children's parties when made to dress up. The village dressmaker, on her knees with a mouthful of pins, had constructed a bright pink frock with an obscene collar of gathered tulle, around her resisting body.

Old Lady Mabel gave the village an annual party at the castle which, until the arrival of that sepia photo, Julia considered to have been one of the most unpleasant experiences of her childhood. Shepherded and bullied by adults into acquiescence, games had to be played which other children appeared to enjoy. That feeling of utter panic, wretchedness and humiliation when given a pencil and a piece of paper and instructed to draw a semolina pudding, and the team having to guess what it was.

She didn't need to play games: she had Betty. Jumping the drainage ditches on the roadside, hearing the roar of applauding crowds, they won the Grand National together, Betty reliving her foal days, wild at her dam's flank, leaping over Exmoor's stony terrain.

At eight years old, Julia had been allowed to ride beyond the boundaries of the demesne established by her maternal great-grandfather. The house had been built in the mid-nineteenth century from the proceeds of men toiling in the huge fire-belching foundries of Shropshire and West Cumberland at the start of the Industrial Revolution. The manhole covers, drainpipes and council ironworks bearing the embossed name of mother's forebears were still in evidence in northern towns. Her home had been a vast red-sandstone mishmash of Victorian Gothic, with turrets to impress, set in two hundred acres. Father called it an ugly pile but it had been the dowry Julia's mother brought to their marriage and he had learnt to love it and be grateful.

Julia had resented those holidays, resented having to relinquish even for a moment that intimacy with the familiar world which was part of her and without which she became a stranger to herself, reinforcing an embryonic perception that she was living in her own personal bubble, detached and absent from the real world.

Amongst the myriad blooms of daffodils appearing every spring, she knew which clump would, without fail, be the first to flower, which fields yielded the most harebells and wild orchids and where the slow-worms could be found, snakes in miniature, exquisitely marked, their gentle, dim-sighted, eye-lashed eyes catching hers. When they were picked up and handled, she felt the rigid, disproportionate strength within their twelve-inch bodies when she had clutched too tightly for fear they would escape.

Lying on her back among the emerging bracken fronds, a sea of miniature green shepherds' crooks, the warm earth beneath her, she would watch the scudding clouds. She listened to the sound of grasshoppers, so close that their vibrating membranes gave away their presence, difficult to find, camouflaged, their green-brown bodies rigid against the bracken stems, turning off the sound if she got too close. If she sensed an eye looking at her, she quickly turned away.

She remembered the huge yew, christened the Octopus Tree, a thousand years old, so Father had assured her; almost half the size of a tennis court, its branches and tentacle roots a labyrinth, an impregnable castle, until as children they found their secret entrance and discovered the hollow cavern within. It was a sibling meeting place for a decade, carpeted with sharp, dry yew needles which clung to clothing. Her brothers laboured on long-term engineering projects, creating an underground sewerage system out of discarded guttering and clay drainage tiles where you peed at one end in the hope that it might reach the other; it rarely did because of lack of volume, gravity and the yew's roots obstructing the flow.

She smelt again the mustiness of damp leaves and soil, heard the bark of the fox giving warning to lock up the poultry and tar the newborn lambs, the frantic squealing of a rabbit caught by a stoat. She saw the horses' graves, where decades of faithful retainers, Wellington, Hadrian, Major and Captain, had been rewarded for their service with headstones, moss-encrusted, hidden by ever-encroaching rhododendrons. Julia's secret feral freedom was to do a 'number two' outside, covering the steaming heap with leaves from the conker tree. It was an enchanted world and, until now, faded like all enchantments.

Her memory's protective immune system had been overridden by receiving a sepia postcard…

Tommy, yes, that was his name, the son of the owner of the seaside riding stables to which she was allowed to walk on her own and ride out on the sands, the pony vetted by her father as suitable. A consolation for having to leave Betty behind.

The smell of Tommy, the familiar aphrodisiac musky smell of horse and man, her father's smell with an alien ingredient, a too-clean soapy smell, out of place in a man. He was smartly dressed in clothes that did not look part of him: brown jodhpurs, highly-polished riding boots, loud yellow and brown check waistcoat and matching flat cap which he filled uneasily. So unlike Father's clothes, fused to his skin, the old stained brown trilby, plus fours and patched sports jacket, the pockets bearing scorch marks where he had forgotten to knock out his pipe.

Julia did not know Tommy's age; to her ten years he was an adult. Now she remembered the fluff, the pubescent covering of the jaw and upper lip. His grinning smile. With her life behind her, she now recognised it as offensive, over familiar, but at the time, with inexperience, she had taken it as friendly. He had lifted her onto one of the unsaddled horses in the stable, placed one hand on her shoulder to steady her as she settled into that familiar, reassuring, warm, silken feel of the horse's coat between her bare legs.

The two fingers thrust upwards, sidetracking the flimsy cotton knickers, penetrating an unfamiliar, yet-to-be-explored area of her body which, until that moment, had been private and from where she weed.

Breathless and weeping, she ran back to the comfortless sanctuary of the rented house, the pain between her legs increasing. It was all her fault; perhaps this was something grown-ups did and no one had told her. But a more reasoned voice told her that this was wrong, like the naughty songs Thelma sang.

As she ran up the path, out of the corner of her eye she caught a fleeting, unfamiliar image of Thelma, a white body stripped down to brassiere and knickers, sitting in a deckchair smoking an illicit cigarette, not expecting anyone to return until teatime as Nellie and the family were still on the beach. She called, 'Are you alright, Julia?'

Her enquiry went unanswered.

In the bedroom she shared with her youngest brother, Julia inspected the blood-spotted knickers. Remembering Father's mantra, his advice when faced with adversity: 'Take control and do the best you can to help yourself', she picked up her bucket and spade from the porch, put the knickers in the bucket and set off to the sand dunes, out of view of the beach, to bury the incriminating evidence.

A warm, strong wind was coming off the sea, churning the waves frothy white, whipping the tough marram grasses horizontal. An ominous black cloud rested on the horizon as Julia, her back to the wind, tried to dig a hole, the moisture-free sand disobeying her spade. As quickly as she dug, rivulets of quicksilver sand slipped back. Her hair blew forward, restricting her vision. The ever-increasing wind lifted her frock up, driving the sharp, stinging sand against her exposed body. Panicking, fearful of being seen, she had hurriedly stuffed the knickers under a clump of lyme grass. She knew its name; it was on one of the cigarette cards her brothers collected.

When she was unable to eat her supper that evening, Father enquired whether she was feeling ill. Mother replied for her, 'Probably too much sun,' and her brothers said, 'Too much time in the saddle.' Julia was grateful that attention had been drawn away from her, for she had been wracking her brains for an excuse not to go to the stables tomorrow without causing suspicion.

At nine o'clock that night nature, always her ally, took charge and intervened on her behalf. That afternoon's dark cloud on the horizon moved west. Rumbles of thunder heralded a storm; torrential driving rain and lightning crashed down upon the small community. The electricity went off just as they were going to bed and by morning the damage was done, there for all to see. The small harbour was submerged in silt and debris, walls of houses were hanging on to their foundations at rakish angles, and the lower part of the village was flooded. The twin becks upstream, unable to cope with the deluge of water, had burst their banks and joined forces, their double strength altering the course of the river, destroying everything in their path. The ancient packhorse bridge, over which she had run eagerly to the stables each morning, had been washed away. It was an omen and Julia said a quick thank you to God.

Not only would they have to go home, the floods would carry her knickers out to sea. She had been unable to sleep, worrying that Ponto, with his awareness of her scent, would nose in the sand dunes, unearth the evidence and take it back to Father. Now her secret would cross the North Sea, to be washed up on a different shore, evidence of their dark history expunged by salt water, flotsam to be found by other children and cause merriment in a foreign tongue. She would get into trouble for losing her knickers and her brothers would rib her, but she could cope with that.

In that last hot summer holiday of 1939, childhood certainty was swept away.

Julia's home, her sanctuary, was invaded by strangers, evacuees displaced by war. The first consignment included Mrs Wilks, a tiny, thin, husk of a woman, old at thirty-two, with bewildered eyes and six children. Marion, twelve, self-assured, confident that her role in life was to bring up her younger siblings, cocky, standing no nonsense. Jimmy, ten, always laughing; Julia fell in love with him – they shared embarrassingly large,

17

gingery freckles. Doreen, nine, pale, withdrawn and thin, her eyes too big for her face. Mother said, 'I think she has worms,' and Julia felt sorry for her. If Mother got her way, Doreen would be subjected to a visit from the district nurse with a special salt solution that would be pumped up the child's backside until she felt she might burst. Victor, seven, an aloof, distant, secretive boy. Frank, five, had somehow never registered. Finally, two-year-old Christine, who lived her life strapped into a huge, unstable, filthy perambulator that stank of urine, from which she was occasionally released by Marion to be kissed and put back.

Julia had seen poor people before – there were some in the village whom mother befriended, the recipients of cast-off clothes and other largesse – but she had never seen poverty. The Wilks' only possessions were the clothes they stood up in, lice, impetigo, family loyalty, the battered pram and the compulsory government-issue, square, cardboard boxes carrying gas masks.

Mother, determined to do her bit for the war effort, assimilated the new family into the household. Ground rules for communal living were established. Her strong Quaker beliefs overrode the inconvenience to her own family.

The billeting officer returned a fortnight later, glanced at her list and said, 'I see you have nine bedrooms. We can squeeze in another four.' Julia's father retired to his study and started to drink.

CHAPTER TWO

Dead for thirty years, Julia's father remained the over-riding presence and influence in her life, his humorous acceptance of the world's idiocies standing her in good stead. She recognised now that the values drilled into her as a child were no longer valid; if she had once been fleetingly in step, in harmony with the world, she wasn't now.

His eyes catching hers, silently shared under-standing, jokes between them lost on others. He lacked pretension, a noble lineage ignored, confirmed only by a simple coat of arms hewn from oak, something tangible and steadfast salvaged from a disjointed home, made unwelcoming and hostile by sibling jealousy and rivalry after the early death of his parents.

Three ravens and a stag surmounted by his family crest, festooned in cobwebs, the stag missing an antler – an over-zealous housemaid. The scroll enclosed a motto in ancient Welsh *HEB DDUW HEB DDIM DUW A DIGON*, translation uncertain, something about God being on your side. It now hung in her home. One day, one day, she thought yet again, she would contact Aberystwyth University and have it translated.

Its presence in her childhood was not to impress

but to fill a space, cover up cracks in the plastered walls of the cathedral-cold entrance hall, alongside the two original Reuben Ward Binks watercolours. One was of Ponto retrieving a pheasant, commissioned by Father; the other a fox cub, the exquisite brush strokes of red hairs more tactile than those of the masks and brushes of the real things hanging on the opposite wall, attached to their wooden headstones, the place and date of their killing immortalised in black lettering. The foxes' companions were an array of antlers and the heads of two moulting buffalo, history unknown, fulfilling a similar duty: covering damp patches of flaking, yellowing plaster. They had caught the attention of moths two generations earlier, leaving bare patches and ears denuded of hair, the light from the great log fire that was lit only at Christmas reflected in their glassy staring eyes.

The fox painting had been given to Julia by Ward Binks, one of the more pleasurable episodes of her childhood that involved strangers. Secretly, to protect herself from brotherly ridicule, the memory of the semolina pudding still raw, she had entered a painting competition sponsored by Raphael Tuck.

Thelma spotted the entry form in an old copy of the *Daily Mail* as she crumpled it up in readiness to lay the fire in the morning room, and suggested that Julia painted a mermaid. Julia decided to paint the mermaid riding side-saddle on Betty. The only usable artists' materials available in the nursery were an over-thick brush, which her brothers used on their Hornby engines when the wheels needed a clean, and the remains of some yellow ochre and cobalt blue in a small battered paint box. Remembering to use a wash to make a watery misty image, she was quietly pleased with the effect of horse and rider emerging from the sea.

Sworn to secrecy, Thelma produced a stamp, made Julia sign an IOU for the postage and entrusted Julia's artistic efforts to the Royal Mail.

Two months later, a parcel arrived addressed to Julia. Thelma, always trustworthy in a conspiracy, intercepted it. They sat together on the bed in Julia's room, undoing the string, carefully removing the brown paper, the door locked against intruders.

Never before had Julia felt such pleasure and disbelief. Second prize. A giant, black, shiny paintbox. Thirty-six miniature white pots containing more colours and hues than she had imagined existed, tiny opaque waxed paper squares guarding their virginity. Six pristine paint brushes of varying sizes.

No longer would she have to be content with her brothers' cast offs, bristles spread-eagled and stiff, rescued from the murky muddy cementing waters of abandoned jam jars, their thinning hairs doing the splits, the metal shanks orange with rust.

She tried to keep her success a secret but Raphael Tuck wanted their money's worth; her name and address had appeared as a winner in Father's newspaper and he had spotted it.

Ward Binks had also spotted it and written her a little note of encouragement. 'Well done. In 1890 when I was ten, about the same age as you are now, I won the Raphael Tuck Competition with a painting of flowers. May I send you one of my animal paintings as a gift?' Julia wrote back, 'Yes please. I would like a fox.'

Father, impressed by the fox painting, had commissioned the portrait of Ponto and the enchanted episode was taken out of childish hands and usurped by adults. Now, half a century later, swanky London galleries were offering Binks' paintings for six-figure sums.

The hall was Julia's favourite place in the house. The sun projected an ever-changing rainbow canvas, a kaleidoscope of colour onto the flagged floor through the south-facing, stained-glass window on the half landing, where the wide dark oak staircase changed direction and Father put up the ping-pong table during holidays. Games were played surrounded by the gradually deteriorating mock-Gothic evidence of Mother's once-prosperous industrial Victorian heritage.

What on earth had made Father love her, Julia, so much? Was it because, having spawned three sons, she had been a girl? He never showed any disappointment in her looks, of which she herself was only half aware at an early age. A lumpish, glum child, straight mousey hair cut in a fringe, a round, belligerent, unsmiling face, featureless, except for an amalgam of pale orange and chestnut freckles that glowered back at her, clearly visible in old black-and-white photographs brought out at Christmas for amusement, before being relegated to trunks in the attics.

One particular photograph was a family joke. Julia at the age of three, her dress tucked into her knickers, Christopher Robin hat, the front brim turned back to expose a scowling face, striding purposefully, disobediently, belligerently, barefoot across the stony beach down to the water's edge of Ullswater, calling out, unable yet to pronounce her name, 'Many tones hurt

Leelo's feet.'

Mother saying, 'That's her first proper sentence.'

Advancing into the water, shouts of concern heard briefly as she disappeared, the treacherous shingle shelf cascading her body down. She remembered the sound, the swish, and saw in a dream the variation of the shingle as it gently carried her body: three larger dark-grey stones, white-flecked and smoothed by their life under water, amongst a muted waterfall of tiny pebbles. Then nothing. Her hat dislodged, floating on the surface of the lake, was all they had seen. Now it gave her pleasure to know it caused such mirth.

From childhood into her teens, had she been aware of a marriage of minds between her and Father? It had all been taken for granted, submerged in a carefree up-bringing of guidance and paternal love. She suspected that Father's own early nurturing had been of a different kind.

He had faced other imprisonments, orphaned at eleven years, the Benjamin of a family of eight. His parents, Julia's grandparents, gone in their early fifties, unknown to her generation; his father from a heart attack brought about by a fondness for the bottle and his mother, so family myth had it, from a broken heart six months later.

It had been his mother's dying wish that the eldest son, Charles, took on the responsibility for his two youngest siblings. Charles, already married, moved swiftly into the family home. His shrewish, purposely childless wife understandably resented the intrusion of childish in-laws into her comfortable, self-centred life and let it be known. At the age of fifteen, Julia's father had absconded from that prison and, giving a false age, joined the Royal Flying Corps.

He never talked about his earlier life. It had only surfaced accidentally when, at the age of eight, she and her brothers were playing a made-up family game called 'dicky ducktails', its origins and rules obscure. She remembered the pleasure and rush of adrenalin whenever the game was suggested. It consisted of not being seen but at the same time racing at high speed through the labyrinth of bedrooms, staircases and corridors. At each end of the main corridor were half-glassed swing doors, their squeaking hinges giving away anyone's presence. The attics were out of bounds and one day Julia broke the rules.

She had been conscious of her brothers shouting, trying to find out where she was but kept quiet until they lost interest.

She remembered the mustiness, the smell of those lightless rooms. The small, moss-grimed, circular windows denying the sun access, outlines of boxes and trunks, curiosity as her immature fingers struggled to push the age-hardened leather straps through the rusted buckles of the largest trunk. Lifting the dusty, cobwebbed heavy lid, revealing yellowing grey-and-white striped material lining and boxes of letters, photos; discarded lives.

And there he was: Father. A sepia image, the familiar roguish eye, pipe in mouth, playing at being a man, his hand embracing its bowl, exuding a kind of self-confidence and love of life so familiar to Julia. But she knew now that that look had hidden demons of self-doubt.

He was wearing unfamiliar clothes: highly-polished Sam Browne and wings sewn onto a military uniform. Julia looked deeper into the trunk, her eyes straining in the semi-darkness, and found other photos of him in an alien setting: barbed wire and high, restrictive fencing, a teenager wearing plimsolls at the end of a line of men.

Owning up to where she had been, Julia asked Father about the photos. She sat on his knee, helping to press tobacco down into his pipe for the ritual lighting up.

His plane, a Sopwith Camel, had been shot down on New Year's Day, 1916, over France. A message dropped by a German plane informed the British that he had been captured and was being held at Le Cateau before being moved to a POW camp at Karlsruhe. Julia, whose only concept of war was Cowboys and Indians, had said what a kind thing for the Germans to do in the midst of battle.

Father had replied: 'There were gentlemen on both sides.'

Imprisoned in a fortress from which escape was impossible, he and friends had dug a tunnel but were recaptured, their exploits recorded in a book, *The Tunnellers of Holtzminden*. Julia listened bewitched, a grown-up fairytale, its authenticity confirmed by Father's pipe.

Trust is such an ephemeral concept, a no-man's-land between belief and hope, like faith in a God.

Julia still found religion ambiguous. Technically she was a bit of a bastard, her father Church of England, her mother a Quaker. Mother's Quakerism had become diluted by marriage and she rarely attended

Friends Meeting. Her forebears were a long line of eighteenth- and nineteenth-century Quaker physicians, fundamentalists willing to bear persecution and ridicule to uphold their beliefs.

There had been a break in Julia's maternal, medical, Quaker family tradition when her great-grandfather had been orphaned at ten and taken in by distant Quaker relatives. With no money to put him through medical school, his intended vocation, he had been apprenticed to an ironmonger. That was a stroke of good judgement, sowing the seeds of the wealth and home which, a century later Julia's mother had brought to her marriage. The Industrial Revolution was at its zenith, the Victorian entrepreneurial precursor of the microchip industry.

But iron mongering was common and beyond the pale. You bought goods from ironmongers; you didn't marry their daughters.

Julia's mother had been the recipient of snobbery and prejudice. The three taboos, Liberalism, Quakerism and Trade, had prevented her from being accepted as a pupil at Cheltenham Ladies College in 1911. Being in trade was a social anathema. The money of industrialists, Telford and Brunel, under whose patronage her mother's grandfather had prospered and who had contributed so much to the greatness of Britain, was deemed a corruptive influence upon the rarefied old money of the aristocracy and academia. A century later, wasn't it new money keeping those seats of learning afloat?

As a child Julia had absorbed a confused curriculum, and nothing much had changed. Self-doubt continued to haunt her in her twilight years. Surely there must be something out there more worthwhile than disorientated frenetic mankind, something you could believe in other than self? She tried to return to the reassuring solace of youth.

Matins every Sunday. The strong smell of chemicals keeping death-watch beetle at bay, tissue-thin pages of the prayer book, given to her on her sixth birthday by godfather Nunky, sticking together when Father helped her find the place. Mosaics of colour streaming through the east window, creating strange pictures on the faces of the congregation; patterns on bare knees from kneeling too long on prickly coarse-covered hassocks, and the myriad dancing dust particles held in the sun's rays.

Memorials on the walls to those who had fallen in the Great War, similar names time after time, names of people in the village. Finding the next hymn from the numbers on the board in good time, so that she could stand up immediately like Father and enjoy the singing. Father leaving her side to take the collection, walking up the aisle, smiling upon the givers, acting a part in a play.

Old Lady Mabel shuffling unsteadily with her stick in stained, red-velvet bedroom slippers, the gold-embroidered coronets on the toes faded and worn, to sit in her solitary feudal pew at the front. Hairs on her chin wart caught by the light, her clown's mask of carelessly applied pale face-powder and rouge, pendulous jowls vibrating as her tone-perfect contralto overrode other worshippers. Her large dark eyes blank, unseeing, until they saw Father and came to life.

Julia loved the exotic look of Lady Mabel. Her clothes the colours of a cock pheasant, iridescent, warm autumn-coloured chiffon plumage awry, floating, flying, following her uncoordinated progress up the aisle. The large red floppy velvet hat, a pheasant tail feather stuck in at rakish angle, making her look like paintings of Henry VIII that Julia had seen in history books.

If Julia ever grew up and could choose her own clothes that was how she was going to dress. Not like mother, corset-imprisoned, restrained and prim in tight, tailored, cold-blue suits, shoes, gloves, handbag matching and over-polished, the pudding-basin hat an embarrassment.

Julia bore witness to the Glory of Lady Mabel but hadn't seen God. Even had He been there, He would have been quickly superseded, discarded for a jolly midday whisky and roast beef and Yorkshire pudding.

Julia wondered what her brothers made of it all. Two out of three were still alive, the eldest, David, approaching ninety-two, keeping in touch on birthdays. On Julia's seventy-ninth celebration, she had received his usual humorous card with a spidery note in his now unsteady hand: 'Do you remember dicky ducktails?' She had wept and immediately written back to remind him of the Octopus Tree.

David had been, and still would be had his fingers not succumbed to arthritis, a talented musician, a gifted pianist, organist and a dab hand on the squeeze box. In later years, a composer. Playing jazz and classics by ear as a small child, he was unable to read a word of music until Mother insisted on tuition. The hours spent round the upright in the nursery singing their hearts out. 'Pardon me, boy, is that the Chattanooga Choo Choo?', nurtured on Fats Waller, knowing every lyric. 'Your feet's too big, mad at you cos your feet's too big.' The guttural spoken aside at the end: 'Your pedal extremities really are obnoxious.' The gramophone which, if you forgot to wind it sufficiently, made the voice on the record descend to a deeper than deep slow bass, and the record of 'Bye Bye Blackbird' which had hiccups caused by warped grooves. 'Molly on the Shore', Mother's favourite. That rare occasion when Mother was moved to tears as they sat on the wide staircase, an unaccompanied impromptu sibling quartet, their parts instinctive, singing 'The Skye Boat Song' and Mother thinking it was the wireless.

Did David remember such things? He had drifted through life earning what he could, his passion for music uppermost until, a bit late in the day, his talent was finally recognised and meagre royalties started flowing. He now lived in contented, impoverished old age in the West Country. Until fifteen years ago, Julia had caught glimpses of him on television, guest organist at one of country's great cathedrals, occasionally forgetting where he was and allowing Louis Armstrong, Benny Goodman or Duke Ellington to join forces with Bach in impromptu Voluntaries.

Nicholas, Julia's youngest brother, was the unexpected sender of the sepia postcard which had kick-started all this. The antithesis of his eldest brother, cautious, pedantic, winning a scholarship to read mathematics at Cambridge, he disappeared into himself, isolated by his own brilliance, his mind unapproachable. On the rare occasion he remembered to send a birthday card, it was never humorous.

It was her middle brother, Jack, with whom Julia had shared an affinity. Always getting into trouble, Jack could do no right and Julia had felt she could do no wrong. She acquired an early recognition of injustice and tried to lessen Jack's burden of being misunderstood. When he had been sent to his room without food as punishment, Julia smuggled some to him, pushing mashed potato and gravy under the ill-fitting, warped bedroom door, the plate becoming wedged, making a mess and Jack blamed. Perhaps her normally compassionate father saw, in his middle son, a freedom of spirit he denied himself and his strictness was a form of jealousy.

There had been other cases of injustice. Jack had been packed off to boarding school at a younger age than his elder brother to 'try and knock some sense into him' but it had backfired. He was home again within the month, having painted the headmaster's dog from head to tail in lime-green enamel paint. It was the premeditation of this act which resulted in his expulsion. He had gone into town, strictly against the rules, and purchased a tin of paint, the colour chosen for major impact. This type of forward planning had not been appreciated and a lesser, more accommodating, boarding school had been found.

How Julia wished she could put the clock back, be given a chance to talk with Jack again, to reminisce. She felt certain he would have become a controversial journalist. He may well have ended up on the editorial staff of *Private Eye*, but he took himself off to Africa in his late teens to make his fortune and, reckless to the end, died in a car crash of his own making.

CHAPTER THREE

Julia's memory was in overdrive. Was she making it work too hard? Asking it how far back it could go with accuracy, pinpoint dates and chronicle them with certainty. That early lesson, learning to tie her shoe laces, the breathless concentration, following instructions to get the bows right; the resulting loose inadequate tangle.

Life mirrored that first lesson and now her fingers had reverted to that confused disobedient state; opening cans, unwrapping biscuits, unscrewing bottles had become everyday challenges for aged, weakened hands. She had read somewhere that ten thousand elderly people were injured every year trying to remove safety tops from bottles.

It wasn't the three Rs she remembered from kindergarten days but fellow pupils. Those first shared attempts at intimacy, four and five year olds, shy and unsure about what was being asked of them. Obedient, disciplined and anxious to please. Julia had caught the eye of a boy sitting two rows behind her, an expanding pool of liquid beneath his chair and seen a look of panic and uncertainty in his face.

His image had returned recently. An unexpected

coverage of a debate in the House of Lords; there he was, snoozing on the Opposition benches, probably still uncertain how he had arrived in the Upper House, something about making a fortune out of privatisation and rewarded with a peerage from Maggie. Julia couldn't remember. At school, had she been nice to him or joined in the laughter?

She supposed she must have been able to read and write before being 'sent away'. Was the decision to offload her into the care of strangers before her eleventh birthday by parental agreement? Had Father tried to intervene on her behalf? It had never been openly discussed, just assumed that she would follow her brothers into the monastic seclusion of a one-sex institution. Perhaps Father, unable to deal with his own problems, had seen it as a way of protecting her from his drinking, still in its infancy, noticeable only by his increased jollity and redder face. Perhaps he couldn't bear the thought of her seeing him as he knew he would become, the memory of his own father lodged in his mind.

It may have been Mother's preoccupation with an ever-increasing number of evacuees, and her growing realisation that succouring the needs of other people's children might be more rewarding and appreciated than those of her own. Mother's death in 1990 had revealed letters. Testimonies, words of thanks from grateful parents for nursing their young through whooping cough, measles, mumps and other childhood traumas.

The sobbing and grief of homesickness was lessened by Father. His love and patience had embraced them all; they sat on his knee, clinging, his shirt dampened by their tears, inwardly weeping himself for their unhappiness. In the twenty-first century men had become wary of showing physical love and giving comforting hugs.

She clearly remembered the weeping, and the in-comprehension of what was being done to her. Standing on the station platform in the grey of morning to catch the early train south, holding Father's cold hand. The smoke and roar of the approaching engine deadened for a second under the bridge, crossed only minutes earlier in the familiar warmth and security of the old Rover; the bridge over which Father would return on his own alone, after her abandonment, her presence still with him. The train re-emerging with a hiss, the steam and noise all-engulfing, hurried good-byes unheard.

It hadn't mattered: neither of them would have been able to say what they wanted to say. Father lifting her into the carriage, trying to hide his own doubts. The guard, isolated between stations in his van at the rear of the train promising, for a tip of half-a-crown, to keep half an eye on her and make sure she got off at Crewe.

Meeting up with the school's representative and other new girls feeling their way into an alien world. Crying herself to sleep in the hard unfriendly iron bedstead, unheard, isolated from other anonymous weepers in the dark, oppressive, wooden-cubicled dormitory.

Mother had told her that she was privileged to be sent away. 'Other children are not as fortunate as you.' But at nearly eleven that was not how it felt.

Now her memory was being too clever by half: it knew exactly which button to press within the nervous system to take her back to the desolation of that first term.

It was almost three terms before she realised that things were on offer other than unhappiness. She missed the male company of her brothers and found it difficult to make friends, her rural upbringing isolating her from the interests of many of the other new girls.

Julia's parents had not visited the school; she had been sent there by word of mouth, Mother's best friend had recommended it, her own daughter a past pupil. Absorbed at home by their commitment to the war effort, her parents never took her out on the two exeats allowed each term. It was too far, petrol was rationed, trains overcrowded, troops blocking the corridors with their cumbersome kit bags, standing room only. Their lack of interest in her progress was not meant unkindly, but they had other priorities.

In the summer term of 1940, and from an unlikely direction, Julia found a friend. The father of her rescuer was an Oxford don, a man of letters who, with his wife, encouraged the gauche, ill-educated friend of their younger daughter Prudence into their home.

Julia had written home about Prudence and the following week Mother's letter had a short paragraph saying: 'What an unwise name to give a child,' but nothing to say that she was pleased that Julia had found a friend.

In hindsight it had been a curious liaison. Prue was popular, sporty and blonde, a jolly-hockey-sticks type with brains. She excelled at languages, was fluent in Spanish and French. Julia's only confidence in a second language was the dialect words picked up from the village children which Mother had done her best to stamp out. She could still count to a hundred if she concentrated: *'Yan, Tan, Tethera, Methera, Pimp,'* – one, two, three, four, five – but it had not impressed the French teacher.

Prue glowed with self-confidence. New girls had crushes on her. Her muscular, bronzed calves were the result of sculling on the River Severn from an early age. On her second visit to Prue's home, Julia was introduced to sculling; it had been mandatory. Without thinking she had let go the scull; in seconds it had disappeared. She looked downstream and glimpsed it racing away, competing with the strong current around a far bend in the river, and heard the irate voice of Prue's father from the bank.

Initially the invitation to stay over half-term was born out of kindness; living within fifty miles of the school, Prue's parents had felt obliged. Prue's home became Julia's second home, a haven from petty restrictions, an antidote for unjust school chastisements. Hers was a large family into which Julia was warmly welcomed.

Each visit was an education, full of love, as was her own family, but with different histories. The hall in Julia's home smelt of dogs, wet tweeds and guns, the walls displaying the trophies of the hunt. The hall in Prue's home smelt of books, the walls literature-lined from floor to ceiling, interspersed with shields and varnished oars, emblazoned with names and Roman numerals in gold leaf, the spoils of inter-varsity boat races over generations. There were no animals visible, dead or alive.

The realisation that, by good fortune, she had wound up with a whole family of different minds hadn't been immediately appreciated but now Julia knew that it was one of those lifelines thrown to you from time to time.

After each visit there was the gift of a book, written or edited by her host in which he wrote, 'To Pudge, remembering another happy visit, love P.A.C.', and the date. Julia had been bewitched. She still answered to Pudge seventy years later. Only recently, as she watched *Flog It*, someone had brought a book similarly inscribed by P.A.C. to be valued. A first edition of one of the many best-selling thrillers Prue's father had written on his retirement.

There were seven similar books in the trunk in the boxroom. It was not their value which was important but the memory of being pointed in the right direction: classical music, politics and poetry. He had introduced her to Cicero, Swift and Donne, made her aware of other questioning minds to whom she could turn for reference and solace and find release from the narrow tedium of the school's English curriculum. He suggested she read Housman and Emerson for a more contemporary outlook. He taught her to ask questions.

Julia didn't doubt that there were such books at home but they had never been brought to her attention. Fed on a diet of Milly Molly Mandy and the latest Amelianne Stiggins in her Christmas stocking, she had lacked the essential inquisitiveness to find things out for herself. Encyclopaedias were at hand and whenever Julia asked Mother a question the answer was, 'Look it up.' That in itself should have been sufficient, but Julia's mother, because she had plenty of her own, had not recognised Julia's lack of motivation.

Mother's letters arrived every Monday morning, full of news of the strangers usurping Julia's home. Never the things she wanted to know. Were the daffodils out, and what were Nelly and Thelma up to? What news of her brothers? Julia suspected that they were the recipients of identical letters. Father was mentioned briefly for his part in collecting the latest five evacuees from the station.

Father never wrote letters. Only on her birthday was there an envelope with his reassuring handwriting on the table in the school hall and inside two lines of tangible love, a ten-shilling note and the remainder of the day spent in a warm glow.

It was only on her return home for the Christmas holidays that she heard the full story of the arrival of the five evacuees from Father. He had gone to the railway station to collect the four allotted boys, round their necks a piece of string, the attached brown label giving a name, their physical presence ticked off the list by the billeting officer, their only luggage a square cardboard box carrying a gas mask.

In the dimly lit station master's office it became apparent to Father that bargaining was going on. Unattractive children were rejected by their prearranged hosts, runny noses going to the back of the queue. A replay of stomach-churning school team games when you were last to be chosen. Father saw in those rejected children glimpses of himself and arrived home with five instead of four: Roger, a self-assured, excitable six-year-old; twins Peter and Michael, aged seven, both with a history of bed-wetting, and eight-year olds, Bill and John.

Bill had an allergy to eggs; if they were ingested in the minutest quantities in cakes and puddings he was violently sick. A challenge for Mother: eggs were the only protein available, other than rabbit, rook and pigeon, to eke out the minimalist two ounces or six pennyworth a week wartime meat ration.

The thirty Rhode Island Reds and ten on-point-of-lay pullets contributed to the war effort, scratching, clucking and laying happily, oblivious to the mess the human species had got itself into. Their spouse was a vicious, macho, scarlet-combed, copper, shiny cockerel named Marmaduke who ruled his wives by domestic violence and abuse. Father called him the Marquis de Sade. Mother said in her cross voice, 'Don't call him that in front of the children. I'm not in the mood to explain.' When Marmaduke turned his aggression to humans and attacked six-year-old Doreen Wilks, Mother gave instructions that those evacuees on egg collection duty must arm themselves with a broom to fend off attacks. Eventually Marmaduke breached the defences and drew blood, at which point Father said he must go.

'Going' meant Mother wringing his neck, a quick twist and pull. Julia remembered an uneasy feeling that Mother might have enjoyed it. From a culinary point of view, the Marquis turned out to be a disaster, his breastbone twisted and fractured, the result of too many encounters with the broom. Even simmered slowly for almost a day, he was so tough to eat that in death he was even more of a challenge than in life.

Of the latest evacuees, it was John with whom Julia felt most at ease. During the holidays she formed a liaison with this gentle boy who sought her company. Overweight, with adenoidal problems, unable to breathe through his nose, his mouth was permanently open, releasing a constant flow of saliva that made him look half-witted, but Julia knew he wasn't. Breathless, unable to keep up with his peers, he was bullied mercilessly until Mother, on discovering that both his parents were doctors, became angry and wrote a letter. John disappeared for three weeks. His adenoids and tonsils removed, he returned.

Mother threw herself into this new career with her usual determination, creating nutritious meals out of almost nothing, dealing with ration books, registering all newcomers with grocers and butchers, believing every word that emanated from the lips of Lord Woolton, head of the wartime Ministry of Food, whose radio broadcasts spurred people on to Dig for Victory, making certain the nation was adequately fed. Mother and he did a pretty good job, their efforts probably the reason Julia and her two remaining brothers, with a joint age of two hundred and forty seven, still had their teeth and, other than the odd arthritic twinge, were fit and lithe.

There had only been one rebellion against wartime food. Boiled nettles with dumplings made from flour and water. It may have been Mother in a vindictive mood. The beneficiary of that largesse was Dolores, the house pig, her long eyelashes resembling those of a popular American film star of the day. Quaffing that unexpected treat of green sludge from twenty plates hastened her fattening and the date when people from the village came to participate in her slaughter. All hands on deck to make sausages and brawn, salting the prime cuts to break the monotony of meatless weeks ahead.

When petrol coupons ran out, Mother purchased a third-hand milk float and broke Betty to harness. They drove the six miles to the nearest market town to do the shopping, stabling Betty at the auction mart. This transport enabled her to continue her work for the Red Cross, raising funds and organising first-aid classes. At times, after a frantic knock on the door in the middle of the night by an expectant father, she acted as village midwife when the district nurse on her bicycle wasn't going to make it in time to a home confinement. Mother worried that things might go wrong but it was her duty to help. There were two boys in the village named after Father.

Father's domain also suffered a wartime sea change. The farm, livestock and arable had run smoothly for decades, the labouring work in the capable hands of two stockmen who lived in the village. Within two months of war being declared, the men had en-listed and Father's help dwindled to Thompson, aged seventy-seven.

At fourteen, Thompson's apprenticeship to the head gardener in Julia's maternal great-grandfather's day had given him a thorough grounding. Now, sixty years on, he was trying to maintain the same standards with which he had been brought up. The only evidence of those glory days was the skeletal remains of the vast greenhouses, the sharp shards of broken glass stubbornly clinging to the wooden frames weakened by dry rot and woodworm, still resisting the final onslaught of the elements. The gnarled old trunks of the vines struggled to survive, ignored by man, sprouting out their last spring messages of hope and nature's optimism.

Julia had been unsure about Thompson. Since Tommy, she had felt uneasy in his company. His unsmiling comments and ferret-mean face, the yellow-stained crotch of his coarse heavy-duty trousers, had put her on her guard. But, when the weather was bad and she wanted to escape from helping in the house, she sat with him in his undisputed kingdom, the harness room, as he cleaned tack for imaginary horses yet again and had his ten o'clock, enjoying together the pungent smell of polish on leather.

She liked listening to Thompson's tales, aware that most of the stories were fantasy. Just as she lived in her imagination, so did Thompson. His surprising rare kindnesses; he allowed her to take strands of red, cream and blue raffia to plait into Betty's mane, their faded presence hanging on a nail, reminders of days when the stables had been fully occupied and he had decked out the farm's Clydesdale horses, braiding manes and tails for village May Day celebrations.

Thompson lived at the end of the front drive in a mini grace-and-favour, three-roomed Victorian bungalow. He had never married. His strange and gently demented spinster sister Edith, who talked to herself all day, was his housekeeper and companion. As children, Julia and her brothers had been frightened of Edith. Mother said, 'Edith lost the person she loved in the

Great War; you must be kind to her.' In Julia's world, losing something usually ended in chastisement.

War brought Thompson into his own; always a complainer, he now had something to complain about. Just before the war started, in deference to his age, a new kitchen garden was suggested nearer the house and a quarter acre allocated. It was the final nail in the coffin of the old, walled kitchen with its three-seater ash privy, secretly used by Julia and her brothers, yellowed remnants of torn-up newspapers with their print still visible, dated 1899, hanging by a string from a rusty nail clinging to the loose-puttied limed walls, the splintered seats covered in rubble and rat droppings preferable to the long walk back to the house.

The speed at which Thompson created a new vegetable garden, armed only with a spade, fork and wheelbarrow, bore evidence to the excellence of his early training. Not a weed was seen between the im-maculate rows of beans, peas, cabbages, lettuces, cau-liflowers, Brussels sprouts. The strawberries bedded down on their thick straw ignored by slugs, raspberries, black and red currants bearing fruit within two years. He taught Julia to grow marrows, how they liked to be king of the castle on their high mound of compost.

The lawns had already succumbed to the wartime absence of petrol and were grazed by sheep to keep the grass down. Thompson tut-tutted a bit but it would be an invasion of a different sort which hastened his decline.

The two farm workers had eventually been replaced by six Italian prisoners of war. They had a reputation for being easy-going. Gossip had it that it took twenty

'Eyeties' two weeks to plant twenty acres of potatoes whereas it took ten German POWs a week. Neighbouring farms, which plumped for Germans, found them difficult, arrogant and hard-working. Father chose Italians; his experience of life and Mother had taught him that confrontation was not the way to achieve peace of mind.

Julia suspected Father resented not being called up; at forty-three he was considered too old to serve king and country again. Reluctantly he accepted, as the next best thing, an appointment as CO of the Local Defence Volunteers, forerunner of the Home Guard. Father certainly saw the humour of it all. Those pseudo-military manoeuvres, trying to instil some sort of urgency and understanding of possible danger into a rural community so remote from the killing fields.

The human material out of which Father tried to create a fighting unit to take on and repel an invasion by Hitler's crack Panzer divisions, was sparse. The elderly, a handful of men who had failed their medicals, colour blindness the most common cause of rejection (a disadvantage in any occupation but hazardous with a gun in your hand), the odd school teacher in a reserved occupation and boys under the age of eighteen. That was it. The only weapons available were pistols and shotguns lent by locals and kitchen knives attached to staves.

There were exercises to guard the hastily erected steel and asbestos aircraft hangers built on farmland, camouflaged to confuse the Luftwaffe. The artistic efforts of the Air Ministry were effective and beautiful. Huge murals of idyllic rural scenes, farmyards, haystacks and cow byres, gave lie to the Hurricanes, Mustangs and Spitfires within. Even neighbours were taken in: 'Didn't know so and so had a barn in that field...' so realistic were the paintings. Summer scenarios were replaced by snow scenes in the winter.

Julia was bewitched by this cleverness, this adult make-believe, the vast rectangles of sheaves of corn boldly painted in Van Gogh hues of yellow. Once, when she was riding Betty, she witnessed the imitation straw burst open and, like a genie in a pantomime, an aeroplane suddenly appeared and flew off into the clouds. Father's Home Guard were the stagehands on call to replace the scenery, wooden cows on wheels and lengths of hedgerow on rollers. Father explained it all as a sensible precaution. Should the Germans destroy all the airfields in the south, we had our own secret fighters to shoot down enemy bombers when they ventured north.

Most of the evening exercises ended up in the pub in the optimistic hope that there might be some beer left for half a pint all round. The contraband whisky under the counter was for locals only. Rumours of spies abounded, gossip and the radio the only source of information, strangers approached with mistrust. Land Girls working alongside Italian and German prisoners of war were not exempt from suspicion.

Everyone shared the domestic inconveniences and denials that war brings: rationing, blackouts, sacrificing aluminium saucepans, propaganda telling the patriotic that theirs would be turned into Spitfires, the savvy suspecting that wide boys got hold of them and flogged them on the black market. 'Make Do and Mend' and 'Sides to Middles' when someone stuck their toe through a thinning sheet were already part of Mother's domestic policy. She was an avid darner and patcher, creating small masterpieces out of holes. Woollen socks were her speciality; she darned them until there was little left of the original sock, exposing the hole on a well-worn wooden mushroom, creating a warp to be woven, small loops of wool left at the end of each line of weft to allow for shrinkage. Today there were still pairs of Father's wartime socks in family use in Wellington boots.

School holidays became a lottery. Julia never knew who would be living in her home or if there would be any space for her. She became a temporary squatter. At least the house and land had not been commandeered by the military, the fate of some of their neighbours. Mother's work for the Red Cross and Father's appointment as CO of the LDV may have saved the day. Nellie and Thelma now slept in the attics, the original servants' quarters, the purpose for which they had been built a century and a half ago in less egalitarian times.

Father dug his toes in and insisted that he and Mother retain one of the bathrooms for their private use. Julia and her brothers were only allowed access and permitted the luxury of piping-hot water and pre-warmed towels when they were recovering from illnesses. Except for those times, they joined the queue with the twelve evacuees and Nellie and Thelma for the other three bathrooms; one had been brought into emergency use, unused for thirty years, the bath stained yellow, the reawakened water from rusting pipes brown, tepid and uninviting. There was alarming banging as the pipes tried to free themselves from decades of trapped air. The plug system was an antiquated three-foot high cylinder which defied understanding and had now come full circle, the latest thing in flashy twenty-first century interiors' magazines.

Wartime rituals became second nature. Weekly gas mask drill; struggling into the tight suffocating rubber apparatus, the younger evacuees hysterical and frightened, Father trying to make a game of it without success.

In peaceful times, illumination from the big house had beamed out shards of light, giving assurance and guidance. Now they turned traitor, leaking information to an enemy. The forays of German planes droning over the house to bomb the factories and shipyards of Glasgow were guided by chinks of light which had evaded the ARP warden's eye, confirming to the navigators in their Heinkels and Dorniers that they were on course.

The nightly routine of blacking out the windows. Whoever was in the house at dusk was responsible for the evening routine of fitting the made-to-measure, black, material-covered wooden frames into the fifty windows. If it was left too late, Julia floundered in the dark, her mouth dry with fear, ghosts around every corner as her fingers tried to engage the hooks into their keepers.

But when her brothers were around it had been an adventure, patriotism and pulling together. They were the goodies, so all would be well.

CHAPTER FOUR

Against government advice, less than a year after their arrival, the Wilkses returned home to the East End of London, lulled into a false sense of security by months of phoney war when nothing much had happened on the home front. The British public were starting to believe that nothing ever would.

The Germans had not yet bombed London as expected and Father Wilks was missing his family, as they were missing him. They pined for the familiar: smog, pawn shops, chippies, a pub around the corner, noise and overcrowded neighbourliness. The countryside was too isolating, nocturnal scufflings of nature frightening, a flushing WC a challenge and the realisation that milk came warm and frothy from a cow disquieting.

Their decision was perhaps hastened by Jack, whose inability to foresee the consequences of his actions stemmed from his early literary diet, an over-consumption of Richmal Crompton's *Just William* books from the age of five telling him that anything was within bounds.

There had been an occasion when Mrs Wilks, her slight body tightly encased in a floral wrap-around pinny, her dull, lifeless, mousey hair contained in a snood, little strands escaping through the wide mesh, contentedly humming to herself 'The Lambeth Walk', singing – when she remembered the words – '*Run, Rabbit, run Rabbit, run, run, run, Don't give the farmer his fun, fun, fun,*' as she worked her way through the dozens of dirty plates every meal produced. Happily conscious that one of the sons of the house had placed his hand on the draining board and joined in the singing, unaware that hidden within his sleeve was a ferret looking for a way out. It emerged on to the edge of the sink from the wrist of its owner, paused, its inquisitive nose sniffing the air, exploring to see whether it was on familiar territory.

Mrs Wilks fainted. Nellie rummaged through the kitchen drawers hoping to find one of the small glass perles of amyl nitrite to break under her nose, left-overs from the time Julia's grandmother had lived with them in the thirties until her early death from angina.

Julia remembered that that had been a quiet time, the game of Dicky Ducktails forbidden, replaced by childhood responsibility, to carry at all times the torpedo-shaped glass phials to be broken quickly under Granny's nose if she had a dizzy spell. The unfamiliar pungent sickly smell of approaching death and Granny's departure in Mother's bed where, as a very small child, Julia had been nursed through scarlet fever, the coal fire lit and stoked throughout the night by a vigilant Mother to lessen the dark cold of the vast bedroom, the shadows of dancing flames casting frightening, sinister fingers on the ceiling, compounding delirium and fever.

Misunderstandings between town and country

were mutual. Victor Wilks had found a box of matches in the harness room and set fire to a neighbour's hay barn, destroying the building and twenty tons of fodder.

Victor's explanation was plausible: he had lit it on purpose in the belief that his fireman father would suddenly appear and put it out and they would be reunited. In all probability, at the age of seven, his explanation might have been the truth.

It had the desired effect. Father Wilks made the long journey north to stand with his son before the Juvenile Court to witness him charged with unlawfully and maliciously setting fire to a barn containing hay and two wooden loose boxes, the property of one Joseph Platt, at four p.m. on April 1940.

Julia's mother was called as a witness, tried to intercede on Victor's behalf, attempted to keep the family together, but there was opposition in the village. The malcontents were supported by the Clerk of the Rural District Council. Victor was banished to a juvenile offenders' institute.

The incident greatly distressed Father. He felt responsible. The Wilks lived a confused parallel life, their living quarters the old servants' sitting rooms, everyone coming together for meals, Mother having decreed that it was as easy to cook for twenty as two and it would keep friction out of the kitchen and make the rations go further. All the children, Nellie, Thelma, Marjorie and Mrs Wilks ate in the nursery. During term time, the four eldest Wilks children, Marion, Jimmy, Doreen and Victor, walked two miles to the village school. Victor had been playing truant.

Father had taken it upon himself to educate the

Wilks boys in the ways of the countryside, aware of the divisions between town and country, the certainties and traditions of rural life, set in stone for generations, under threat. He formed a strong attachment to eight-year-old Jimmy, admired the child's resilience and Cockney humour, saw beyond the cheeky freckled face and answering-back to a mind longing to be informed. Father took Jimmy under his wing, taught him along-side his own sons the disciplines and responsibilities of carrying a shotgun, the skill to shoot rabbits and crows. Ferreting, looking for used burrows and netting the holes, making sure the stake was firm and would hold a bolting rabbit. Handling the ferrets, Marks and Spencer, slipping them into the fresh dunged holes, aware of their presence underground, the excitement and expectation, keeping eyes open should the ferrets surface and escape and cause havoc in a neighbour's hen run, returning them to their box, their job done, the flushed rabbit speeding towards the trap, its quick despatch with a wooden club.

In that first wartime November, Father introduced Jimmy to the hounds of the local farmers' hunt. Fa-ther's mount, Spartacus, was an army horse from the time pre-war when he had overwintered equines for the army. Spartacus had developed a bog spavin; such imperfections were unacceptable in the Blues and Royals and he had been left behind for Father to nurse back to soundness. Julia riding Betty and Jimmy on David's bike completed the trio, joining an egalitarian, depleted gathering of neighbours, the doctor, the local bobby Patrick, the greengrocer and old Tom who was a lengthman on the railway; the remnants of those men of the soil already conscripted, those left awaiting their draft into factories and coal mines.

They didn't follow the hunt that day. It was a social occasion for Jimmy to be introduced to the hounds. Julia promised that next time, after Father had taught him to ride, Jimmy would ride Betty. But there never was a next time.

Returning home, they encountered a fox sitting on top of a wall grooming himself. Jimmy asked why the fox wasn't running; in the distance the hounds were already giving tongue. Father explained: 'The fox is far cleverer than the hounds. When he feels threatened he will be into the stream to kill his scent and up into the hills and away.'

As they sat watching him on that cold, crisp, hoar-frost November day, not a cloud in a surreal blue sky, they could not have foreseen that one day this natural balance between fox and hound would be banned and foxes would be subjected to the gun, dying a lingering gangrenous death from a poorly aimed bullet.

There was a kill that day, not their passing acquaintance but an old rogue dog fox without a mate. The huntsman knew him well, a long-standing adversary, the culprit for mutilation and random slaughter amongst local lambs and poultry.

Jimmy was also a favourite with David and Jack. They co-opted him to the board of the still-secret, officially-named Octopus Sewage Company; his creative engineering skills and Cockney nous enabling a more ambitious system to be constructed. His initiation to the club was to steal a spade and some rusting flange pipes from the disintegrating greenhouses without being seen by Thompson.

Jimmy could keep secrets, a challenge, for the Wilks children shared the large, corner bedroom in the west wing, and exchanging stories was a temptation during sleepless nights.

It had been a distressing goodbye. Father's strong paternal attachment to Jimmy was about to be severed; he had pleaded with the child's father that he be allowed to stay but Fireman Wilks, having already lost one son to the juvenile courts, was not prepared to chance another. When the time came Jimmy had sobbed, clinging to Julia's father. He had found his Utopia, witnessed fleetingly his salvation.

Although enquiries were made, nothing was heard of the family again. Two weeks after their return, the Blitz on London began, blanket bombing the East End with incendiaries, the horrific fireballs recorded by Gaumont British News and Pathé. Julia and her brothers cycled six miles to the local cinema to see Disney's *Snow White and the Seven Dwarfs*; there had been newsreels and they began to understand why their parents had opened their home to strangers and offered succour. This was a different war, not the sheltered one they were living.

Looking back, Julia wondered how her mother had kept going. Nellie, Thelma and Marjorie were still there, but only just. They had begun to show signs of discontent at the extra burdens placed upon them, the never-ending cooking and laundry. Marjorie's red-raw hands, old before their time, submerged twice weekly in the dolly tub in the outside laundry room with its damp, cold, sandstone flag floor, scrubbing out stains by hand. The mangling and carrying of heavy wet sheets to be hung outside to dry, rows of them caught in the wind, billowing like galleons in full sail. In bad weather the old reopened kitchens were filled with giant clothes horses, ceiling racks of steaming laundry in front of the huge iron kitchen range, resurrected and lit for the duration of the war. Marjorie took pride in its black leading. On its oven door, there was the embossed name of Julia's maternal great-grandfather, whose industrial prowess had built the house.

During 1940, Mother did her best to keep alive pre-war village traditions. The twice-yearly hops held in the hall, all-comers welcome, in aid of a car for the district nurse who, now she was getting older, was finding hills on her bicycle heavy going. The frayed Persian hall carpet rolled back to rest against the wall; the local dance band sitting on the stairs, Joe Loss in the mood, free beer and Marjorie giggling as Father flirted with her. As small children, they would creep out of their bedroom to peer between the stout wooden landing balustrades at the jollity below, wishing to be part of it.

They became part of it all too soon. The band was called up and music came from the old nursery gramophone, belting out Glenn Miller, Vera Lynn and Anne Shelton, supplemented by a group of evacuees sitting on the stairs with combs and Bronco lavatory paper, backed up by Nellie and Thelma on ocarinas. Tom, the village blacksmith, acting ARP Warden, was on guard at the front door, preventing the slightest glimmer of light escaping as people entered and left the house, creating a no man's land in the vestibule like a submarine's escape hatch, denying the Luftwaffe guidance. Mother had to keep a closer than usual eye on Thelma as soldiers from the nearby camp had heard there was a party.

Mother looked for additional help in the village and found Mary, whose husband was away at the war. She was prepared to come in term time when her three children were in school. Mary had a gamine beauty rarely seen in country women, an ethereal quality of shy gentleness. Julia's brothers said she looked like Merle Oberon and fell in love with her

Within two weeks of the Wilkses exodus, a different invasion took place. A military despatch rider roared up the drive with a message for Father. The house and grounds were to be taken over temporarily, requisitioned by the military, a tank battalion on training exercise. The officers and chaplain would be billeted in the house, the hall converted into a dormitory, other ranks in tents on the lawns.

Thompson gave in his notice.

For Julia and her brothers this was high adventure; having to return to boarding school after only one week of this occupation caused resentment.

Almost as quickly as they had come, the military moved on, leaving behind a devastation which Thompson had envisaged and for which he had no wish to be responsible. The acres of lawn so lovingly tended over decades were now deeply rutted. The immaculate grass tennis courts from where, on warm summer peacetime evenings, the distant laughing voices of adults and the comforting muffled thud of ball against racket could be heard through the children's open bedroom windows, were destroyed.

Everywhere was a quagmire, the zigzag of tank tracks dissecting the carefully white-limed boundary lines of the courts. The hill dividing the top lawn from the lower one down which they had rolled their Pasch eggs was now an assault course. The tanks accelerating up the steep incline, the metallic noise of war now in charge, had churned the earth into a mini Somme.

Nellie still insisted on the ritual of Pasch eggs, keeping onion skins and left-over pieces of coloured wools to wrap around the specially chosen white eggs before they were hard boiled. Father made it a competition for the prettiest, most colourful, most unusual. Two eggs each so as not to show favouritism and spread the prizes. The unexpected geometrical patterns, hues of autumn. Julia was always reluctant to roll hers, not wanting to break them.

The stable block became the outside catering area for the troops. Portable ovens were erected in the yard, steel cauldrons of soups and stews heated on giant gas rings, the roar of the flames frightening Betty. Queues of khaki men holding out tin bowls for two ladles of something which smelt more appetising than anything being cooked in the house.

By the time Julia and her brothers returned for the Christmas holidays, the military had left. The places vacated by the Wilks family had been taken by five members of the Womens' Land Army working in the nearby forestry plantation.

It was Father's nemesis. He never lost his temper; that he did so twice in one week made Julia realise that he too had his breaking point.

It was unusual for Mother to discuss domestic matters with Father. They had their allotted parts to play in keeping the family on the road. Father never entered the kitchens, felt out of place in them.

Mary had come to work her face puffed up, bruised and bicoloured, one of her lovely eyes invisible beneath a swollen mass of flesh. She was weeping. Nellie sat her down with a cup of tea and tried to find out what had happened. The answers to her questions were incoherent, immersed in sobbing. Mother was called for. She took Mary into the drawing room, away from inquisitive prying eyes, and closed the door. Julia, who had been in the kitchen getting a drink of water, witnessed this and told her brothers. They sat on the stairs, trying to hear what was going on. Mother came out and said, 'Find Father and tell him to come,' so they knew it must be something serious.

Mother eventually confided in them, used it as a lesson that they were fortunate to have such a happy home; some people didn't.

Mary's husband, home on leave, had listened to malicious village gossip: his wife had been carrying on with one of the officers recently billeted at the big house. The two had been seen talking at the dance. Rumours abounded and sides were taken, Mary's mother-in- law, who lived with her, adding to the vitriol against her daughter-in-law.

That gentle, innocent Mary had been subjected to a violent physical assault enraged Father. They had never seen him so angry. He walked to the village to confront the perpetrator of such falsehoods. He felt it was his duty. What was said and whether it had any effect, Julia would never know.

The cause of Father's second outburst had all the makings of a French farce. Of the five Land Girls, four were cheerful assets to the household, pulling their weight, helping with the youngest evacuees. The fifth imagined herself to be a cut above the rest; having failed to get into the Wrens, with its glamorous uniform and proximity to naval officers, she had been unceremoniously drafted into the Women's Land Army. She had, however, the determination to make the most of it. Wearing her green issue sweater three sizes too small, her bust became a major feature from which it was difficult for anyone to escape, and a cause of disbelief and physical disturbance in Julia's adolescent brothers. Her face was caked with make-up, surrounded by a halo of peroxide blonde hair.

Mother said, 'I have to admire her,' and christened her The Doxy. Julia thought that a pretty name. She also heard Mother say, to no one in particular, 'She's setting her cap at James.' She didn't understand many of Mother's comments.

Father had had a heavy day. Since Thompson's departure he had additional duties: stoking the boiler, its huge belly needing to be fed regularly to keep the house moderately warm in winter; raking out the clinkers which dropped through the grid onto the floor of the boiler house; trying to ensure that the farm cats had not chosen the warm ashes as a maternity ward, once inadvertently gathering up a spluttering mass of tiny dusty bodies.

Father returned to the house looking forward to his one remaining privilege, his private bathroom.

Undressed, his heap of dirty, farm worker's clothes left in the bedroom for Thelma to clear up, naked, he walked into his adjoining bathroom and saw The Doxy in his bath. She had discovered the key hidden under the carpet and known only to the maids. Before he had time to react, she purred at him, 'I knew you wouldn't mind, James dear.' But he had minded and arrived in the kitchens where supper was being prepared, a hastily-thrown towel around his shoulders, and shouted, 'The bloody Doxy's in my bath.' It was the first time anyone had heard him swear. Later he laughed it off, but his image of The Doxy in his bath remained. 'Her hair was tied up in a red chiffon scarf and she had bright scarlet lipstick on.' He added incredulously, '… in the bath!'

Mother, as always, dealt with it. The Doxy had disappeared by the end of the week.

There had been desperately sad departures. Nellie gave in her notice, not because she really wanted to leave; Julia's family was her real home. She had arrived eight years previously, thin, sallow-faced, fourteen years old, small for her age, with a mouthful of rotten teeth and very little self-esteem. Mother had turned her into an excellent cook who smiled all the time.

Nellie was engaged to be married. The courtship had lasted three years; a local farmer's son whom Mother encouraged as a thoroughly good match. He was allowed to visit at weekends and Julia adored him. His name was Harry and he greeted her as his conspirator when he sneaked in a mid-week visit, hugging her and saying, 'How's my second favourite girl?' Julia experienced jealousy for the first time.

Thelma departed a month later. Lonely without Nelly, she joined the Auxiliary Territorial Service, returning often to see the family, smart and flirty in her new uniform, her curly hair carefully arranged around the khaki issue cap. She later married a bookie from Newcastle upon Tyne and, by all accounts, lived happily ever after. Having no close relatives nearby, she brought her intended to be vetted by Mother. Julia answered the front door and there was Thelma, laughing on the doorstep with a jolly, portly, red-faced man in a brown suit and watch chain, a twinkle in his eye and fifteen years her senior. Mother pronounced him spot on.

CHAPTER FIVE

So many anchors of childhood dragged and gone, the clouds of war overshadowed the next two years, creating a hazy no man's land between home and school.

The Allied invasion of Italy from the Mediterranean in autumn 1943. Unknown to Julia, that part of her life yet to come, her future brother-in-law was captured in Sicily during the first hours of the campaign. Within days the Italians surrendered. 'Giving in' might protect their treasured architectural heritage from the ravages of bombing. A forlorn hope, for the Germans were happy to continue the fight, to pillage someone else's homeland. As the Allies moved north through Italy the Germans, in retreat, fought blitzkrieg battles of such ferocity that decades later, on her annual pilgrimage to Italy, Julia marvelled that so much beauty had escaped the plunder.

It was the last week of the summer holidays. On hearing the news of the Italian capitulation, Julia raced across the recently harvested fields, the stubble stalks piercing her sandelled feet and ankles, her heart pounding, lungs bursting, to the potato fields where the Italian prisoners of war were working. The large yellow dinner plate patch on the back of their chocolate brown battledress was a familiar and trusted sight. Julia needed to be the first to tell them that they no longer had to hate one another.

Rules of fraternization, the government edict forbidding contact with the enemy, were not taken seriously by her parents. When the Italian POWs first arrived, to be on the safe side, Father said, 'Sit on the wall and say *buon giorno.*'

Initially they had not responded until one day the eldest, Guido, his greying hair and academic, aquiline features setting him apart from the others, had straightened his back from a morning hoeing potatoes, picked a buttercup from the edge of the field and slowly walked over to her. With a slight bow he presented it to her.

'*Grazie,*' she said.

They all looked up and smiled and she felt happy. They called out '*Bella, bella.*' Julia was aware of pleasurable, unfamiliar stirrings, inner flutterings, an awakening, a contradiction of the continuous calling of names by her brothers. 'Fat, freckle-faced baboon' was the usual accepted endearment; loving sibling verbal abuse confirming the advantages of large families and putting the brakes on pretension.

Her brothers tried to scare her into believing that the yellow patch was where Father would aim his gun if they tried to escape but Julia knew with certainty that Father was incapable of shooting anyone. He had seen too much slaughter in a different war of which he seldom spoke other than to say, 'It must never happen again.' However, Julia knew with the same childish certainty that Mother, given the right circumstances, would have had no hesitation in squeezing the trigger.

The Italians had no wish to run away. They counted themselves lucky to have been captured and allowed to do what many of them had been doing in their homeland. Conscripted peasant farmers, they had been dragged into a war they didn't understand by an unhinged Il Duce, exchanging their meagre native hectares of hard sun-baked blocks of earth for the rain-soaked mud of northern England to grow potatoes instead of pasta maize. Figs, olives, cyprus and poplars were exchanged for gorse, heather, oaks and ash. The roaming scattered flocks of Swaledale, Rough Fell, Scottish Black Face replaced the regimented belled Maremma sheep of their homeland.

Within a month of their arrival on the farm, Mother had taken pity on them. She saw Guido searching the bottom of the hedgerows and asked what he was looking for. In perfect English he replied, 'A large edible snail to supplement my diet of a quarter of a loaf of bread,' the working ration for the day handed out as they boarded the bus at six thirty each morning from the POW Nissan huts to surrounding farms. Guido knew the Latin name of the snail, *Helix Pomatia*, and informed mother that it had probably been introduced into Britain by the Romans.

From then on the 'Eyeties' were given a hot midday meal, however simple. Nellie was instructed to double the quantities of mashed potato cooked daily, adding to them as many of Marmaduke's embryo offspring as could be spared. She sacrificed a few of her own precious ration points to make up a thermos of meaty broth.

There was competition between Nellie, Thelma

and Marjorie to take the bucket of food across the fields. For Thelma, the opportunity to be close to so many men must have been an unexpected bonus of war and probably the reason she didn't give in her notice earlier. Julia noticed an increase in whispering and giggling and Mother had to lay down ground rules to prevent 'shenanigans', a word Julia hadn't understood at the time. Fifteen minutes there and back and they must always go together.

Later in the afternoon of the Italian surrender, Father went down to the cellars and brought up two vintage bottles of wine laid down pre-war. Julia took some glasses from the kitchen, secretly, for she was never sure how Mother might view things. Together she and Father went to the fields. She had never seen grown men weep before.

Julia was beginning to believe that life mirrored her school reports: 'Could do better if she concentrated.' She had already accepted her part in the Alice in Wonderland concept of education on offer. Those excelling at a subject got the coaching, the eyes of teachers on the kudos and acclaim which would rub off on them if they produced an Oxford or Cambridge candidate. The average struggled as best they could. It was the same with hockey, lacrosse and tennis; she waited with baited breath for who would be picked for the next away match (second team) but it was never her. Even when half the team were in the san with chickenpox her name was never called. She was invisible.

But there was an exception. Miss Caleb was meant to teach history as in the history books but taught about life instead. Her father was an Indian doctor and her mother the wayward daughter of a white colonial. Their liaison in a different century produced this remarkable woman who had been denied a place at an English university because she was a half-caste. Brought up by her father and rejected by her mother and her family, she had inherited a remarkable love of life and people. Her face, which looked like the shell of a walnut, bore a permanent smile and occasionally her body shook with mirth, an inward chuckle when her mind was elsewhere. With no official qualifications, she had only been taken on by the school because everyone else was at war.

Julia loved her. She smelt of the vicar at home, a sort of insulin smell. She knew it was insulin because mother had explained about diabetes when Julia had asked why Canon Paterson had that strange odour when he came to tea.

Miss Caleb must have been about seventy years old. There was hardly anything of her. She looked like one of those stick insects which inhabit the bottom of fast-flowing clear rivers and which Julia and her brothers caught in the fishing nets they purchased for a penny from Woolies. Her pure white hair, bobbed western style, contrasted with the dusty coffee colour of wrinkled skin. Summer and winter she dressed in brown twinset and threadbare tweed skirt, almost through at the knees where her skeletal joints had rubbed against the fabric. Her bony hands and arms clasped stacks of books which she rarely opened in lessons, preferring to read out loud from *The Times* and gaze at the ceiling with her large spaniel eyes and talk about her experiences. Every lesson was prefaced by the story of how

65

her father had discovered penicillin a decade before the world had heard of Fleming.

She bore no grudges, talked about her idyllic childhood in India, the love for her father and the beauty of her native land, but when asked when and why she had come to England she changed the subject, so her life became an unfinished jigsaw to her pupils with all the centre pieces missing.

When careers were mentioned by other members of staff, Julia did not really listen, toying in her imagination with the idea of going to an agricultural college until she discovered too late that chemistry was a necessary requirement. She had been advised to drop it before School Certificate, been told there was little chance of her passing and in order to matriculate in six subjects she should concentrate on something she was good at. Miss Caleb listened and said, 'You do not need to pass exams to succeed in life, just try to understand people and learn the word "percipience".' Julia had looked it up.

Domestic science had been offered as an alternative. Julia was comforted by the thought that she might achieve a credit mark. All those hours spent with Nellie skinning and cooking rabbits and making ginger biscuits should have rubbed off.

On the day of the examination fate was not on her side. The written part was easy: 'Describe how to make a sponge cake'; the practical something she had done a hundred times before: scrambled eggs on toast garnished with parsley.

She was proud of her effort, spent a little too much time cutting the toast into a circle for artistic impression and just had time to grab an unwashed piece of parsley from the communal bowl. As she stood behind her chair listening to the complimentary remarks of the examiner as she approached, 'Well done, Susan. Very nice, Jean', Julia became aware of a caterpillar emerging from one of the compact parsley fronds which she had placed with such care. Just as the examiner arrived, it rose to its full height, balancing on its rear suckers as it decided where to go next. There was suppressed giggling from Julia's neighbours and the rebuke from the examiner: 'Slovenly work.'

A secretarial course was beginning to look like the only option. Prue, on the other hand, was sitting a scholarship to read history at Oxford.

One hot weekend during Julia's penultimate summer term, she and two accomplices had, for a bet, taken off their clothes, climbed through a window onto the flat roof outside the classroom and pranced around naked, embarrassed by their own stupidity. They had been seen but only Julia, as tail-end Charlie, clambering back through the window, had been recognised.

She was summoned to the headmistress's study the following day and immediately thought of David, who was now in the army. He must have been killed in action. Girls were only called into the head's inner sanctum for three reasons: to be congratulated on being part of the winning team in the inter-schools tennis, lacrosse or hockey matches; to be told they had won a scholarship (neither of those could happen to her), and to be told that a brother or father was a casualty of war. The recipients of such news returned to class fifteen minutes later, their faces swollen, wet from weeping. The stupidity of war as a way for mankind to settle differences was already clear to Julia, but she said nothing for it would have seemed unpatriotic and it was compassion that was needed at such times.

In the five years she had been at school she had never been invited into the head's Holy of Holies. Prue had been, many times, as the recipient of congratulations.

Julia was to be expelled as a corrupting influence and an example to others. Her parents had been informed. Julia's body reacted strangely; abandoned and disowned by her mind, left to fend on its own, it went weak and she thought she might faint, but her mind knew exactly where it was, receiving mixed signals, the lessons of her childhood misunderstood.

She and her brothers had enjoyed a rare freedom which would nowadays be seen as parental neglect, but of course was no such thing. It had been a lack of awareness of their bodies in the exuberance and innocence of youth. Until they were in their teens they had run naked together in those privileged private surroundings, the boys' flaccid willies flapping from side to side as they ran to hide in the long grass as callers approached the house.

Now she knew that on receiving the letter from the headmistress, Father had asked for a full account of the reasons for his daughter's expulsion. When the triviality of her misdemeanour became apparent, Father demanded an interview. It was his only visit to the school and one of which Julia had been totally unaware at the time.

The story of her deliverance unfolded during the holidays. A hasty judgement had been made against his daughter and he was determined to put the matter straight. He caught the next train south. Mother scribbled Beatrice Tomlinson MA (Oxon) on a piece of paper which she tucked into his breast pocket, mindful of Father's inability to remember names, and suggested he take a bottle of vintage wine from the cellars to oil the wheels of introduction. By the end of the interview Father and the headmistress were on Christian-name terms. Of course Mother already knew he could charm the hind legs off a donkey.

Julia was summoned to the Holy of Holies again two days later. The headmistress hugged her and said, 'What a brick your father is. We'll forget about it shall we? He's a brick, an absolute brick.'

Julia had no idea what she was talking about but knew that Father had somehow come to her rescue, as she would to his years later.

Thereafter, when the headmistress passed her in the school corridors, she stopped to ask after Father. After six years at the school, Julia had finally been recognised.

Of course, at the time Julia had not appreciated the significance of the school's proximity to the recently arrived American Army camp located on the other side of the school footpath and the fact that three naked girls might be seen as provocation.

A late developer, sex never really registered until she was sixteen when she had had a brief, all-consuming crush on the head girl. Photos taken secretly on her Brownie Box camera of her beloved playing tennis were the closest she came to any kind of relationship. The out-of-focus prints were a disaster, the girl a tiny unrecognisable white speck. Julia settled finally for a studio photo of James Mason under her pillow, torn up when she discovered he was married to someone called Pamela Kellino.

The significance of the Yanks hadn't registered. They were over here a bit late in the day to help Britain get rid of Hitler. They were friendly like her brothers but slightly older; they whistled and shouted, 'Hiya babe' or 'Honey' but appeared to be no threat, unless you had an adult mind and responsibility for 330 pubescent girls.

In hindsight Julia could see the head's dilemma, but for many of Julia's generation, sex and its implications were never talked about. She had no doubt there were cliques of girls in the school who talked about nothing else but she always avoided them. She was aware of a clandestine copy of *Forever Amber* going the rounds, its centre pages grubby and worn, and she hoped for a quick glance to see what was causing the giggling but she never seemed to be at the front of the queue.

Julia was taught that sex was private, something to be kept to yourself. Living on a farm she knew all the technicalities but had never associated them with humans, thought it took a different form.

Somewhere along the line Mother felt it necessary to have a little talk. It was short, to the point and effective. Having a baby outside marriage brought disgrace upon the family and the way to avoid this happening was to say 'no'. If you flirted and tempted a man, you were as much to blame and men, once aroused, found it hard to stop.

That last commandment she knew was true. She

had been present when Thompson requested the services of the travelling stallion to cover Mother's cob mare. Thompson had suggested she return to the house but she hid round the corner and watched, fascinated by the two-feet-long rigid membrane seeking the hindquarters of the mare, the stallion's roar of anger if the mare kicked out to dissuade him and the frenetic mounting, teeth bared as he roughly grasped the mane and neck.

Contraception was not mentioned. Julia, because she felt she might not get another chance, plucked up courage and asked Mother whether she had done it with Father only four times because of the four of them. Mother mumbled something about coitus interruptus and that was that.

But it wasn't really. Mother was not all strictness and spanking, leaving the imprint of her hard hand on their bottoms. That, perhaps, was the face she felt she should show to the family and the world. Inside her were contradictions. When fifteen-year-old Edna in the village produced an illegitimate baby, which Julia's brothers, who were just beginning to understand such things, unkindly called the 'immaculate conception' since the poor girl had no idea what had happened to her, Mother gave her full support, against the prejudice and ostracism on offer from neighbours, and counselled her parents to keep the child. Perhaps this was what Father had seen in her which others hadn't.

Julia, curious to see for herself what all the fuss was about, picked some bluebells to give to the new baby, knocked on the cottage door and was welcomed inside.

By the fire, suckling her baby, was a child Julia

knew from Sunday school, her large inflamed breast protruding into the mouth of a pink object. Julia had never seen a mature breast at close quarters before and, for some unknown reason, felt embarrassed at being so close to something so personal. What she remembered most of all was the mass of tiny hairs in which it was covered.

She knew now how Father, with his quiet reasonableness, could win anyone around yet he himself, so full of self-doubt depended on a bottle of whisky to see him through the day.

CHAPTER SIX

People say that you never forget where you were when something momentous happens. Julia was outside on the school terrace underneath the magnificent cedar, the thick carpet of dry discarded needles beneath her feet reminding her of the Octopus Tree, the weekly letter from Mother unopened in her hand. She decided to wait until morning break to read it.

Could the sudden loss of a home be classed as bereavement? Julia knew it should be. Reading Mother's letter, she was overwhelmed by grief. She ran to the bursar's office and asked to be allowed to use the school telephone to ring home, having been told that a bereavement in the family was the only circumstance for which permission would be granted. She could not explain that she was about to be bereaved by the sale of her home.

The letter sounded final. If she could get through to Father he would stop it happening for, although it was Mother's family home, she was certain he would never agree to such as thing. If she could speak to him, decisions could be reversed; whatever had precipitated her parents' actions could be talked through. Her father must have been coerced in some way.

73

Love for her home and its surrounding acres was all-embracing; not only bricks and mortar, it had a soul, it was her refuge. She had mistakenly believed it would be there forever, a haven to which she could return at any time. For the past six years, school terms were made tolerable by the knowledge of it. She was about to be severed from herself and she must try to prevent it. She reread Mother's letter, her vision blurred by tears of disbelief.

The letter to Father would take three days; if he answered immediately, another three days to receive a reply. It was the first time she had written to him personally, letters home always addressed to Mr and Mrs. The waiting was unbearable and, when his reply arrived, she knew she would have to accept a decision already made and, for Father's sake, make the best of it.

Secretarial college in London was beginning to feel like an escape route.

Father's explanation bore his familiar reasonableness. Hostilities with Germany had ceased, the evacuees and Land Girls had gone home. Julia and Nick, eighteen months her senior, would be leaving school at the end of that summer term, David and Jack had already flown the nest.

Father's most compelling reason was his concern for Mother. Only forty-six years old, she was physically exhausted. Six years tirelessly and selflessly helping others during the war had taken its toll and, for her, the prospect of carrying on in that huge house with no help, trying to maintain the gardens, was too much.

Perhaps her parents needed money? Money was

never talked about; as children they were given no pocket money, never requested it. The value of money was appreciated only when a dropped coin, a farthing or halfpenny, was found and they raced on their bikes to the village shop for an ounce of rat tails, Julia choosing the red ones to moisten and use as pretend lipstick.

That a war profiteer was buying her home added insult to injury. He had made a fortune from the manufacture of military uniforms. Julia met them only once; the wife looked like Thelma without the laughter and fun, all make-up, cheap scent and flounce. He was bald-headed, large, with a loud voice, the cigar hanging between his teeth affecting his speech. He wore a shiny double-breasted suit and had small feet which turned outwards in brown and white shoes which Father called co-respondent, an adjective Julia did not understand but knew was derogatory by the way Father said it.

Julia wondered what her home would make of them; perhaps the ghost would materialise, his crunching invisible feet on the gravel beneath the window of bedroom seven would be made flesh. At least the horses would rest in peace, their graves safe, hidden beneath the mass of overgrown rhododendrons.

Julia wanted to share her own joy of the garden with the new owners, to point out its hidden treasures, but instinctively felt she would be wasting her time. The initials of family members over four generations planted in daffodils on the terrace, invisible to the uninitiated amongst that glorious spring blaze of yellow. The corky bark of the tulip trees, their yellow upturned delicate flowers sluggish to open in a colder climate, the walnuts and Wellingtonias, trees planted by her maternal great grandfather. One Wellingtonia had been struck by lightning and christened The Wet Hen by locals, its distinctive shape a guiding beacon. The cavern under the Octopus Tree. What was the point? They didn't have children, only a chauffeur who didn't look as if he would be happy scrambling about in the undergrowth.

Julia was beginning to feel nostalgia for Thompson. They would need a Thompson but village rumour had it that the new owners had their own supply of lackeys recruited from the wartime factory.

For the time being her parents would live in a small rented property on the outskirts of the village, a characterless house, jerry built between the wars, intrusive amongst its mellowed neighbours.

A clean break with the past would have been easier. Julia stopped looking up at the old home when she passed, imagined the windows to be weeping with her and imploring her to return, like a faithful jilted lover wanting to go back to the way things were.

It was made more difficult by Father's retention of shooting rights over the land, a concession to his children. From an early age Julia and her brothers had been taught how to handle a shotgun. It was a long and disciplined apprenticeship: walking miles over muddy fields with frozen hands with an unloaded gun for months before being allowed to fire a shot, until safety had become instinctive and second nature. Then they would be permitted to help control the vermin, crows in particular.

Julia hated crows; those sinister black shapes sitting on the drystone walls, watching labouring ewes, swooping down, plucking out an eye from the slowly emerging lambs head in a split second; Julia's realisation that she wasn't running fast enough, wouldn't make it in time, a searing burning sensation in her chest as she ran devoid of breath across a field to reach the sheep before those evil forms descended. Arriving too late, only to see what she dreaded, the empty, bloody eye socket, the lamb still cocooned in the bright yellow mucus of birth struggling to its feet.

Julia could see things from the crow's angle, that contradictory unsettling trait of understanding both points of view. The crow had its own young to feed and, unlike humans, had no concept of cruelty. How misguided those sentimentalists who teach children that all animals and birds are cuddly; her own experiences had taught her otherwise. She still bore the scars on her left hand from when she was attacked by a badger at the age of four: opening the hen house door to collect the eggs, confronted by brock who had got there first and didn't like the competition.

Sitting in her kitchen now, Julia's mind and memory were going AWOL. Memories beget recollections, she was trying to sieve them, the grain from the chaff; she hoped her memory wasn't being discriminatory, remembering only those things that suited her current frame of mind.

Those tacked on, still-trying-to-belong, days, pro-longed Julia's agony. The anticipation and challenges of London were becoming more inviting.

Julia was aware that she possessed an unsettling misfit gene that guided her thoughts away from those of her peers. In the year she became sixteen, Father's friends had started making comments, 'You've got a Bolshie one there, James.'

At that stage in her life, other than those heated, friendly discussions over mealtimes she had witnessed when staying with Prue's family, when Mary the elder sister, already at Oxford, had returned at weekends with a succession of radical left-wing boyfriends, Julia had been unaware of politics. Her beliefs sprang from an intuitive source. Her maternal grandfathers and great-grandfathers were self-taught men of letters. They had a discipline and determination which she lacked and she was beginning to experience that grey cloud of self-doubt, that feeling of standing on the sidelines looking on, absent from the world, a spectator. It was the forerunner of that formidable enemy, that overwhelming black cloud of depression which would sneak up many years later and carry her off into the underworld.

But there were decisions to be made. That her parents allowed her to go to London aged barely seventeen, a country innocent, was, in hindsight, a most remarkable statement of trust. They must have known that they had instilled values into her which would stand her in good stead and give her a resilience to fight her own battles. She had not recognised it at the time but now knew it was so. She would meet the same conflicts again, frailties and decencies witnessed in the people who had sought sanctuary in her home during the war years. The war was a quick, harsh and enlightening crash course in life and communal living. Learning to bite your tongue and count to ten before saying anything which might cause friction or hurt to others, this lesson overseen by Mother who, at all times, kept the peace but perhaps in so doing had sidelined her own family.

Unless you lived in or had contacts in London, hostels were the only place for single people to live. Accommodation was at a premium in a city mutilated by bombing. The bursar sent a list of possible lodgings within walking distance of the college and a place was found in Vauxhall Bridge Road. A jumping-off ground. The shared dormitories and iron bedsteads were reminiscent of school; the inmates students, minor civil servants, shop workers, nurses, secretarial temps, males and females all ages.

Julia had already learnt not to make hasty judgements or assumptions. After the first week she put her name on the waiting list for a two-bedded room and was fortunate; within six weeks she had some sort of privacy.

David announced his engagement. The wedding would be in Woking. Julia, invited to be one of four bridesmaids, knew this was not her scene. She hated being on display, however minor the role, but was prepared to go along with it for a day for the sake of her brother, hoping that the dress would not be pink. That was the first of many lessons she would learn from her new room-mate: 'With your orangey freckles don't wear pink.'

The colour chosen *was* pink, not a sophisticated coral or lilac pink but a strawberry ice-cream, in-your-face pink, the material sharkskin, headdress to match, stiff and unflattering, determined to make a statement on its own, whoever wore it.

The wedding day was autumn balmy. She tried hard to enjoy it but felt like a fish out of water. The three other bridesmaids, happy to be imprisoned in pink sharkskin, were two cousins and a friend of the bride. Other than her parents, Jack acting as best man, Nicholas an usher, there were few familiar faces on the groom's side from the North. Petrol was still rationed and friends were unprepared to make the three-hundred-mile, ten-hour train journey south standing in a corridor.

David was demobbed with the rank of corporal. With no other qualifications other than his gift for music, he had landed a menial job with a minor publishing company on the outskirts of London and met his future wife, a model, at a launch party. Models were called 'mannequins' in those days and had dignity as well as elegance, the odd one marrying a peer of the realm.

Julia liked her future sister-in-law. She was gentle and friendly, tall, with a beautiful figure and deportment. She worked for a minor Paris fashion house, re-emerging and reinventing itself after five years of Nazi occupation. Julia couldn't understand what her new sister-in-law saw in David. She should have realised and understood; he had inherited Father's genes and charm and that, coupled with ability to play jazz like no one else, made him irresistible to anyone outside the family.

Somewhere in a box in the attic there were black-and-white photographs of a bride and groom in a church porch and four bridesmaids wearing sharkskin. She remembered little of the day. Long trestle tables, wartime austerity still overlapping into peacetime; perhaps it had been Snook sandwiches, a home-made cake and champagne. What she had been aware of at the other end of the room was Father's voice above the rest, his whisky voice, the outward sign that he, like her, felt unsure of himself, unhappy in the social role he was being forced to play. Or was she imagining it, creating her own discomfort, the looks of disapproval misinterpreted: 'Is that the father-in-law?' As his voice became more strident, people were laughing in an embarrassed way. She wanted to stand up and say to those strangers, 'That is not the real him,' but she herself didn't feel real. She was wearing ghastly pink fancy dress and didn't want to draw attention to herself.

Mother didn't appear to have noticed or, if she had, was turning a practised blind eye.

A disturbing thought struck Julia. One day Father might have to play a major role in a similar play in which she would be the leading lady.

CHAPTER SEVEN

The choice of secretarial college was a good one, selected from four on offer, hidden under more impressive higher-education prospectuses aimed at cleverer pupils on the school's careers table. It had a prestigious list of politicians, authors, cabinet ministers, judges and diplomats who promised ready employment if you made the grade, which persuaded Father to foot the bill for the eighteen-month course though Julia doubted her own ability to complete it.

No such doubts amongst her fellow students, daughters of authors, politicians, and those with diplomatic parents studying the course in a second language. They already had a head start, a pied-à-terre in London, confident of the kind of people who would eventually employ them.

As she sat typing 'The quick brown fox jumps over the lazy dog' to music going too fast, she found it difficult to take the course of her education seriously. The hilarity of the situation got to her and she chuckled inwardly as her fingers lost control. The tutor shouted, 'Julia, keep your eyes on the script. Do not look at the typewriter.'

Her fingers were happier exercising other skills:

untangling a mass of unborn legs, heads and tails which had knitted themselves into a ball in the womb of a ewe trying to give birth to triplets. Julia's small hands under Father's patient instruction, sorting them out. Seeking a head, running her fingers down the shoulders, establishing which head belonged to which legs, concentrating, eyes closed, on her stomach in the cold wet grass, gently, so as not to rupture the ewe, the contraflow of contractions pushing to expel her arm, one finger hooking a leg forward into the birth canal. The reassuring click as it made its forced passage through the pelvic bone. Julia's hand, her fingers and mind in perfect harmony, pushing back two siblings to await their turn, slowly pulling until that slippery, slimy miracle shook its head and spluttered.

She never mentioned this skill; it seemed in-appropriate, might have been misunderstood, even ridiculed. It would be thirty years until her fingers would be permitted to rekindle that feeling.

In addition to the mandatory Pitman's shorthand and typing, she studied civics, a smattering of law, presentation of formal legal documents, scripts of plays and how to address the Archbishop of Canterbury, members of the nobility and various legal bigwigs, face to face, on an envelope, formally and informally. It was a finishing school without the flower arranging, cooking and deportment classes. Julia sometimes still referred to those browning, faded sample documents kept in the attic trunk, unable to throw that part of her past away, anachronisms, from a time when life was polite and restrained.

She accepted her position as dunce of the class,

the butt of amusing comment. She was used to it; her brothers had seen to that. It did not worry her, she almost took it as a compliment. She knew she was liked, that knowledge confirmed by invitations to stay for weekends at grand country houses and smart suburban villas. The introduction to parents: 'This is Pudge. Her parents live in the North,' sufficient to ensure a warm welcome and return weekend visits.

Evenings in the hostel blossomed under the tutelage of Elsa, her newly-acquired room-mate. A worldly seventeen year old, with wide-apart grey-green eyes and honey-coloured hair inherited from her English mother, a pale perfect olive skin from her Italian father, she turned heads. An impoverished noble family on her father's side, domiciled for many years in the UK, interned during the war, his wife and daughter left to fend as best they could in a hostile and suspicious country. Bilingual, Elsa earned her living as an interpreter at one of the embassies.

Clothes were still rationed. Elsa's clothes had once been fashionable. Passed down from her mother, adapted and patched chic, they still bore the elegance, cut and style all couture clothes retain. Julia, used to hand-me-downs, jumpers and shorts from her brothers, appreciated the offer of a frayed blouse or skirt in exchange for cash. Father had agreed a subsistence allowance until she was self-sufficient. Elsa and she pooled their resources to purchase a bottle of garish bright-red nail varnish, giggling as they tried it out. It made Julia feel tarty. She could hear Mother saying something about fallen women.

Seven years of wartime clothes rationing and

austerity contributed to the extravagant indulgence of the New Look. Long full skirts and small, tight-waisted jackets began to appear in the shops. Julia was adapting to a new awareness of herself.

Glimpsed from the top of a bus, a yellow dress in a newly-opened shop in Kensington Church Street, the skirt spread out to fill the whole window. She got off at the next stop, walking back to see whether on closer inspection such feelings were warranted. They were.

The colour was palest lemon with tiny blue and white flowers. Her freckles would be happy with that. The material moygashel, a mixture of linen and cotton, the top half sleeveless and gathered on the shoulders, the swathes of material crossing over the bust to the waist.

She had sufficient clothing coupons but insufficient funds. The secretarial course had finished but it would be at least two weeks before she could find a job and a pay packet.

She tried on the dress, stared at the stranger in the mirror in disbelief, asked the assistants whether they would keep it for her, admitted her impecunious state. They ignored her, looked down their noses.

The high flyers on her course were snapped up by the great and famous. Julia bore no resentment. Like Father, she never felt at ease too close to pomp and circumstance. She was offered an interview with a Commonwealth Scientific Institution based in Queen's Gate. The director, for whom she would work, was a bumbling, white-haired bear of a man, old enough to be her grandfather. She felt at ease, at home with him. He was a brilliant entomologist, working to find a chemical to eliminate that tiny lethal mosquito *Anopheles gambiae*, the malaria carrier, still on the rampage sixty years on.

Throughout the interview, her prospective boss tried to dislodge something from his ear with a finger. When this failed, he picked up a pencil and dug around in his left orifice. Hypnotised by his eccentric manners, Julia couldn't remember anything that was said, but his behaviour so endeared him that she accepted the job offered on the spot. Her instinct proved right.

She could still feel in her hand the independence of that first pay packet and see the wage slip: £4 15s. The frock was still in the window, the assistant aware that this time she may have to take the customer seriously and accept the £2 deposit that was offered. It would take four weeks' wages to pay off.

After a year, Julia escaped from Vauxhall Bridge Road, moved upmarket to a hostel in Holland Park. A dilapidated Georgian house, it was war damaged, paint peeling, falling stucco, unloved, too near Shepherd's Bush, Notting Hill and the notorious 10 Rillington Place to be considered a salubrious neighbourhood. The rent took a third of her wages and this extravagance led to a curtailment of the weekend visits with friends to Lyons Corner House, Marble Arch or Piccadilly on Saturday evenings where they would queue on the wide marble stairs leading down to the restaurant, hear the sensual evocative sound of the orchestra playing in the distance until they reached the foot of the stairs with the 'Wait Here' sign. Then the sophistication of being led to a table by a waiter with a black bow tie and being called Madam.

To fill in a weekend on her own, she accepted a kind invitation from a quiet, shy girl called Ruth, an inmate of the hostel, who went home on Friday evenings to Sleaford to spend Saturdays and Sundays with her parents.

They were met at the station by Ruth's father, unsmiling and brusque, a retired army major who owned a prosperous family firm producing pet foods. Julia felt unwelcome. At dinner that evening she felt uncomfortable, a replay of pink sharkskin in a different dimension. The conversation was unfamiliar, crude, a put-down of women by the father. Ruth and her mother were subdued, reluctant to contribute. It was one of those experiences which Julia's own mother warned her about. 'If you feel ill at ease in a situation, get out, trust your instincts.' But Julia had also been taught good manners and these two were in conflict. She couldn't just get up and leave, would not wish to embarrass her friend in any way.

Ruth remained in the kitchen talking with her mother. Julia, making her way to bed, was accosted by the brother. She had disliked him at dinner. He sneered at his sister, but not in the way Julia's brothers ribbed and teased her with laughter and love, hugging her if they felt they might have overstepped the mark.

He pinned her against the wall and, uninvited, pushed his tongue down her throat, his hands groping. She heard Jack's voice from beyond the grave: 'If a bloke tries to get fresh with you, Sis, knee him in the groin.' Julia obeyed with such force that she almost dislocated her hip and left her assailant writhing on the landing.

Panicking, she went to her room, locked the door and sat on the bed, shaking for an hour, hoping no one had heard. Desperate to go to the loo, but too anxious to attempt a foray along the landing, she had decanted the hyacinth bulbs and soil from their bowl on the window sill into her suitcase and peed in the vase. After a sleepless night, as dawn approached, she camouflaged the bowl under her towel and dispensed its troublesome contents down the loo, replanting the hyacinths on her return, hoping no one would notice.

At breakfast the following morning, the brother didn't appear. It was raining. Walks on the sand had lost their appeal. An early return to town was suggested and Julia gratefully agreed; she had been worrying about how to combat a further onslaught from the brother.

That encounter had other repercussions. The experience with her bladder so dogged Julia that, now approaching ninety, she never stayed overnight anywhere without taking with her a family-sized, used, plastic trifle case from Tesco.

Father was appointed to sit on a committee dealing with rural and agricultural affairs which necessitated visits to London, staying at the Constitutional Club in Northumberland Avenue. His twice-yearly visits became major events in Julia's calendar. Now with her own income, she was determined to show him that his faith in her had been justified. On their first outing together he considered the Constitutional to be a bit stuffy and suggested they meet at the Savoy for a drink before going on to the theatre, a nightclub and meal.

She made every effort to impress him. He had not

seen the transformation from tomboy to womanhood. The uncomfortable high-heeled, black suede, peep-toe, sling-backs, the expensively acquired frock, now fully paid for, pert little hat with a half-veil, no coupons required.

Having been brought up to believe that being late for an appointment was bad manners, she arrived ten minutes early. Sitting self-consciously in the foyer of the Savoy, she told the hall porters that she was waiting for her father but felt they did not believe her. Fifteen minutes passed. They were watching her suspiciously, discussing her; she was beginning to feel uncomfortable. Perhaps they thought she was soliciting. She had watched this happen at the Regent Palace in Piccadilly when waiting in the foyer to meet up with friends before going to a theatre. Father was twenty minutes late and, on entering, did not immediately recognise her.

He had two front centre stalls for the latest Ivor Novello musical, *King's Rhapsody*, rekindling the buzz of excitement and anticipation of childhood visits to the pantomime. When they were children Father always managed to acquire the best seats, front row of the dress circle, chins and small bare arms resting on the velvet-cushioned rail, minds carried off into a make-believe world below and the added enchantment of coming out of the theatre into night-time, a myriad pin-pricks of light reflected in wet pavements all part of the magic. Now, in the stalls, she sat back in the comfort of a plush seat, different smells, cigars and perfume. One or two couples were in evening dress, long frocks and dinner jackets re-emerging from wartime mothballs.

Vanessa Lee sang, 'We'll gather lilacs in the spring

again, and walk together down an English lane.' Julia glanced at her father. Tears were trickling down his face. She smiled and thought, 'What an old sentimentalist,' then suddenly realised it wasn't that. For the whole of his life, had he held things back?

After the show they went on to the Bagatelle with Edmundo Ros and his Latin American Band. Halfway through the evening Father thought he recognised someone sitting with a girl on the other side of the room. They went onto the dance floor to get a closer look, glancing between quicksteps at the couple in an intimate alcove. It was the husband of Mother's greatest friend. Father said he had a feeling they didn't want to be seen and perhaps they should go and sit down, but it was too late. The two men's eyes met in surprised recognition. Father said that, in these situations, it was best to be open and they walked over.

'Hello, Keith, what are you doing in town?'

'Well, well, James. Wasn't expecting to see you two here.'

The girl looked like Thelma, but with more make-up, her dimpled plump elbows resting on the table (Mother's voice again, 'Elbows on the table will be carved,'), her chipped scarlet nails caressing a wine glass. When introduced as Miss Jones, she replied, 'Pleased to meet you, I'm sure,' and giggled. Of the quartet it was only she who was at ease.

Returning to their table, Father said, 'I think we should keep this under our hats. Don't mention it to Mother,' and she never had.

She saw her father safely into a taxi and took the tube back to Notting Hill. She lay in bed unable to sleep, wishing Father had a Miss Jones waiting for him at the Constitutional Club.

CHAPTER EIGHT

In her final year at Oxford, Prue came up to town occasionally. They met for theatre outings, joining the multitude for a sixpenny seat in the gods to see the current heart-throb, Lawrence Olivier, in something Shakespearian at The Old Vic. Bagging a claiming stool in the queue outside The Albert Hall for the last night of the Proms, Sir Malcolm Sargent conducting. Julia was unsure which she preferred: the good-natured Spartan headiness of the gods or the warm cosseting stalls.

Once or twice she was invited to an Oxford college summer ball when females were in short supply. An alien amongst the hedonistic clever, Julia dreaded the question, 'Which is your college?' Giving a truthful answer, she tried to make her job sound more impressive than it was: Secretary to the Director of the Commonwealth Institute of Entomology. It usually produced what she suspected to be a look of boredom in her transient partners and a feeling of regret in her. If only she had worked harder...

Weekends on her own she fed on the minds of others, walked through Hyde Park to Speakers' Corner, joining groups of dirty-mackintoshed men listening to the thoughts of the eclectic mix of orators, would-be prophets, tub-thumpers and religious fanatics. The fun of being able to heckle anonymously. Dingle and Michael Foot inspired and reaffirmed her pacifist and leftist tendencies. Julia had always admired those prepared to be 'agin the Government', a criticism her mother used of her and Jack when, as children, they had enjoyed being argumentative, questioning the status quo.

At a loose end one weekend, she joined the crowds thronging Waterloo Station to see off the Royal Family on the first part of their journey to South Africa aboard HMS *Vanguard*. It was a bridge-building exercise to unite and reassure those parts of the Commonwealth which had come to Britain's aid during the war, those loyalties and allegiances now wearing thin.

A flash image of the King's haunted eyes staring from the window of the limousine, a quick glance seen through the myriad moving heads in front of her, the same beseeching eyes of Father when he felt he couldn't cope. A thin, haggard face dwarfed by regalia, gold braid on his naval uniform engulfing the frail body, thick tan make-up reassuring the public that all was well; their monarch wasn't dying.

Reality was close behind; a man moaning, rubbing his erection against her bottom, the crowds dense and rigid, escape impossible. When she had tried to get out of his way her movement was interpreted as encouragement. Above the cheering, heaving, solid crowd Julia thought she heard a voice, 'Is that man bothering you?' and, emboldened by the knowledge that maybe out there was a knight in shining armour, she shouted,

'Yes,' and quickly turned to face her abuser. He was gone, lost in the crowd, his escape route planned through experience. She remembered his pale blue, watery eyes.

The job was going well, her colleagues were congenial and her work valued. She was enjoying London. Then something unexpected caught her off guard.

She had been working overtime, helping organise an international conference of entomologists coming to London to pool their fieldwork. Papers on their research arrived on Julia's desk for filing and copies were sent up to the top floor to be translated and edited before publication.

Copies taken up the narrow, steep carpetless, stairs to the book-cramped dark rooms on the upper floor where, cocooned from the outside world by their own brilliance, the four scientific translators worked. Elderly gentlemen, of whom Julia became fond, shuffling around in worn-out bedroom slippers, the room reeking of intoxicating oriental tobaccos. Between them they spoke fifty different languages.

The expert in Middle Eastern tribal tongues was a grand bearded White Russian for whom she saved the leftover milk after making the tea. It stank, hidden in the bottom drawer of the filing cabinet in Julia's office, until it was deemed sufficiently soured and solid, mildewed and matured to be eaten with his morning Russian tea.

The conference went well. Julia, her shorthand notebooks and pencils at the ready, sat at a small desk in the lecture theatre, struggling to keep abreast of all that was discussed, foreign accents difficult to interpret;

at the end of the day trying to make something comprehensible out of her almost unreadable Pitmans to hand to *The Scientific Press* and *The Lancet*. Her boss was happy. He suggested she took a long weekend break. As she hadn't seen her parents for some months she decided to go north for five days.

Her parents had been invited to Sunday lunchtime drinks with neighbours. Julia was included in the invitation. As she entered the drawing room, the view across the border country was obscured by a group of men talking, framed in the window. One in naval uniform, three rings of scrambled egg on his sleeve, his back to her...

Taking her arm, Julia's hostess had said, 'There is someone you must meet, he's staying with friends in Hexham,' and guided her towards the figure at the window. 'Hugh's at The Admiralty in London.'

On hearing his name he turned. Julia found his close proximity unsettling; she was reliving those first stirrings at twelve years old when she had sat on her favourite sun-drenched stone on the wall of the old kitchen garden and heard the words *'bella, bella.'*

She was tongue-tied but he put her at ease, asked about her job. He had bachelor chambers in Petty France, Palmer Street, near St. James's Park tube station opposite the Passport Office. He asked if she knew the area. She didn't and explained that she lived in hostel land.

He had been mildly humorous about the vibrations from the underground trains upsetting his tea, something a former resident, Milton, had not had to contend with. To keep the conversation going, Julia mentioned seeing the Royal Family at Waterloo Station at the start of their visit to South Africa.

'What a coincidence,' Hugh said. 'I was at Southampton on board *Vanguard* waiting for their arrival, accompanied the Royal Party to Cape Town.' He laughed, remembering something. He told her that Bill, a fellow officer, had availed himself of the overwhelming hospitality on offer when they arrived in South Africa, and within a week had become engaged, his bride to be an heiress to one of the finest Cape vineyards. 'He never looked back,' Hugh added.

Afterwards, Julia tried to dismiss the encounter. It had left her with a confused uneasy feeling, a yellow-dress yearning.

Two weeks later in Holland Park, the communal telephone rang. A shout: 'Pudge there's some bloke on the phone for you.'

It would be Father or one of her brothers.

Hugh was back in London; what about a show? Over the phone they decided on *Oklahoma* at the Theatre Royal in Drury Lane, Quaglinos for a meal afterwards.

A goodnight peck on the cheek. A phone call the following evening requesting a repeat performance. She had been walking on the surface of life quite contentedly and suddenly she was falling in. This was no studio photo of James Mason to be put under the pillow, this was real flesh and blood and she wasn't at all certain that she was ready for such intimacy.

Life was now happening too fast, becoming unreal. She thought of the unsecured scull, saw herself being swept away by a strong current, joining it, floundering in some ocean.

'Is there anything in particular you would like to see?' Hugh asked.

There he was, on time, the taxi's engine purring, meter ticking; self-assured, holding the door for her, chatting with the cab driver, at ease.

A couple of weeks previously, Prue had mentioned a play at The Globe by Christopher Fry, rave reviews, a Tennant Production in association with the Arts Council of Great Britain. *The Lady's Not for Burning* with a newcomer, Richard Burton, making his stage debut. Julia was bewitched by the performance and its message and assumed, mistakenly, that Hugh felt likewise.

When they said goodnight, he put his arms around her and kissed her gently on the lips. The closeness of him and the aphrodisiac smell of masculinity were pleasurable, giving the lie to the unwelcome violations she had come to expect.

Father had tried to warn her in his gentle way. Now, in hindsight, his sound advice on every subject had never been found wanting; at the time it was given, and with the impetuosity of youth, she had questioned it. On the subject of marriage, she rejected it.

Reluctant to say an unkind word about anyone Father had, on being told of her impending engagement, said: 'Be careful. There is no doubt he's in love with you but I feel he is not the type of man to make any woman really happy, least of all you.'

That was all he said but the accuracy of his judgement would be confirmed soon enough. Julia's memory hadn't got there yet, it was still basking in the euphoria of her engagement, the congratulations, the 'lucky you' from friends and the 'how did you manage that' from the bitchy.

Julia had been as surprised as they were. Just as she had been unable to see what her sister-in-law saw in David, she was at a loss to see what Hugh saw in her. Perhaps his love affair with naval ships named *Illustrious, Formidable, Indefatigable, Indomitable* had seen in her Endurance, another ship to command.

That she was about to participate in what was considered a good match had been of little consequence to Father. It certainly looked good on paper, top of the list of social engagements in the *Daily Telegraph*, and had probably impressed his friends.

That she was to marry a man of the world, twelve years her senior, whose good looks and uniform had overwhelmed her latent hormones, was now accepted. Everything was done to welcome the future son-in-law into the family fold.

The large country wedding. It was a crisp November day, not a cloud in a surreal blue sky, a re-enactment day of that long-remembered meet of the hunt. Sitting with her father in the chauffeured limousine on their way to the church, her veil held in place by force-fed freesias, he suddenly said, 'This doesn't feel like me. Does it feel like you?'

Julia had to admit it didn't and his answer was, 'Let's stop the car and go fishing.'

She knew it was a last desperate attempt to save her, to remind her of what was about to be severed.

Fishing was symbolic, it was one of the threads which had bound them through her childhood into womanhood. They enjoyed each other's company, a natural father–daughter relationship, but there was more to it than that, those threads that had endured for three-quarters of a century.

She could still feel his left arm holding her body, resisting the current, the river wanting to sweep her away. Standing behind her, his right hand guiding her right arm and the rod, teaching her to cast, that flick of the wrist which released the line from the spool with the rapid soft clicking whirr to take it skimming as far as possible, gently caressing the surface of the water to reach the still pool under the far bank where the trout were rising.

Those fishing expeditions were etched into both their minds. The choice of fly, which stretch of water to be fished first and that solitary quiet togetherness they both needed.

When the waters were running too deep for her or her waders, she sat on the bank watching as he, battered trilby, pipe in mouth, cast expertly. When a trout was landed, the shared acknowledgement of the beauty of the fish, those iridescent spotted markings and slithery feel, which made it difficult to hold before it was placed into the creel to slide over the bodies of those already caught. Above all, the smell, a freshwater smell, like all nature's smells, pungent and honest. Smell had always been her favourite sense.

A bedecked church awaited, well-wishers seated. They both knew without saying a word that it was too late and they would have to go through with it. Mother would not understand.

Mother had prided herself that there had never

been a cross word in their marriage; she was anchored to efficient domesticity, unable to lift up her eyes unto the hills. Father prided himself that he had kept it that way by acquiescence.

She remembered now her father's grey, gaunt face, his eyes withdrawn, the result of foregoing his usual pre-lunch bottle of whisky at the time he most needed it so he would not let her down on her wedding day. Julia had almost longed for the jolly, red-faced, unpredictable, embarrassing person she had grown to understand.

The wedding was a success, enjoyed and talked about afterwards. They walked down the aisle clutching each other. Father whispered, 'Remember they are all on your side,' and Julia felt an unaccustomed ripple of pleasure at being the centre of attention.

Prue was one of four bridesmaids, together with two other school friends and a little-known cousin whom Mother felt it would be diplomatic to ask. Their dresses were understated pale blue; pink sharkskin still haunted Julia. They left before the party in the evening, as was the custom, guests seeing off the bride and groom in a shower of teatime confetti and hope. As the car drove away, Julia was overwhelmed by a feeling of isolation.

According to the mores of the day, the man she had married had been a good husband. A material provider. On the practical side he was a genius, no technical problem beyond his knowledge and ability to solve; indeed, his philosophy was 'the impossible takes a little longer'. But he was unable to accept that the human brain, that unattractive grey lump of tissue, that vulnerable part of man's make up, contained a cornucopia of feelings. She wondered now to which part of her he had actually said 'I will' at the marriage service. He was oblivious to what was going on in her head.

His understanding of her virgin state had been another thing. His gentleness, patience, respect and love as he coaxed and caressed her unawakened body had been a rare privilege. She longed for the evenings and night-time and the closeness and smell of his naked body and the ecstasy and blossoming of physical love.

When she looked back at her sexual flowering, she remembered as a very small child of three or four hearing her grandfather say to Thompson, when deciding which stallions to put with which mares, 'Put the old stallion with the two young fillies, he'll teach them a thing or two.'

Her father had not been the only person to warn of the impending mismarriage of minds. Comments Hugh made during their engagement bore significance later: small things, criticism of how she dressed. Even her brothers' behaviour found disfavour; the fact that they laughed and enjoyed life appeared to upset Hugh. It niggled Julia at the time but seemed unimportant.

To avoid putting a spanner in the works, her father-in-law left his comments until after the ceremony, anxious to see his second son wed in order to produce much longed-for grandchildren which his elder son had failed to provide. He patted her on the shoulder and said, 'Good girl, you'll deal with it.' Something about the whole world being out of step except him was lost on her at the time. With the optimism of youth and love, she felt there was nothing to fear.

Reared on a diet of tolerance, good humour and a self-effacing ability to have a good laugh at herself, the realisation that these qualities were lacking in the person to whom she had entrusted the rest of her life had come as a shock. Julia now realised that there was a lot to be said for shacking up together before marriage; you got a warning. But when Julia was young, particularly if you were middle class, it turned you into a social pariah, made you not nice to know. The aristocracy and the working class happily got away with it; the aristocracy did it openly and the working class pretended they were married.

The drip, drip of irrationality and unpredictability interspersed with bouts of normal behaviour caught Julia out. She had tripped whilst carrying a hot teapot, fallen, scalded her hand and hurt her head on the corner of the bureau. Hugh had ignored her, angered that she might have damaged the bureau, a family heirloom. Raised in the age of marital stoicism, Julia was confused; and there was her father to protect – he would never, ever say 'I told you so.'

Father must have suspected that something was wrong; once he had asked and she had said how blissfully happy she was. It was the first and only time in her life that she lied to him.

David and his wife produced a son within a year of marriage, a grandson for Father. Julia felt pressured by Hugh's family and, just before her twenty-second birthday, produced a daughter.

She heard the click of the lock on the cage in her head.

CHAPTER NINE

Ambition, that eager desire for distinction, power, fame and money, is a curious phenomenon. Animals possess it in a different form, wanting to be top of the pecking order, but humans are capable of reasoning and those with happiness in mind should learn to reject it as a false god, a double-edged sword which, unless you accept its down side – the abandonment of contentment – is a cruel master.

Hugh was ambitious. Julia was unsure what drove him. It may have been the realisation that he was not going to make First Sea Lord that persuaded him to resign from the Royal Navy and look for acclaim in other directions.

The post-war, short-term, government-sponsored engineering degree course at Cambridge, open to those returning from active service, slotted well into his carefully planned use of time between asking Julia to marry him and the wedding. He had excelled, been awarded top marks. The business world beckoned. His good looks, self-assurance, technical know-how and gift of the gab brought a flood of offers.

Julia's mind went into cold storage, lost in Hugh's focused pursuit of being a success in a material world to which Julia knew she did not belong.

His first appointment with a city export and import company, representing major British firms in the Middle and Far East, offered good prospects but a meagre salary.

Julia was beginning to have disquieting thoughts that marriage was not the be-all and end-all of life that her parents' generation had cracked it up to be. Her freedom, so willingly given, was now imprisoned in the stultifying social niceties of suburbia. Not any old suburbia but affluent, five- and six-bedroom suburbia, with nannies in blue-and-white striped uniforms from Harrods, as well as gardeners and children who were discouraged from building sewage systems and using them in their parents' large, manicured gardens.

The small house they rented predated its smarter and grander neighbours. It had once been the gardener's cottage of an estate which, pre-war, had allowed its lands to be designated ripe for development.

Although they could not afford it, Hugh suggested a nanny. They now had a second child, the longed-for son. Hugh, Julia suspected, had not suggested a nanny to help her. It was more a status thing to give her more time to entertain his business friends. Julia declined the offer. She enjoyed having her home to herself, hated the intrusion of someone living in; there had been too much of that during wartime. Like Father, she enjoyed her own company and was happy to make do with occasional daily help. When required for a walk-on part in one of Hugh's theatrical career productions, she learned her lines and stage directions well. In conversations with wives of senior management, the most common topic was what their husbands had been up to during the war.

These wives were older than she, proper service wives, who had suffered separation. They had been called up themselves, hearty, confident ATS, VADs, and Wrens, doing men's work packing and maintaining torpedoes in Inverarey, the clever ones decoders at Bletchley Park. The company secretary's wife, a small cheery woman with a shiny complexion and raised veins in her cheeks, reminded Julia of a robin redbreast, darting to and fro, inquisitive. She had been a Land Girl on an arable farm in Norfolk. Julia felt a usurper in their company, encroaching on their real experiences of war, a schoolgirl amongst them. She was certain that it hadn't been their husbands who had taught them how to kiss.

She took the trouble to find out about Hugh's wartime experiences, so when confronted with, 'Hugh was in the Navy, wasn't he?' she was able to reply with confidence, 'Arctic Convoys in 1943,' whilst her mind was on one of those mercy missions taking food and military supplies to Russian allies; hazardous cruel journeys of frostbite and death up to Murmansk and Archangel in the long dark winters of the Northern Hemisphere. The ships in danger of capsizing from the weight of the ice forming on superstructures, the continual hacking away at ice to keep the ship upright. Shark packs of lurking U-boats beneath the waves waiting to strike. Ninety-eight merchant ships sunk, twenty-one naval convoy vessels lost, sucked down to their resting place on the seabed with thousands of men, the blessing of the anaesthetizing icy water giving them a quick death.

Another voice cornering her: 'I hear your husband was in the Far East at the end of the war?' Julia's reply: 'Yes, with the British Pacific Fleet, one of the task force of the American Third Fleet under the command of Admiral Halsey.' Seeing Hugh's description of his aircraft carrier, the heat rising from the four-inch-thick steel flight deck so intense that eggs and bacon could be fried on its surface and the ship's cat had to be fitted with paw protectors to enable it to come up on deck.

This time the enemy came from the sky. Tiny specks of aircraft so small they could be mistaken for skylarks by a sailor on watch dreaming of home. Kamikaze Japanese airmen, their minds conditioned by patriotism and reverence for a divine emperor. Screeching raptors dispatched to incinerate themselves and their prey in an Armageddon of destruction and glory.

The final obscenity of man's condition, the secret instruction to the British fleet from Washington to stand back from Japan, clearing America's way to drop the bomb from Enola Gay, obliterating half a million women and children, in the name of freedom, democracy, the Stars and Stripes, and God.

The carrier's guns hushed, her new cargo the sick skeletal bodies from the Japanese death camps, Australian prisoners of war and civilians captured at Singapore almost half a decade before, lying in rows on the flight deck, hanging on, hoping to make it back to Sydney.

Did the company secretary's wife, sipping her martini, ever doubt?

All that human displacement and misery. Could war ever be justified? Could the deaths of sixty-two million people and the suffering of their families be balanced against the saving, an eighth of that number from the Nazis? If Chamberlain had not declared war and allowed Hitler a free run, would the suffering have been statistically less?

And here she was, fifty years on, still worrying as Blair made his pseudo-Churchillian speeches and oversaw the slaughter of yet more innocents in the quest by one half of the human race to be understood by the other half. Where had all the statesmen gone? Those wise, fine-tuned minds, the privileged products of our top universities. Gone to the City everyone? Had they been seduced by the Big Bang?

She could do nothing to change things; it was not her responsibility. Better to allow her memory to try and make sense of those years of dutiful, unsuccessful motherhood.

There had been the miscarriage, a common occurrence happening to hundreds of women daily, another statistic, but when it was happening to you, it didn't feel like a statistic.

They had been up to London for the company dinner, a formal affair which aspiring managers took as a barometer of their prospects. The closer you were seated to the chairman, the higher your chances of being made a director.

Julia searched the seating plan, unable to find her name. It never occurred to her that she might be on the top table and she had thought it presumptuous even to look. She was beginning to sense that she was playing a game for which others knew the rules but she didn't.

Hugh wasn't at hand to help her. He was too busy

talking to the right people. A wife whom Julia hadn't known came up to her and, unsmilingly, said, 'You are on the Chairman's right.' She sensed hostility, had an uneasy feeling that she was entering an unfamiliar world of petty jealousy and intrigue. Smiling, she thanked the woman and asked which was her husband?

'Oh, I thought you knew. He's the company accountant.' Without pointing him out, the woman walked away.

Julia liked the chairman. Easy to talk to, they shared a love of the countryside and field sports; they laughed together. Hugh, sitting opposite, gave her anxious glances. Did she sense mistrust? There were cold stares from the wives. The chairman called across the table to Hugh, 'You're a lucky man, Hugh,' and looked at her. Hugh heard but ignored the remark.

Towards the end of the evening, Julia felt unwell. Too much to drink, she thought, but in the car driving home, she was aware of a trickling down the inside of her leg. Nothing to worry about. They would be home shortly and she would rest the following day. She didn't mention it to Hugh; he probably did not want to be reminded that she was pregnant again. His career had had a good evening.

In the morning Julia did mention it. Hugh replied, 'I've got a busy day. Don't phone the office. I shall be in meetings all morning. I'll phone at noon to see how you are.'

Julia drove their daughter to nursery school, young John on the back seat. On her return, she had difficulty lifting him out of the car and decided to go straight to bed, taking him with her. She began to feel vulnerable, not for herself but for the children. She wished noon would hurry up, when Hugh would ring, but when it came and he didn't, she dared not phone him. She was beginning to read his mood swings and become fearful of his reactions.

By one o'clock she knew she would lose the baby. She felt it coming, rushed to the bathroom but, unable to get there in time, deposited what looked like a pound of fresh liver with gristle on the new, pale yellow, landing carpet. Her first concern was the carpet; Hugh set great store on material possessions. She flushed the liver down the loo, remembered Mother's advice about blood stains – salt and cold water – and got down on her hands and knees and did her best to scrub the carpet clean, hoping it would dry before Hugh's return. Perhaps he would be held up in traffic.

John slept through the drama. Sarah needed to be collected. Julia was no longer thinking straight. She should have phoned the school. They would have helped, but her immediate thought had been neighbours. They really had none with whom they were intimate.

She remembered the elderly couple who lived in a large rambling house with an ill-kept garden three doors away. She had met them whilst taking the children for a walk. They were friendly and Julia liked them immediately. She believed they were titled but preferred it not to be known. She had heard tittle-tattle; they had recently experienced their own mini-drama, apocryphal and reported with glee and malice by neighbours. They had given a party, a fairly big do. The housekeeper had drunk most of the gin, substituting water

109

and everyone had been too polite to say anything; the evening had not gone well. Julia had warmed to them when she heard this story and it was perhaps this that persuaded her to phone and ask if they could possibly collect a child from school. They neither hesitated nor questioned why. Julia left the front door unlocked and, exhausted, went to bed and slept.

They were still in the house, looking after the children, when Hugh returned from London. She heard raised voices downstairs. She wanted to get up and explain but felt too weak. Hugh appeared annoyed that Julia had invited strangers into the house. He took it as a slur upon himself that she had sought outside help. She had dented the brilliant husband image he put on to impress everyone except her; he mumbled something about disloyalty. The damp patch on the carpet went unnoticed.

The following day, determined not to make an issue out of what had happened, she arose early to test herself physically, for she knew there would be little sympathy on offer.

The only words addressed to her since his arrival home the previous evening had been at breakfast.
'Glad you're feeling better. I've got another busy day, may be late home.'

Hugh was with the City company four years, rose rapidly to the post of managing director, and was now looking for further challenges.

He was headhunted. In the late fifties headhunting was a new concept, companies created to flatter the successful, tempt them for a large fee, playing on people's imagined worth and aspirations.

Julia was expected to participate. Wives were interviewed to see if they were up to their husband's job. For wives, there were no terms of reference, no job specification. She imagined diplomacy might be high on the list of requirements, had there been any, unpaid corporate entertaining, or just someone who knew how to hold a knife and fork correctly.

Hugh learned to play each interview by ear, giving them what he knew they wanted to hear. Julia decided that the best course of action was not to treat any of it too seriously. Political correctness was unheard of but class and how you voted were. Julia's candid response to questions probably amused. Her outspokenness may have been the catalyst which brought Hugh a succession of high-powered offers but Julia would never know; any contribution she made went unrecognised.

Hugh finally accepted the post of export director with a prestigious, internationally renowned British manufacturer based in the North West. In his eyes he had made it; Julia was pleased for him. In her eyes, the move a hundred and sixty miles north would bring her closer to her spiritual home, the northern hills and its granite people. Still a hundred and fifty miles from her roots, but at least they were going in the right direction.

Julia would miss the places she had grown to love. The soft, gentle beauty of Sussex and Kent, visits with the children to Bodiam Castle, Petworth, Sissinghurst and Knole House, where she had pulled three-year-old Sarah by her reins along the polished oak floors of long galleries, the child gazing upwards at the walls, taking in the Van Dycks, Gainsboroughs and Reynolds which would become part of her memories.

Now, on a salary commensurate with their former Surrey neighbours, they were ambitious in their choice of home and put in an offer for a large, dilapidated Victorian house in two acres of land on the outskirts of a market town. The former owners were an elderly couple, local worthies who had recently died.

Nothing had been done to the house for thirty years and Julia saw it as a challenge. It had the same smell as her old childhood home, the tell-tale mustiness of fungi and dry rot. Hugh was less enthusiastic and would have settled for a smaller, well-maintained, character-less property. It was one of Julia's rare victories but she had an unexpected ally.

Having looked around the gardens, they were crossing the lawn to return to the house when they were approached by a lady in her late fifties. She apologised, hoped she wasn't speaking out of turn and introduced herself as Elsie, daily help to the previous owners for twenty years.

'Will you be needing help in the house?' her voice a gentle Lancashire burr.

Julia immediately said yes.

That evening Hugh said, 'You know nothing about her.'

Julia would soon discover that God had sent her a guardian angel, a Nellie and Thelma rolled into one. Of course, God knew what was in store.

CHAPTER TEN

Could the death of a child be more distressing than witnessing the suffering of an infant pleading for help? Julia hadn't thought so at the time but now, so many years later, the question resurfaced. She was not an advocate of life at any price, did not support pro-life groups who kept severely premature babies alive artificially, whatever their future.

Her childhood close to nature had hardened her. Animals bereaved, standing sentinel over an inert small body, allowing a peaceful drift into coma, instinct telling a mother that there was nothing to be done. Returning at dusk to make certain, walking away.

She was given the task of getting rid of the numerous, unwanted, day-old farm kittens found in the cat's maternity ward of warm ashes beneath the huge central heating boiler at the old home. Holding down those tiny, squirming, protesting, sightless bodies in a bucket of water until gradually movement ceased, Julia had felt relieved that their suffering and her guilt were over.

They were aware of the toddler rash behind John's knees. Chamomile sufficed. Friends were reassuring, 'Childhood eczema. He'll grow out of it.' His beauty, blonde hair, blue eyes and perfect skin were much commented upon. In cafés, waitresses cooed and carried him into the kitchens to show him off to other staff.

A year later that gentle innocent was invaded by demons, his body encased in raw weeping extrusions, small hands gloved to prevent the tearing of skin. There was no ease to the torment, a body in a frenzy of scratching, wild eyes beseeching, demented, staring. Night after night she sat at his bedside, gently stroking, easing and comforting until exhaustion and the release of sleep took over.

Lotions and bandages. Soaking in the bath to dampen the stiff, matter-encrusted dressings to remove them less painfully. Endless trips to specialists and hospitals searching for answers, doctors trying but unable to help. The arrival of that other affliction asthma, in league with the eczema, taking turns to torture. 'I've had a good fortnight, now it's your turn.' When the eczema receded, the asthma stepped in to fill the gap. The coughing and fighting for breath, the over-use of nebulisers.

Hugh's patience was unexpected. He took his turn to comfort during sleepless nights, though his mind was dealing with pressures elsewhere. Julia admired him for it. He showed a compassion which he denied her and Sarah. He understood physical suffering but could not accept that minds could be ill too, scratching away in distress. His assessment: you were either on the ball or mad, and you had to decide which you wanted to be.

Elsie became Julia's tower of strength. Her love for both children and her compassion for John were the crutches on which Julia depended. Elsie understood suffering. She had done suffering as a child, learnt to live with deprivation and poverty. Coal mines and cotton mills were the backcloth of her upbringing. Her father was a Lancashire miner and her mother worked in the cotton mills of Oldham from the age of thirteen. It was from her mother that Elsie inherited her revolutionary streak, witnessing her early struggles for better sanitary arrangements for women mill hands.

Elsie's God was socialism and she was not going to break faith. She had absorbed working-class solidarity, and the physical stigmata that go with it, at an early age. The humped back and twisted leg bore witness to childhood TB and rickets and walking five miles with her siblings to a neighbouring town when rumour had it that potatoes could be bought for a farthing cheaper.

At eighteen Elsie had married Jim, a miner at the same colliery as her father. Thirty-five years on, after a lifetime underground, the dust from that black gold had permeated his lungs. Childless, they lived to the sound of coughing in a semi-detached council house on the outskirts of town, a tiny palace lovingly maintained. Hugh and Julia's offspring became the children Jim and Elsie never had.

Hugh complained that Julia and Elsie were getting too close.

A specialist in Harley Street was recommended. People were beginning to talk of steroids as a magical cure-all. Julia made the train journey south without Hugh. Strangers stared and looked away, disfigurement in a child a threat. John was already familiar with this strange anomaly in adult behaviour. At school his peers accepted him for his gentleness and joviality; it

115

was the older children who showed their cruelty.

'We're not going to sit next to you, your skin's rotten.'

Julia liked the consultant, she believed in him. He said he could help. Yes, steroids may be the answer but there might be problems later in life. Later in life was a long way off. Anything to alleviate the present suffering.

'In my opinion, it is as important for your child to have steroids as it is for a diabetic to have insulin,' clinched it, and Julia entered into that Faustian agreement. At the time, had she accepted it for their son's sake or for her own? Later, when payback time had come early and his immune system gave up any pretence of being active, she couldn't answer that truthfully.

The resurfacing of two scribbled childish poems tucked inside old letters brought it all back. Pencilled, poignant pleas about matters he was unable to discuss with his parents. To read them again was a shock. She couldn't remember how she had reacted at the time.

Under earth high ceilings,
Pausing, meditating,
Overwhelmed by downtrodden feelings,
Seeking revelations.
Seeking after lost concentration,
Searching the field of medication,
Grovelling for some kind of healing,
Finally degraded and kneeling.

The second must surely have disturbed her at its first reading.

From nowhere thoughts arise,
Deep depressing and hidden,
From somewhere relief must come,
But from where, from whom or how?
These feeling that worry so, on what have they
been founded?
I as the victim do not know,
Confusion ousts all reason.
Just yesterday, not a care,
But today it has all swelled,
All I want is peace, freedom,
Freedom from worry and rule.
And they claim they understand
'Think of others worse than you,
Fight and keep to present arms!
What are you trying to do?
Bring an end before it is due.'

The improvement was miraculous; the eczema
was still present but manageable. The asthma attacks
became less severe, enabling John to walk upstairs
normally. No more stops halfway up the stairs to rest,
whilst Sarah raced ahead three steps at a time.

Hugh's progress up the greasy pole took him away
from home more, trips abroad lasting months rather
than weeks. He was on the up and up and Julia was
happier during his absences than she had been for a
long time. She was released from criticism and the
burden of corporate entertaining, having to invite
people for whom she had little respect into her home,
fearing that if she refused some big contract might be

in jeopardy.

Now she had time to devote her energies to the ne-
glected, rambling house which was a half-recompense
for the loss of her childhood home. Apprenticed to
Elsie, she learned plastering, painting and papering.
The damp, dingy, billiard room, abandoned and used
as storage space for decades, was transformed into a
playroom where the children and their friends could
roller skate when Hugh was away. In defiance, Julia
painted each wall a different colour, brash fashionable orange and turquoise. She bought black-and-
white posters of an up-and-coming group called The
Beatles. Hugh would disapprove.

On the day of his return from one trip, Sarah was
allowed the day off school to go with Julia in the company's chauffeur-driven Rolls to Manchester Airport to
meet his plane and have grown-up lunch in the VIP
restaurant.

It was to be a treat, Julia hoping for a happy family
reunion. That first glance as he emerged from the ar-
rivals exit made Julia instantly regret bringing their
daughter; she recognised his mood. Although she
was beginning to find the strength to deal with his
bad temper, she knew it would be their daughter who
would bear the brunt of it. He hardly acknowledged
Sarah's presence.

They ordered lunch, Julia requesting a small
portion of something which she hoped Sarah could
manage. The child couldn't, and left half of it. Hugh's
nastiness surfaced, back in control, damned if he was
going to see food wasted. Julia implored him with her
eyes but his were unseeing, oblivious to her message,

blind to the hurt he was inflicting. The silent sobbing and distress were an additional irritant to him as Sarah tried to swallow another mouthful to please; her childish guilt that she was responsible for everything going wrong.

Julia tried to lessen the disillusionment when they were alone in the Ladies and said, 'Mummy didn't enjoy it very much either.'

Sarah replied, 'Daddy isn't as nice as I thought he was.'

They drove home from the airport in silence. Sitting in the back, Julia caught the chauffeur's eyes in the mirror and saw sympathy in them. They were her father's eyes, capable of speaking without a word being said. In order to break the tension he asked, 'Was it a successful trip, sir?' and was rewarded with a grunt.

His name was George. He was one of the perks of Hugh's job, on call when needed, a friend and disciplinarian to the directors' children whom he chauffeured daily to the elitist private school which had been recommended by the chairman. So as not to rock the boat of Hugh's career, Julia had abandoned any thought of the local village school.

That night Julia played Judas. She longed for his lovemaking, the tenderness and understanding which he gave her body but denied her mind. Her whole being in ecstasy, she remembered murmuring something about a condom but it had got beyond that for both of them. Her mind repeated Donne's elegy to his mistress, 'Licence those roving hands, and let them go, before, behind, between, above, below.' By morning she knew she was pregnant.

Elsie was overjoyed by the news; an addition to her family.

It was a good pregnancy. Julia sailed through it, her looks blossoming as they had with the other two. She continued to entertain Hugh's business friends until she sensed that the enormity of her belly was becoming an embarrassment to some of the Middle Eastern businessmen who were more inclined to keep their women under wraps at such times.

She was going to have this baby at home; she did not wish to be overlooked again by overworked midwives. There was a mild altercation with her GP, who said it was unwise at her age, advice which Julia already knew bore no relation to nature. She was only thirty-eight.

Father had had a couple of old mares put to the stallion, their ages the human equivalent of sixty-four. They had dropped and nurtured their foals, no problem. Homo sapiens' breeding patterns, Julia convinced herself, evolved not from nature, but social convenience.

To reassure her GP, Julia engaged a midwife-cum-nurse through a London nursing agency who would deliver the baby and stay a fortnight. This good soul arrived two days before the baby was due. She looked very old, her tiny, thin, frame brittle, as though some unforeseen force had sucked all moisture from it. Pressure wrapped, hermetically sealed in a grey uniform, ankles protruding like sticks from beneath the hem, the stiff white headdress resting on her eyebrows, apron, collar and cuffs over-starched, crackling when she moved.

Hugh was concerned. Would she be capable of

holding a baby, let alone delivering one? But her references were from the highest in the land, extolling her excellence. Julia's immediate impression was that she was disappointed in them. This was not the grand domain to which she had become accustomed; no nanny or cook and the brash playroom/nursery not to her taste.

It had been made clear by the agency that demarcation lines were important. She was there to deliver the baby and keep it alive for a fortnight. Elsie had never heard such rubbish and announced that she was not going to kowtow to anyone who was not prepared to muck in.

The terms of employment were rigid: no duties other than those immediately connected to the baby, and she was to be called Nurse McCracken at all times. She instructed Elsie to sterilise everything within sight as if entering a house of pestilence and Elsie took it as a personal insult.

It was an infringement of rules which solved Julia's concerns.

Jim was unwell. Elsie had gone home early and Nurse McCracken kindly offered to walk the three hundred yards to collect John from a birthday party. It was January, there had been a hard night frost and those parts of the pavement where trees had denied the sun access, remained frozen. Nurse McCracken slipped and broke her tiny, fragile wrist.

It was one of the few occasions when Julia felt justified in phoning Hugh at work. She was torn between her concern for Nurse McCracken and the baby, four days overdue, which, by hanging in there, was giving them breathing space.

Under certain circumstances Hugh could be relied upon and this was one of them. It was like planning a naval operation: ring the agency, explain what had happened and request a replacement. The agency was justifiably frosty and unsympathetic; strict rules had been broken but, as always, Hugh pacified and charmed someone on the end of the phone, as he did everyone except those who lived with him. Yes, they would send a stand-in, but it would be in two days' time. In the meantime, would he please send Nurse McCracken back to London and pay all expenses?

Mother was sent for, a difficult decision. Keeping an eye on Father's drinking had become her full-time occupation. She agreed a maximum of three days or until the new midwife arrived.

And arrive she did, as promised, two days later. Julia looked out of the dining-room window to see, walking up the drive, a young, plump, rosy-cheeked, dishevelled person carrying a battered suitcase and wearing ankle socks.

They hit it off immediately. Her name was Mary, Irish Catholic, the eldest of nine children. All she had ever wanted to do since childhood was deliver babies and this was her first assignment since training, though she admitted to some unauthorised experience delivering younger siblings. She was amusing, light-hearted and helpful, her whole philosophy the antithesis of Nurse McCracken's. Childbirth should be fun and Mary was determined that her first solo effort was going to be just that.

Mother, seeing Julia was in safe hands, left that

same afternoon.

Their second daughter, having sensed happier thoughts on the outside through the placenta, decided that evening to chance it and leave the warmth of her trouble-free world and enter a troublesome one. Mary hardly had time to wash her hands, let alone sterilise anything. She insisted that Hugh be present, which was not considered the done thing for fathers of his generation, but his presence had, in a strange way, added to the jolly repartee and trusting, bawdy, natal banter between Mary and Julia.

'Come on, you can push harder than that.'

'What the bloody hell do you think I'm doing?'

The children had been denied welcoming their new, unwashed, bloodied sister. Immediately after the birth Hugh quickly gained control, and put a stop to their boisterous excitement, unable to appreciate what was in Julia's mind nor accept her assurance that she was not tired and wanted them with her. His 'leave your mother alone' attitude left them deflated, that precious never-to-be-repeated moment gone forever.

Having made the brief acquaintance of his latest child, Hugh left early the following morning. A meeting in London on which, if he was to be believed, the whole Western capitalist system depended. Julia was grateful for his absence; it gave her the freedom to welcome her newborn into the world in the way she wanted.

As the sound of the company limo receded, Mary produced a half-bottle of Irish whiskey from her nursing bag to wet the baby's head   .

Ten days after Anna's birth, Hugh was due to go

abroad for some weeks on business.

Even Elsie's love and support failed to withstand the grey cloud which slowly descended upon Julia, obliterating all reasonable thoughts. That horrendous, insidious invasion of her mind by the fearsome black hound of gloom.

When the children were difficult and grumpy, Julia chided them and laughed, 'Whoops, you've got a big black dog inside. Let's get rid of him,' and tickled them till their giggles were in charge. How easy it would be if adults could be treated in the same way, but the black hound was not easily assuaged. He bit the throat and wouldn't let go, shaking the mind like a rat until he was in total control. Self-doubt and despair were accepted and every thought and action open to his ridicule.

Julia did not recognise him immediately. She just thought she was losing concentration, the self-doubt normal. His warning signs were petty, insignificant, the feeling of distance from the world around her and a reluctance to push the pram across the road, her senses unsure from which direction the traffic came.

She walked into town to buy a face flannel for Hugh, who was leaving the following morning. The choice was between maroon, green, blue or white. Julia chose maroon. Halfway home, the doubt set in. It was the wrong colour, Hugh wouldn't like it. She retraced her steps and exchanged it for blue, giving some feeble excuse. She'd hardly left the shop before doubt over-whelmed her again and she returned to the counter for the green one and felt like a small child about to be chastised.

She knew it should have been the white one but

was too frightened to go back. During the afternoon the anxiety became obsessive; she dreaded the sound of Hugh's key in the door. He was surprised when she greeted him with, 'I've bought you a green face flannel.'

His reply: 'A white one would have done,' finally tipped her over the edge.

Perhaps the precursor had been an incident the previous day, the trigger which had upset her already fragile mind. Hugh had been packing for his trip and misplaced his nail scissors; he immediately blamed Sarah. She must have taken them for cutting out.

'Go to your room and find them.'

At eight years old, being accused of something you haven't done had yet to be accepted as part of growing up. There were tears and denials and, when the scissors were eventually found in a compartment of Hugh's suitcase, there was no apology.

It was Sarah's helplessness which made Julia go into the drawing room and kick the grandfather clock with such force that the mahogany lower case split. Her remorse was instantaneous. Craftsmanship and love had gone into making this beautiful object by one William Tickle Senior of Newcastle in 1723; it had belonged to Hugh's grandfather. Now it had been subjected to a childish temper tantrum by a woman who was unable to communicate with her husband.

Hugh's assessment of the situation was understandable; his wife was unstable, had lost her mind. But Julia's mind knew exactly the reason for its behaviour. Hugh was mentally abusing something she loved and she was going to abuse something he loved. It was simple. Julia's mind, in its confused state, was seeing certain things more clearly. It understood that Sarah was bearing the brunt of her father's displeasure, his sarcasm, the constant 'don'ts', his built-in disapproval of the human race now being visited upon his first-born. The child was the one person least able to deal with it, her sensitivity and trust a barrier, working against her emotional defence mechanism.

Julia knew she must remove Sarah from the firing line. She mentioned boarding school and Hugh agreed. Julia's own cowardice in not leaving him was buried beneath her burden of dual loyalties.

Elsie guessed all was not well. Julia longed to confide in her but felt it would be disloyal to Hugh. It was her secret unhappiness and she had no wish to infect others. She wept daily and alone. The children noticed her lack of fun and light-heartedness and showed concern and love beyond their years. She kept going, coping with the bad attacks of asthma and eczema and sleep-less nights, staying in bed and sleeping during the day when Elsie was in the house.

Elsie, no fool, insisted she seek medical help, but Julia doubted that she would receive understanding from her doctor. He might be one of Hugh's 'pull your-self together' brigade. But he listened sympathetically and prescribed a new drug: Valium. It became Julia's crutch.

By the time Hugh returned, Julia was almost on an even keel and did not mention her lapse, but kept taking the pills. He was full of his success; a further four weeks of business trips to the States were in the pipeline and Julia would be expected to accompany him, together with the chairman and his wife.

The itinerary was daunting: being entertained by and entertaining strangers from Boston, Chicago, Vancouver to Los Angeles, staying at the smartest hotels. Other wives would have been over the moon. Julia thought, 'If I can't get a face flannel right what hope for an entire wardrobe?' She felt out of her depth, happiest in old familiar clothes, anything sophisticated was dressing up to go on stage with the added anxiety that she may forget her lines.

Life was becoming a big act. Julia would have liked to ask the wives of other directors for guidance. They were much more into this sort of thing, but she knew sour grapes were part of their agenda. She sensed it at those company Christmas 'dos' when the chairman stood up and said, 'This company has always prided itself that we are one big, happy family,' a statement which would later prove to be way off the mark.

Elsie and Jim, now well-acquainted with eczema and asthmatic attacks, offered to live in whilst they were away. Dot, Elsie's youngest sister, would join them for extra support. Sarah would be in her first term at boarding school and baby Anna had already accepted Elsie as her real mother.

In panic, Julia cobbled together a wardrobe of clothes which didn't really suit her.

Flying the Atlantic and her first visit to America should have been memorable, but Valium dented her perception. She passed through the airports and hotels of Boston, Chicago, Vancouver in a state of torpor. Only when they reached The Ambassadors Hotel in Los Angeles did her mind clear. She started to enjoy the heady luxury of her surroundings. Seduced by the hotel boutiques, beauty salon, swimming pool and Tony Bennett at the Coconut Grove.

Years later, under very different circumstances, she would vividly recall every detail of those trips to California.

It was the forerunner of many months of world travel, waving the flag for British manufacturing. Julia became quite good at it, an unpaid company ambassadress versed in the complexities of hydroelectric schemes, the oil industry and centrifuges. It was the small talk when lunching with the wives that she found difficult and isolating.

Hugh managed to say 'well done' once or twice and commented on her ability to get on with everyone. Those war years were paying off again.

The chairman wrote a personal letter, thanking her for her hard work on behalf of the company, complimenting her on her ability to say the diplomatic thing at the right time.

It was when Julia said the right thing to the wrong person that their lives fell apart.

CHAPTER ELEVEN

Somewhere in the box room, Julia still had the photos of those heady days when they had been top of the heap. They lay, with those of Father, waiting to be rediscovered and their contents remembered.

She could hear again Mother's impatient voice, 'Go and look it up.'

'Dissent': a word without guidelines. To Mother, dissent had been straightforward, its meaning specific. She called it being 'agin' the government, but to Julia it was like loyalty, challenging, open to interpretation according to circumstances. The image of an elderly gentleman, a dissenter, a victim of Nazi oppression manhandled by a couple of black heavies in dark glasses, who looked like nightclub bouncers. A flickered image thrown from a TV screen and half-caught, a Labour Party Conference, rekindling the word in her mind.

Julia's own dissent years earlier had been at small-town level, unrecorded, but its consequences life changing.

She had sensed Hugh's withdrawal some weeks earlier. He was lacking his usual self-confidence and built-in conviction that he was always right. He was feeling uneasy about something. She put it down to pressure of work. For some months the company had been negotiating a merger with one of its major competitors, buying out the shareholders and betraying their workforce, wheeler-dealing in lives.

Hugh voted with the board for the merger, unaware at the time of its close association with the arms trade which had been hidden by the chairman in his cleverly worded, half-truth statement to the board. When Hugh uncovered the real source of his family's future income, he uncharacteristically mentioned it to Julia, and Julia mentioned her concern to the MD's wife at their weekly get-together over coffee. A casual comment over cream cakes at Betty's.

Two days later Hugh returned home early. It was a Thursday, Anna's after-school ballet class day. He had been asked to clear his desk and leave the company by lunchtime the following day. No explanation given. At the time, Julia didn't connect what was happening to him with anything she might have said. When no other reason was forthcoming she assumed that it was her fault. Of course, she could never know; boardroom intrigues were kept under wraps, no insight articles in *The Times*, no Wikileaks then, that might affect the share price.

There was no golden goodbye, no severance pay. Hugh would be given half a year's salary if he went quietly. That men were the providers was the ethos on which he had been reared. The stark realisation that, approaching fifty, he may be on the scrap heap, unable to restart a career, was humiliating. Fine if you were still being headhunted, but if you had lost your job and no one was prepared to tell you why, you were seen as yesterday's man.

Hugh was prepared to go quietly in return for six months of financial breathing space. Julia was not. Her adrenalin went into overdrive, anger took over. She got in the car that evening and drove to the chairman's home. Hugh's shortcomings as husband and father were overridden by Julia's certain knowledge that in business dealings his integrity was flawless, his ethical values could not be bought. His word was still his bond.

The front door was unlocked; she walked straight in. The chairman and his wife were giving a small dinner party. She heard the buzz of agreeable conversation and laughter coming from the dining room, a beautiful room, tasteful, the set of Gillow chairs giving it local provenance. It was a room Julia knew well, where she had helped the chairman's wife entertain and flatter business associates.

Her anger made her articulate, sidetracked her normal reticence. 'Betrayal … shabby treatment of a decent man … hypocritical claptrap of those one happy family speeches …' She was a tigress protecting her wounded mate.

Vaguely familiar, staring, shocked faces; Julia's vision blurred by anger making them unrecognisable. Forks poised in midair, returned to plates. She wondered whether they might send for the police but knew instinctively that they would not: too much bad publicity.

Realising that she would not easily be placated, the guests had left quietly. Julia was glad they had heard. After ten minutes her adrenalin surge abated but the anger remained; it was with her still. Offered a cup of coffee, she refused. She was not going to let her guard drop. The chairman tried to distance himself; it was a board decision. Julia no longer trusted anyone. Perhaps Hugh's philosophy of mistrust was the sounder one. There were reassuring platitudes, 'Great opportunities for someone with Hugh's expertise…'

When she returned home, Hugh asked where she had been and did not believe her. What a strange thing loyalty is, Julia thought, emotions pulling in different directions, the mental equivalent of the rack, husband versus wife, family versus family, child versus child, husband versus child, wife versus job, state versus faith, the permutations were endless. She decided late in life, when her time had almost run out, that there was only one set of loyalties which were compatible, God and Truth, and she wasn't absolutely certain about those.

Hugh's loyal secretary phoned the following day to tell him that directors' wives had been issued with an ultimatum. There was to be no contact with Julia. The children asked why George no longer took them to school. Hugh and Julia, too busy with their own shock to be truthful, made up some cock and bull story to placate them and Julia prayed that the imagined sins of the father were not being visited upon their two youngest.

Two days later, the phone rang again. Julia answered hesitantly, suspicious. Was this a trap? Now unsure of herself again. It was a company wife with whom she got on well, whose five-year-old daughter was a special friend of Anna's. She had broken company ranks, shaken by what had happened, aware that a similar fate might await her husband. Her voice was kindly and concerned.

Would Anna like to spend a few days with them at their weekend cottage at Abersoch on the Welsh coast, be introduced to sailing? Their daughter was keen and had asked if Anna might come with them. It might help. A kindly telephone call, but in her confusion, Julia rejected the offer and added that misjudgement to the list of life's regrets.

She tried to put things right many years later, a long letter written at a time when she was feeling low. There had been no reply.

Julia was certain of one thing. Never once had she regretted that intrusion into the chairman's home. It may not have achieved anything but it had made her feel better. Then, a week later, there was the letter, that reaffirmation of kindness.

It must have been a difficult letter to draft and still keep in place its writer's dual loyalties. It was from a couple they hardly knew, Tom and Maureen, guests at that aborted dinner party, a letter of condolence and an invitation to lunch. They accepted, unsure what to expect.

Tom's family were well known, fourth-generation mill owners who had built the huge, sprawling, red-brick buildings, now grimed by soot and part of the industrial heritage, their chimney spires reaching heavenwards to the worship of worsted and tweed, littering the valley bottoms of West Yorkshire and East Lancashire.

Tom had recently sold his share in the family textile firm for a rumoured ten million, a wise move, so those in the know had said. The rapid expansion of Far

Eastern textiles industries was already having a detrimental effect on Lancashire's cotton mills.

He had sold at the top of the market and now lived a comfortable, carefree life, indulging his passions for shooting and fishing. They still lived in the mansion built by his grandfather with its superior elevated position at the head of the valley overlooking the mills, but recently a tide of new development, characterless, cloned, two- and three-bedroom homes was creeping upwards towards the house.

Tom was the same age as Hugh. A big man, bluff, loud, with an earthy sense of humour and a good business head. Maureen was Julia's senior by seven years, petite, blonde, her movements birdlike, quick and nervous as though some predatory feline was about to catch her. She and her home, so it was said, were immaculate at all times, earrings in by nine in the morning. Busying herself non-stop, she polished furniture, something Hugh admired and Julia never had time for. Maureen was amiable; whatever was going on in her head or around her, she smiled. Julia had heard that during the war, she had been in the WRNS, an acting Petty Officer stationed at Inverary and later sent to Brighton on an electrician's course. She must have looked stunning in the tricorn hat. She and Hugh would have lots in common.

Tom and Maureen had married in the same year as Hugh and Julia, giving the new acquaintance a kind of stability. In normal times they would not have become friends, their interests too diverse, but it was not normal times and up until then, both couples had judged each other by outward appearance and gossip.

Hugh was not into shooting and fishing; his pursuits were sedentary, books and history.

As they climbed into Julia's second-hand Mini Traveller, Hugh said, 'I bet they just want to know what happened, spread the gossip.' But, when they arrived, Julia immediately felt friendliness and concern.

Maureen said, 'I saw you across the road last week and you looked so ill. I know Thomas is concerned for Hugh. He has seen this kind of thing happen before. Good men headhunted to improve a company fall foul of petty jealousy and boardroom intrigue.'

Later, Julia heard Tom's voice offering Hugh a brandy, 'If there is anything we can do to help, let us know,' and Julia knew they both meant it.

It was a pleasant, informal meal. She could sense Hugh mellowing and, whenever his hurt tried to surface, their host changed the subject, disallowing bitterness to take control. Did they like music? They had four tickets for The Hallé. 'It would be lovely if you could join us.' Then Hugh remembered a story from his Navy days when, just before D-Day, officers and Wrens had been billeted at Roedean Girls' School in Brighton. The school and its pupils had been evacuated to the Keswick Hotel in the Lake District at the beginning of the war. Above the beds, in the dormitories where the officers slept, were bells with the inscription, 'Press for a mistress'.

Maureen said, 'What a coincidence. I must have been billeted there at the same time. If you had pressed the bell, you might have got me!' The laughter started a lifelong friendship.

But nights continued to be sleepless. The closeness

of their bodies, which had once upon a time been so important to her, was ignored. For the first time, they were free to discuss what they hoped for in life, had, for a fleeting moment, allowed themselves to be honest with one another.

Julia was adamant that never again would she and the children be beholden to the whims of big business and its masters. She was no longer prepared to chance her life again whatever the odds, however many hundreds of thousands Hugh imagined he could demand if he found another opening. It would have no value in her eyes. She was surprised when Hugh, now free from the burden of ambition, understood. From now on, they would stand on their own feet.

His practicality took over. The major outgoings, the mortgage and private education, were no longer sustainable. A letter to Sarah's school received an immediate response. They valued her as a pupil, considered her an academic high flyer and were happy to forego the fees for her final two years, confident that she would get into Cambridge and bring credit to the school.

Elsie and Jim heard rumours but hoped they were just that. When a move became inevitable, Julia and Elsie sat on the sofa, their arms around one another, weeping. The physical contact between them was unexpected and pleasurable. Elsie's soft, warm, mildly-scented skin smelt like Mother's powdered face when, as a child, Julia had tried unsuccessfully to get close to her and give her a kiss. Jim said little, but they knew that to him the loss of his children was a bereavement. And Julia felt again the burden of guilt; something she had said was the cause of all this unhappiness and her,

'We promise to keep in touch,' was meant but somehow sounded false.

Her determination was tested within four weeks when Hugh was offered a lucrative position in London and she said no. There was no way she would allow herself to be subjected to the humiliation from which she was struggling to escape. She was not prepared to go against her migratory instinct. If she had to move anywhere, she was moving further north. She knew that she was playing on Hugh's vulnerability, but it might be her only chance.

The house went on the market in a flurry of local inquisitiveness and anticipation. The agent's board appeared overnight bearing the message 'Ripe for development'. Hugh and Julia had not sanctioned this wording. They were naïve in believing that there were people out there who would appreciate the beautiful gardens they had reclaimed and nurtured over thirteen years. The old English climbing roses the children had chosen and planted for their scent were just coming into their prime. Etoile de Holland and Albertine would, in the estate agent's mind, become six building plots for superior executive houses.

They queried the 'ripe for development' angle and were informed that whoever bought the house would cash in on the garden. It was a no-win situation, a reappearance of the war profiteer who had bought her childhood home. This time there was a desecration of nature, a concrete covering of beauty, and Julia couldn't prevent that happening either.

CHAPTER TWELVE

They delayed telling parents but, as Christmas approached and there were arrangements to be made, it became inevitable. The format for the past eight years had been open house and Julia had tried to emulate and give to her parents and in-laws a taste of the Christmases given to her as a child, ignoring Hugh's indifference and boorishness when his daily routine was disturbed, his determination not to enter into this charade. He wasn't into fantasy.

To Julia, it was a return to childhood when her parents had striven to keep the onslaught of puberty at bay and their children's minds free for as long as possible from the despoiling that awaited them. They, as she did now, had probably tried too hard. Julia felt she was losing the battle, innocence was becoming a dirty word, expunged by reality TV.

Once upon a time sex had been the preserve of adults. If you were lucky, its mysteries and secrets were jealously guarded by courtship and wooing, the love poems of romantic poets hinting at pleasures yet to come. If you were less fortunate, it was more carnal lust and little else, but at least it had been kept in its place.

She vaguely remembered, as a child, sneaking into the out of bounds downstairs men's lavatory to spend a desperate penny, her arms struggling to lift the large, square, heavy, mahogany wooden cover in time, clutching its edges for fear of slipping down into the cavernous bowl with its pretty blue patterns of birds and flowers before releasing the contents of her bladder in panic.

On the walls, alongside black and white framed Bateman cartoons, were brown photos of plump, semi-naked ladies with large bottoms and tiny waists tightly corseted, crisscrossed in whalebone and black lace, hair piled high, flowers tucked behind ears, an elbow resting on a stand with a potted plant, an aspidistra. Julia knew it was an aspidistra because in the nursery, they had a gramophone record of Gracie Fields singing, '*It's the biggest aspidistra in the world*,' and there was a picture of a similar plant on a table, next to Gracie's face on the cardboard sleeve.

Unlike the photos in the drawing room, familiar aunts and grandmothers in high lacy collars and mous-tached, bewhiskered uncles and grandfathers in velvet frames, the photos in the men's lavatory were unfamil-iar. She didn't recognise any of them. Her natural desire to ask who they were was overridden by her conscience telling her she should not have been there. There were books and magazines in dusty heaps, back numbers of *Punch*, *The Illustrated London News*, faded, forgotten French publications yellowed at the bottom of the pile, *Gazette du Bon Ton*, which her great-grandfather must have browsed through once upon a time. Men-only magazines which she didn't understand, hidden from view and under which, two decades later she would find Father's bottles of whisky escaping detection.

Had her grandfather had a mistress? Had Granny, like many wise Victorian wives, conceded that men were randy by nature and must be humoured and the discreet mistress tolerated, accepting an agreement made, keeping her side of the bargain: his kindness, chivalry and financial support within marriage in exchange for the odd peccadillo outside it?

Julia admired her grandmother's generation and now wished that, during those final days when Granny lay dying in the family home, she had taken more trouble, made time to get to know her, but then her mind was still a child's. She hadn't yet appreciated the importance of being too late for something...

She remembered the stillness, broken only by laboured, shallow breathing as her podgy, small hand held the wizened fingers resting on the eiderdown, the joints arthritic, hard and swollen, the tissue-thin skinned, blackened hand, the raised purple pipe veins barely pumping their weary contents. Sunken closed eyes in a parchment face, the few remaining wisps of white hair hardly visible against the white hand-embroidered pillowcase. An overpowering scent of lavender water which, for the remainder of Julia's life, she associated with death and refused to have in the house, although people still kept giving it to her for Christmas. Julia, so many years later, hoped she would find that stillness at the end.

Anxiety had followed Julia into old age and, though she despaired about the state of the world, she had no wish to leave it just yet. It was curiosity. She wanted to be around when the world imploded, wanted to see how people would behave when faced with God's final solution, find out whether she had got life right in any way, understood its purpose.

Would it happen gradually, a slow erosion of law and order until feral instinct ruled and dog started to eat dog? Sometimes fear overwhelmed her, awoke her sweating in the night. Better not to read 'Revelations' with its famine, pestilence and religious wars. From now on, she was determined to resist the temptation to watch BBC twenty-four hourly news. God appeared to be having a trial run and she didn't blame him.

Maybe her own confusion was the problem. Maybe she had been living in an imagined world of innocence. It was she who had sentimentalised childhood, allowed it to become cemented into her brain until she could no longer go to carol services at Christmas for a good sing song. Nostalgia overwhelmed her vocal chords, restricting the muscles in her larynx until she was unable to open her mouth for fear of weeping and causing embarrassment.

When she awoke, troubled, at three in the morning she tried to write down what she was feeling. In the morning she was unable to decipher pencilled notes written on scraps of paper and the old magazines which littered her bed.

Her thoughts were being blown off course again, getting too far out to sea, pulled by a strong undercurrent of immediacy, far removed from the Christmases past that had been uppermost in her mind five minutes earlier.

Father had revelled in Christmas, and this was now

part of her problem, part of her inheritance. He determined that his children should enjoy the excitement which had been denied him in childhood. The ritual of Christmas Eve, writing to Father Christmas, burning the letters on the huge drawing-room fire, watching the delicate blackened wisps of burnt paper rising, caught and guided in the chimney's up-draught, the sluggish ones given a helping hand by the poker. Calling up the chimney, 'Are you there, Father Christmas?' The distant, believed, reply of 'Yes' as Father muffled his voice in a cushion. The torment of not being able to sleep until the early hours and then that heavy hard lumpy stocking, the familiar outline of a book, the latest Amelianne Stiggins stretching the top, confirming belief.

Christmas morning. The drive to church, after the service, handshakes and goodwill amongst the gravestones, even, Julia noted, towards those who she knew Father disliked. Returning home to the smell of roasting turkey which escaped from the kitchen into the hall. The celebration of Christmas dinner, the name miraculously changed from lunch for that one special day. Father carving the turkey, unable to wait, eating small crispy bits with his fingers which he called 'carver's prerogatives', Mother tut-tutting, and Father licking his fingers. Nellie and Thelma coming to collect their plates and take them back to the kitchen, joining the family for crackers, the King's speech and the anticipated arrival of Father Christmas.

Julia's godfather, Mother's lonely bachelor brother Nunky, alias Father Christmas, was always a guest, his presence loved.

In the afternoon, promptly at half past three, as the early winter nights were beginning to darken the sky, he would appear theatrically from under the trees at the far end of the lawn, a sudden splash of red and white against the dark green of the yew hedge. Padded and magnificently costumed in scarlet, by kind permission of some agency in London, unrecognisable beneath beard and wig, a huge hessian sack over his shoulder, his performance planned and perfected over many years, his contribution to the festive spirit. It was a flawless act. She remembered the huge red leather boots. When they were very small, she and her brothers had been overawed by his presence, his ability to have a present for everyone including himself to reinforce the myth; Julia's distress that Nunky was always missing at the crucial moment of present-giving, the explanation that he was looking after the reindeer in the stables, Father's restraining hand resting on her arm, lest she went to look for him.

Now all those generations of make-believe had come to an end. There were cloned Santas everywhere, they were around every corner from October onwards, offering cheap plastic thrills made in China to entice unsuspecting parents into their grotto to purchase expensive hardware, perished elastic trying to hold in place polystyrene beards and whiskers, soiled Nike trainers clearly visible.

Even dear Nunky Santa Claus had not been allowed to go gentle into that good night. His lifetime of service and kindness to others was made fun of, ridiculed by the cancer that invaded his body. Julia had loved him and hoped her presence had helped in his solitary struggle towards an agonising early death in 1970. The whole of his life had been lonely. A devout Quaker, during the First World War, he was ostracised, a conscientious objector, joining The Friends Ambulance Service on the front line in France, injured by shrapnel.

There was a photo of him on Mother's dressing table, laughing, in his teens, sunburnt, his inherited family freckles clearly visible, sitting on a rock in the Lake District, dressed only in a pair of shorts, his arm around the shoulders of a similar young man. Mother said, 'His friend died and all that happiness left him.'

He had been a true godfather, though an honorary one, godparents not being part of Quaker religious ritual. He was always at hand with advice. During those dark, early days of John's illness, his letters of comfort, their compassion and understanding, helped to lift Julia out of despair.

As he lay in the hospital bed, at his request, she had touched the amorphous rock hard lump which had usurped his stomach space. When he had cried out in pain for morphine Julia had gone in search of the duty doctor, to be told he had had his injection ten minutes earlier. She beseeched the doctor to help. He had looked at her closely, pressed her arm for a moment and whispered, 'I'll see what I can do.'

Nunky died gently that night, holding Julia's hand.

Julia had tried to make that last Christmas in her second beloved home memorable, but there was tension. Hugh's parents were unable to accept the change of course their son's life was taking and probably, deep down but unsaid, blamed Julia for it. The pride in their son's achievements, basking in his success, showing cuttings from *The Times* business section to friends, was about to be taken away.

Julia felt sorry for them.

CHAPTER THIRTEEN

Their home sold quickly, too quickly. It gave them no time to find anything remotely habitable which would fulfil their requirements and plans for the new lifestyle of moderate self-sufficiency they had in mind, and at the same time provide some kind of stability for the children. They both needed somewhere remote, solitude, to hide away, adjust and restore their minds. A local school within striking distance for young John and Anna.

Finding anything affordable with land was a nightmare and, in desperation, they settled on a large derelict farmhouse with outbuildings and five acres of land halfway up a mountain. No mains water, electricity or sewerage, a third of the roof fallen in, empty of humans for four decades, the hardened heaps of sheep droppings and wool daggings evidence that it had been a long-term refuge and shelter for hardy Swaledales overtaken by blizzards on those treacherous wintered hills.

The agent had been helpful, anxious no doubt to offload the property which had been hanging on his books for some time. As a sweetener, he mentioned a chance to buy additional land, ninety acres of rough enclosed hill land with grazing rights on the adjacent open fell.

Hugh refused to burden himself with any kind of mortgage for this additional real estate. He had never been a risk taker or a gambler, unlike Julia's father, who was happy to put a tenner, which he could ill afford, on the National for the thrill of it. In their present predicament, Julia understood Hugh's reluctance and did not question it.

The following day, without telling Hugh, she approached a local bank, asked to see the manager. In the old days, Hugh would have dealt with this sort of thing but Julia felt empowered, confident she could go it alone.

It never crossed her mind that a request for a loan might be rejected. Land, she imagined, would be viewed as a safe investment by any bank. But that was before the age of sexual equality; it was bank policy never to lend money to further the dreams of impecunious females. The ambitions of women in business were destined to be thwarted for a further two decades until the anti-discrimination bill reached the statute books. Julia wondered at the time how Mary Quant was getting on in Knightsbridge; had she got a loan for her fashion house?

However, the bank manager seemed sympathetic and suggested a male guarantor. Julia had the impression that, had she gone out onto the street and dragged in any passing vagrant, providing he was male and prepared to vouch for her and carry the can if her farming enterprise went pear-shaped, he would have been acceptable. Hugh refused to budge; he appeared to have little faith in her ability.

'How do you intend to pay off the interest?' he asked.

Asking Father was not an option: it would be an admission of her lack of judgement in the marital stakes.

As she walked across those ninety acres the following day, the earth beneath her feet urged her on, sending messages. It wanted to belong to her for the love and custodianship it knew she would give. It also knew that it was far more important to Julia than the heap of stones that would eventually be her home. Nagging away was the certain knowledge that if she procrastinated, those additional acres would be eagerly snapped up by neighbouring farmers. It was the yellow frock all over again.

Julia phoned David, overriding his impecunious family reputation. His reaction was instantaneous: 'No problem, Sis. Send me the form.'

Hugh found a local builder who exuded enthusiasm and was prepared to ignore the inaccessibility of the site and the extra cost involved in transporting building materials across the rocky terrain. His only physical help, other than Hugh, was a fifteen-year-old apprentice stonemason, Fred.

The three of them shared an optimism that they could, if the wind was in the right direction, resurrect those unprepossessing ruins into a home. They discovered, buried beneath the rubble, evidence of a former, struggling human existence. The flagged floors and central hearth, the ashes of peat and wood were still visible among the sheep shit. Old oak timber beams were rock solid beneath a surface invasion of woodworm and layers of early twentieth-century plaster. The huge vernacular roof stones were intact, lying among a forest of six-foot-high seeding nettles. Their presence confirmed the original builders' understanding of the elements, pitting their wits against nature's strength to hold the roof down during the accepted north-wind storms.

In the rubble, they discovered the rusting remains of a huge cast-iron kitchen range, its original crane and ratten hooks still attached, the oven door hanging drunkenly by one hinge, embossed with the maker's name. It was Julia's maternal great-grandfather's name, forged in his foundry a century ago. It was an omen and from then on, its resurrection and reconstruction as part of the house became Hugh's obsession.

They were warned that the place was renowned for its severe weather conditions and inaccessibility in winter. A fierce, local, easterly wind known as 'The Helm' would announce its presence and intentions by creating a cap of ominous dark cloud, known as 'the bar', ruler-straight along the summit of the fells, its strength legendary though discounted as myth by those who had never experienced it. Julia had read somewhere that a similar phenomenon was encountered on Table Mountain in South Africa, where the geological formation of the mountains, the slipstream of the winds, met turbulent, hot and cold temperatures and together they funnelled a destructive force into the valley below. The strength and myriad icy stings of the wind invaded lungs, taking breath away, stripping off the struggling new shoots of spring grass, making animals search for shelter and humans, if they were foolish enough to venture out, hold tightly to the nearest secure object.

The warning proved accurate when one of the most severe winters on record took everyone by surprise. The snow started to fall silently, gently covering and caressing the small concrete mixer and heaps of stones, its beauty giving lie to what was in store.

They had laid in what they thought was an adequate emergency supply of Calor gas cylinders and tinned food to see them through the winter. The temporary cooking stove and heating appliances would have been adequate under normal circumstances. Water was carried in buckets from the nearest stream after the surface ice was broken. The Elsan portable loos, in constant need of emptying, became a problem when the earth became too frozen for holes to be dug. When there was a brief semi-thaw Hugh, with the help of the children, dug ten deep holes, advance planning which they had hoped would be sufficient. But a further hazard arose when 'The Helm' whipped the already lying snow into a frenzy of movement, depositing twenty-foot drifts into the roofless part of the house and totally obliterating the presence of the ten holes. Fred fell into one. Hugh made markers out of sticks and old towels, multicoloured flags fluttering in the wind. Against the blinding white snow it resembled a Tibetan village on the high fell side. Villagers in the valley gossiped that the newcomers were some weird religious sect.

It had been foolhardy and naïve to imagine that Anna, John and Sarah would adapt to their new life as backwoodsmen without some resistance. To begin

with it had been an adventure and they shared the pio-
neering spirit, up to the point when they saw that their
parents' optimism had been unrealistic: the building
would take far longer than anticipated and winter approached. Life in sleeping bags on camp beds with only
hot water bottles for warmth was not what they had
in mind. Hugh's precious grandfather clock, furniture
and family heirlooms were safely in store, tucked up
warmly and comfortably in some repository.

Before the bad winter showed its hand Sarah, now
sixteen, sensibly accepted a school friend's invitation to
stay with her parents during the Christmas holidays.
She was at that age when friendships, if not worked at
and maintained, could be lost. John and Anna just had
to make the most of it, and did.

The nearest inhabited dwelling lay half a mile down
the fell side. Their neighbours were a farmer, Sidney,
his wife, Vera, and two teenage, strong-muscled, cheery
sons, Harry and Frank, who had left formal education
behind at the age of fourteen and did all the work,
scraping a living for the family from the land and
maintaining the uplands for ramblers to enjoy.

When the snow started falling, they made their presence known, offered assistance and introduced Julia
and her family to Jack, their other neighbour, whose
land half encircled theirs, sharing a boundary across
the stream with the ninety acres Julia had purchased
on the fell top.

Those friendships would endure when others
hadn't.

CHAPTER FOURTEEN

For six weeks the snow continued, the roaring winds at night whipping it into icing-sugar sculptures, drifts obliterating reassuring landmarks and any sign of the track forged by Frank and Harry's tractor the previous day. On minor roads the council's snowploughs were already impotent. Julia and Hugh were grateful for the kindness of their new neighbours. Stores of tinned food and groceries were generously shared.

Sidney warned Hugh not to venture out on his own. Blizzards in those hills could descend quickly. Walk two hundred yards and a sudden change in the direction of the wind would, within five minutes, cover your tracks, leaving no trace of the direction from which you had come. Local shepherds, who knew those hills like the back of their hand, had become disorientated during a white-out and perished.

Julia thought, 'If we can survive this we can survive anything.' She had an inbred respect for the elements; though at times they were harsh masters, she felt in tune with them, they were the real world.

There were magical days when the wind dropped and the snow ceased, allowing the sun to shine with an extra intensity in a clear sky. Hugh made snowshoes for the children, fashioned from sticks, branches and used bailer twine found hanging from nails in the semi-derelict barn. This evidence of a thriftier age, when nothing was thrown away, was a reminder to Julia of the yellowed newspapers hanging from their nail in the wall in the double-seated gardeners' privy in her first home. Hugh's cumbersome inventions enabled the children to walk over the crisp outer surface of the snow drifts without plunging through to the treacherous soft powdery snow beneath.

Hugh's ingenuity under pressure was impressive. Julia had to admit that he would be a good person with whom to be marooned on a desert island. If only their minds could learn to navigate from the same map.

Her mind was becoming troublesome. Free now from two decades of servility to Hugh's career and trying to be some kind of mother, it slipped into fifth gear and was cruising away at high speed. Hugh also redrew his map of life. He appeared to be oblivious to the interests of others if they were not his own and, having already distanced himself from his family, he was now putting a great deal of energy distancing himself from the world, railing in particular about big business, to which, once upon a time, he had been in thrall. In his eyes, capitalism was now corrupt; of course, Julia had suspected that for most of her life.

She remembered going to matins with Father, trying hard to sit quietly and not fidget for twenty minutes so as not to let Father down, her mind wandering, the strong shafts of coloured sunlight containing specks of moving dust shining straight at her from the face of an angel in the stained glass window. It was then that she heard the words: 'Lay not up for yourselves treasures upon earth, where moth and rust doth corrupt and where thieves break in and steal.' She hadn't understood it at the time, had seen it through a glass darkly, but now it was face to face.

The planned purchase of ewes in lamb to start their farming enterprise was postponed by the cruel winter. The decision had been fortuitous; the loss of sheep amongst their neighbours was horrendous. Thousands suffocated, buried alive. The children watched as the bodies emerged from beneath the melting snow, their matted fleeces still bearing the assorted colour marks of ownership; shovelled into trailers to be taken to the renderers, the farmers' income going with them.

Julia and Hugh accepted that they were seen as a couple of foolhardy urbanites. Rumour had it that the locals had given them six months before they would be off licking their wounds. There had been hefty bets laid but that winter taught them both that they were made of sterner stuff. Julia's teenage dreams of being a farmer, which had not been taken seriously, were being given a second chance. To give in now would be confirmation that her detractors had been right and that she hadn't been up to it in the first place.

Then spring arrived, suddenly, with blinding beauty. The sun penetrated the massive snow drifts and the drips from the thawing icicles became more and more rapid. The cold hostile earth brought forth an abundance of snowdrops and Lent lilies, their place taken later by wild primroses, aconites, celandines, harebells, wild violets, field orchids and rare wild gentian. A miracle of nature and an unexpected bonus, a reaffirmation that, by chance, they had chosen the right place.

Julia kept quiet about the almost-forgotten knowledge of livestock she had acquired as a child. Hill sheep were different to the large, docile sheep of her youth. Mountain sheep were small, horned, limestone-hardy, independent and wild. It was said amongst farming folk that a sheep's ambition in life was to wake up dead. Prone to more than two hundred ailments, all difficult to diagnose, they were hardly the best thing to put your dwindling cash reserves into. And those cash reserves had been dwindling; the half year's salary was long since gone, the dole their sole income.

A bonus of that winter was the improvement in John's asthma. The cold, bracing, rarefied atmosphere of the above-the-tree-line, semi-permafrost landscape enabled him to reduce his steroid intake slightly and he appeared to thrive on the physical challenge of that first year.

Hugh quickly realised that, to survive and keep in touch with the outside world and progress the building work, a telephone line was essential. The GPO was helpful, quick and expensive. Hugh went cap in hand to the bank and, against his initial instinct, secured a loan to pay for it. Electricity would have to wait a few years.

Hugh was confident he could harness the peaty brown waters of the stream which tumbled through their land above the house and which they depended upon for water. His knowledge of designing and manufacturing hydroelectric schemes and overseeing their installation worldwide was one of the bonuses of his business career. He purchased a small generator and pump and laid a pipeline to the house. It was a brilliant piece of engineering, enabling them to enjoy a washing machine and dishwasher when electricity eventually arrived. Two families of dippers, nesting in the stony outcrops near the intake pipe, were a sure indication of the purity of the water flowing from its mossy, boggy source in the hills.

Having already gone back on his word not to borrow money, Hugh made the sensible decision that some kind of farm vehicle was necessary and plumped for an old, grey Ferguson tractor. He had already exchanged Julia's Mini Traveller for a canvas-topped, ex-army Land Rover into which he had fitted a Perkins P 3.4 diesel engine purchased from a scrap dealer. It was illegal but gave the vehicle such power that it could have been driven vertically to the top of the Empire State Building. It was still going strong, giving valiant service forty years on. Like its owner it was rusty, temperamental starting in the morning, its canvas shot and leaking.

The purchase of that first flock of sheep was under the watchful and knowledgeable eyes of Sid and Jack. It wasn't just a question of going to the local auction mart and buying a hundred for starters. To maximise their land, it was essential to buy a hefted flock. The land Julia had purchased carried fell rights, that right of commoners to graze their sheep on the unenclosed mountains during the summer months, leaving the lower land free to produce the hay necessary to feed animals in winter. It was a right steeped in time, enabling farmers to earn a living, dependent upon the amount of 'in bye' land owned, roughly two and a half sheep per acre.

It wasn't straightforward reintroducing a flock onto the mountain. Unless you were prepared to sit with them twenty-four hours a day, with a dog to prevent them straying, it meant buying sheep which had been there before, who knew the terrain and wouldn't wander too far. All that was on offer were broken-mouthed ewes, which some other farmer was trying to get rid of before they died of old age. The other possibility – gimmer shearlings – were flighty young females who, having spent one year on the fells as lambs with their mothers, had a vague inkling where they should be within their ten-mile radius.

Because of the tremendous winter losses, young sheep were in short supply. In the end they purchased an assortment of elderly ewes and flighty shearlings, borrowed a tup, took a lot of good advice from Jack and climbed onto the steep, precarious learning curve of sheep husbandry. They awaited their first crop of lambs.

Shortly afterwards they received a confirmation of faith. A letter arrived from a solicitor advising Julia that probate had been granted to her godfather's will. Dear old Nunky Santa Claus had left her a legacy. It was exactly the amount she had borrowed for the land.

Chapter Fifteen

For two years theirs was the only telephone within a four-mile radius. When news of this spread, they became the clearing house and means of communication for all the scattered farms along the fell side. They realised that their telephone number was being given to all and sundry and that they were to receive and pass on messages; it was taken for granted. Jack was in constant demand. The phone would ring and a dialect voice would say, 'This is so and so. Tell Jack I'm coming over with a yow this evening.' If it was holiday time, one of the children would be despatched to deliver the message. Julia hoped they were not acting as go-betweens for some sheep rustling syndicate; such things still went on in that Border Reiver country.

They made enquiries. Jack, blessed with knowledge and skill handed down by his forebears, could cure 'Sturdy' in sheep, the cystic stage of the tapeworm, carried by dogs. Its sinister, complicated life cycle had been cleverly thought out by evolution or God, its millennial existence perfected. An infected dog defecates in a field, a sheep eats the grass, picking up the eggs. They enter the blood stream and travel to the brain, where they turn into a grub. The symptoms are blindness and a circling gait leading to death. If the fortunate sheep got to Jack in time, his huge, sensitive, gnarled fingers could locate the grub beneath the skin at the top of the skull. A small incision with his penknife released the larvae and ensured the sheep recovered.

His success rate was phenomenal. But within ten years of Hugh and Julia's arrival, the canker of officialdom descended upon the countryside. No longer were you allowed to alleviate animal suffering unless you had gone through the proper channels, got the correct paperwork, called a vet and notified Defra, by which time the poor sheep had long since gone. Julia felt sympathy for the sheep, but what saddened her more was the loss of that human skill. Once it had gone and Jack died, his gift would be usurped by drugs, and hearsay and folk lore would be the only proof that such men had existed.

They got to know Jack well. He was a dog-and-stick farmer of the old school, her father's school, with the same values, an unsentimental oneness with nature and animals. Hugh and Julia felt, and hoped, that he enjoyed their company, for he would walk the mile and a half to their house many an evening for a kitchen crack, a few whiskies and a curiosity to see how the building was progressing.

Of course, it may have been the need to escape his wife, a dour, non-drinking, hard-working, godly Methodist, who wore the trousers. They would recognise his step in the yard, the strong strides, his clinkered clogs striking the newly-unearthed cobblestones, the purposeful banging on the door. They looked forward to his impromptu visits.

That second full summer and third autumn when, at last, they had something resembling a home, Julia did her best to re-establish friendships which had gone by the board when survival had been the priority.

Elsie and Jim came to stay. Never having owned a car, to be met off the bus by Hugh in the old army Land Rover was an adventure, a safari into the unknown. Other than going to Blackpool for a weekend, they had never had a holiday.

The weather was glorious. Jim was now visibly failing, his years underground hewing coal catching up with him, his breathlessness a strain on everyone. He spent his days sitting in the sun, wrapped in a rug, gazing at the view, absorbed in the stillness of the vast expanse of hills, hearing and marvelling at the calls of peewits, skylarks, and the bleats of sheep, the warmth of the sun on his face. Hugh and he talked about old times from their opposite perspectives of privilege and hard grind. Julia took them coffee outside. Rivers of tears channelled down the deep ruts of grey worn folds of skin. Jim saw what Julia's father had seen in a London theatre: the realisation that they had left living until it was too late.

On her arrival Elsie, seeing the old iron kitchen range in working order, saw nothing else. Still holding her handbag, her fingers picked at the rusting iron flakes on the doors, her work-hardened skin impervious to the red heat roaring from the fire which heated the water in the back boiler. Since Hugh's clever restoration, it supplied the house with an abundance of piping hot, peaty water. Elsie, in a paroxysm of delight, instructed Hugh to go back into town and find some

Zebrite and steel wool.

Hugh said, 'You can't get Zebrite now. It's been banned by the EU. It will have to be something else.'

Elsie said, 'Nonsense. Find a traditional family iron-monger. They will still have some under the counter.' Elsie was in charge once more.

Julia, whose mind had been focused on giving Elsie a break, was thrown off course. Elsie was determined that black leading was how she wished to spend her holiday; she couldn't go home happy, leaving it in that state.

Hugh returned with six hardening, black-and-yellow striped tubes – grate polish, Reckitt Colman of Hull, familiar to Julia from the blackened hands of Marjorie all those years ago as she pushed back stray-ing strands of mousey hair with her thick, reddened, bare forearm, getting black lead all over her face.

Hugh suggested asking Maureen and Thomas for a weekend. Thomas would enjoy a bit of rough shoot-ing and the rabbit population was getting out of hand, digging under the netting defences around the tender hedge whips and destroying them.

Julia was unsure. Maureen's last Christmas card had stated that they had installed a swimming pool in the house; it had usurped the billiard room. She didn't wish to stretch that particular friendship too far.

Julia's invitation carried a warning: no en-suite or electricity sockets for shavers and hairdryers. Thomas and Maureen accepted. They were muckers-in, keen to learn how to lay a hedge and repair a drystone wall. Maureen, amiable whatever was asked of her, helped too much with everything to the point of becoming annoying, washing up every cup and saucer under the tap with its brown water, unable to accept that Julia's interpretation of homeliness was untidiness.

When three rabbits arrived in the kitchen Maureen said, 'What fun. I haven't skinned a rabbit for thirty years.'

Other acquaintances, into whose homes Julia and Hugh had never been invited in the old days, phoned inviting themselves, their curiosity having got the better of them.

'We've just stopped at Scotch Corner to find a phone. Making our way up to Scotland. It would be fun to see you again.'

Julia tried to forestall unwelcome guests by pointing out that access to the house was up a narrow, walled, deeply-potholed, rough track with outcrops of stone which caught the sumps of unwary vehicles. Mindful that their Jag may never have encountered anything more challenging than a minor B road, she thought it only fair to warn them. When her warning fell on deaf ears and they hit the mushroom stone, so named by the children for its resemblance to a giant field mushroom, their arrival was tense with blame and acrimony.

Hugh and Julia took childish pleasure in creating a welcoming image which would ensure no further visits. Hugh, in his filthiest ex-army surplus clothing, stinking of sheep dip and Julia, hair unbrushed, impregnated with hay seeds, unwashed hands, offering a biscuit from a packet.

Jack unintentionally contributed to the game. Familiar footsteps and a bang on the door, it was ten thirty in the morning and he had come to report a boundary wall down, rushed by ramblers. Their sheep, believing that the grass is always greener on the other side, had got through the gap and joined his.

Jack accepted his usual whisky, his geniality and dialect tongue misunderstood by outsiders. When he had played his part and departed, their visitors asked, 'Is there no one of your ilk living around here?'

After they left Julia, unsure of the definition of 'ilk', looked it up: 'class', and felt justification for her historic dislike. She had always thought 'ilk' to be a uniting word, rather like clan.

The tentative bond of friendship forged with Prue through unhappiness at school, had loosened over the years. Cards at Christmas kept them in touch. Over the years, her cards had changed, Trafalgar Square in the snow replaced by UNICEF and, for the past three years, the same glossy close-up photo of bright green Brussels sprouts from Oxfam. The last one contained a hurried note with the news that her marriage to that dry accountant had withered and, with the three girls almost off her hands, she was reassessing her life and had become a vegetarian – or was it a vegan? More disturbingly, she was running a shelter for abandoned cats. Julia recalled that book-lined home from home, not an animal in sight. Experience had taught Julia to dislike cats; pretty, fluffy, songbird killing machines which, having slaughtered everything outside, were welcomed into homes mewling for their dish of minced mammal.

Should she just leave that friendship where it was? But she had impulsively written a note. 'If ever you are up north, there is always a bed,' feeling she had done her bit. The response was immediate: 'Coming north at the end of the month. Lovely to spend a few days with you. I have found someone to look after the cats.'

That clever mind, given so much attention in its youth, sat at Julia's kitchen table. Now age had put them on an equal footing, neither could be judged by the expectations of others. Their lives were exposed for all to see, all that promise dissipated. Julia felt that, quite by chance, it was she who was having the interesting life.

Prue, domiciled in the sterile certainty of blinkered suburbia and never having encountered a fox, was vociferous and active in her condemnation of hunting.

Somehow faith entered the conversation one evening and Prue said, 'Good God, Pudge. Surely you don't still believe all that drivel?'

She stayed a full week. Julia perfected her wild mushroom tagliatelle and Hugh's face bore a well-established look of resentment.

The Royal Mail brought other jolts from the past. Hugh's loyal ex-secretary who, since their departure, kept in touch by Christmas cards with hastily written ambiguous notes: 'It isn't the same here now' and 'Things have changed a lot since you left', felt it her duty to write and tell him that the managing director, that self-assured, sophisticated, wine snob with whom they had travelled the globe in pursuit of export orders and in whose wife Julia had mistakenly confided her concerns about the arms trade, had committed suicide.

The letter contained no insight. He'd been found in the kitchen by his teenage daughter, having taken poison. The horror of the news numbed them. Why would a man so worldly and successful do such a thing?

They would never learn the truth, those close to him absorbed in keeping up appearances, putting up a front against the torments raging in their minds.

Julia could not obliterate the image from her mind. That expensive show kitchen, outclassing any of the glossy photos found in *House and Garden*, the envy of others, and that immaculately groomed body lying there, its mind at peace but its face contorted and convulsed by strychnine. Julia wanted to write a letter of condolence for old times' sake, but wasn't sure of her own ground. She wasn't yet strong enough to take the rejection of another unanswered letter. When she did feel strong enough, too much time had elapsed and regret set in.

That glorious summer was the last time they saw Jim. A letter from Elsie; he had died at peace in his sleep.

On returning from the Lancashire funeral Julia was determined to do something to leave her mark, however small, on the land. In the autumn she and Hugh started a planting programme. Julia was driven by hearing a radio interview with Arthur Miller just before his death; he was asked what made him want to write and he had replied, 'To leave a trail of one's own presence.' She needed future generations to stand in her favourite places and sense that, once upon a time, she and others had been there and experienced that sense of awe.

They planted thousands of naturalising daffodils and Lent lilies, supplementing those which had appeared the first spring. It was a rare togetherness, a common goal. The children planted the bulbs to form

165

their initials, just as Julia's great-great-grandmother had done in the gardens of that home they had never known, but Julia had.

The fourth winter, three hundred oak trees were planted. There was evidence that oaks had once been common on those barren uplands. Old maps with the deeds to their land showed small plantations. Iron-hard, hollowed stumps still remained, offering protection from the bitter spring wind to newborn lambs. Jack told them that his father remembered the oaks being hewn in the 1920s during the slump, when rural and urban poverty went hand in hand and the wood had been sold off as a much-needed cash crop.

The fifth year they planted half a mile of hedge-rows, ignoring the advice of local Jonahs who said they were too exposed. They enjoyed the shared optimism of the task, spades slicing into the earth, dropping the thin, flexible whips of thorn, dog rose and holly into the crevices and firming the soil with their heels. In those tender roots they planted the remainder of their lives.

CHAPTER SIXTEEN

The role reversal was gradual. Julia was becoming the one with ambition. Her frustration at Hugh's lack of encouragement, his belittling of her aspirations and achievements and blocking of her enterprise, began to affect her health The culture of 'don't' instead of 'do' which he visited upon their children. There were few 'well done Jocks', Father's favourite phrase of spurring on and being on your side, from him.

Hugh was busy fencing and hedging so she offered to do the auction mart run, taking the fat lambs to the Monday butchers' market. They made a reasonable price. Waiting for the payout to be processed, she wandered into the adjoining part of the mart where cattle sales were in progress and into the ring came two Simmental in-calf heifers. Possessing Father's eye for livestock, she was bowled over by the conformation and honey-coloured beauty of the two animals and, without a second thought, she bid for and bought them. It was the same intuition that had bought the yellow frock years ago and made her ask for that bank loan for the land.

On her way home, she began to appreciate that what she had done might incur displeasure; the sheep money to pay the bills had been squandered on a whim without consulting Hugh but she knew from experience that, had she asked, he would have said no.

By the time she got home, it was almost dark. She drove the Land Rover and trailer as far as possible up the rough track to the enclosed fell land, out of view of the house, off-loaded her purchases and didn't say a word. Hugh's anger was too familiar and best avoided, put off for as long as possible, a rerun of the head-mistress's chastisement when she had gone weak at the knees. In adulthood it made her feel sick and reach for the bottle. She would have to judge her moment – but fate interceded and, before she could confess, she heard the familiar tread on the yard cobbles, the bang on the door and Jack's cheery greeting. 'I see you've a grand pair of Simmental heifers in the top allotment.'

She had to explain to Hugh. It was a double hu-miliation for him. Not only had Julia not told him but he had been put at a disadvantage, made to look a fool. He reacted with his usual charm in front of Jack, pretending to know all about her purchases but when Jack left he started on her. He never assaulted her physically – but he attacked her mind until it could no longer function, pacing up and down in anger, shout-ing, banging the table, reasonable debate beyond his comprehension. Then came the blackmail, insidious, seeking out what he perceived to be her vulnerability, the children, belittling them.

The following morning there was silence, both of them reeling from something that should not have been. Her tentative efforts to regain conversation, to get back to some kind of uneasy normality.

In hindsight, she wondered whether he was ever aware of the hurt he caused her. Probably not; his outbursts were the only way he could come to terms with his own disappointments. She tried never to answer back. Her mind went into its shell, conscious that it must protect the children from discord.

She probably worried about them unnecessarily. They seemed to be managing pretty well amongst the debris of their changed lives; appeared, outwardly at least, amazingly resilient to all the chaos that Julia felt was going on around her. They made humorous, endearing comments to boost her morale: 'Gosh, Mum, it must be like trying to climb Everest with someone shooting at you all the time.'

When she thought about them now, those three had been pretty remarkable. Sarah won a scholarship to Cambridge, the confidence, judgement and generosity of her headmistress had borne fruit and been repaid. John, battling with permanent ill health, had got to university to read Law but, after a year, had to drop out, too much pressure and stress for his body and mind to cope with. But he was content working for a charity for the disabled. Anna married a farmer.

It was the unpredictability of Hugh's outbursts that threw her off balance. The morning following the heifer incident, after a night of frightening dreams, she was awoken by her old adversary, the black dog of depression and that complete sense of worthlessness, its constant companion.

Always a keen riser, looking forward to feeding the livestock, she didn't want to get out of bed; her mind no longer cooperated with her body. Her body finally

169

got up and went through the motions. To the outside world she was functioning adequately, but her mind was somewhere else, trying to hide, longing to find some private, warm, reassuring hole where it could be cosseted by understanding. Then, into this unreal world, the phone rang. Mother. An SOS. Such a rare occurrence that Julia's mind, even in its fragile state, knew the call had to be taken seriously.

Against her better judgement, Mother had let Father out of her sight for twenty-four hours to attend the funeral in Ulster of his eldest brother, Charles. On the overnight Stranraer to Larne ferry he had made his way to the bar. He was discovered by the steward in his cabin the following morning, almost unconscious. His tremors had passed the stage of hallucination and entered the final and fatal sphere of raging, terrified delirium. The police had been called to restrain him, the doctors were doing all they could and Mother could no longer cope.

Hugh's reaction was predictable, 'He had it coming,' but he drove her to the station to get the train to Stranraer from where she could catch the next ferry to Ulster and make her way to Belfast.

She needed to get to Father before strangers bore witness and sentenced him. When she walked into the ward he was asleep, his battle over for a short while. He awoke an hour later and, on seeing her, could not speak. He clutched her hand as a drowning man might, tears streaming down his bloated face, watery bloodshot eyes, his humiliation in front of her complete. However much she tried to find the words to say it didn't matter, to reassure him, they didn't sound right. They were not the words she felt. She wanted to embrace him, to hug him with love as he had done to her as a child, but couldn't get near him; the tubes keeping his body alive were an impregnable barrier.

The doctor in charge was sympathetic, world-weary, having witnessed similar tableaux a thousand times before. He accepted Julia's assurances that, after an agreed time in detox, she would be responsible for him until Mother felt she could cope again. Julia phoned David, supportive as ever; both of them were aware that this latest binge had so weakened Father in body and mind that from thereon he would be a semi-invalid.

When Julia finally got him back to the farm, she took pity on that cold, blue, shaking, drying-out body, the warm familiar joviality gone. To deny him a drink ever again was, she felt, a punishment too far. She had to make certain that he felt no guilt and they reached a compromise. She took him a pint of beer at lunchtime and a double whisky in the evening, and the warmth in his eyes returned. During the day he would sit outside, wrapped in rugs and hot water bottles, a look of near contentment on his face. However, in the evenings he usurped the TV and Hugh's space and Julia knew it could not last. That other adversary, loyalty, was rearing its divisive head. Hugh asked when Father was leaving.

So it was that Father was with them when the time came for the heifers to give birth.

CHAPTER SEVENTEEN

Julia's memory kept regurgitating snippets of the past, newsreels bringing back incidents, episodes in their lives at which they had been watchers, on the sidelines of world events.

Hugh called to her from the snug. It became the TV room when finally they had electricity installed. Julia could hear and keep an eye on what was going on in the world without having to stop preparing a meal.

'Come and have a look. That's where I stood at the May Day parades in the 1950s.'

Julia walked through, her hands dripping. The one o'clock news, China, student rebellion in Tiananmen Square. A picture of tanks taking on a lone protestor.

She returned to the sink to finish scrubbing the sheep shit off Hugh's made-in-China wellies. How rapidly the world was changing, things were turning full circle, they were becoming our industrial masters. Another part of her mind was thinking why had they not planned for an outside tap when they did up the house?

Hugh had been one of the few Westerners allowed into China, invited by Mao during his regime of brainwashing, fanatical Communist ideology. The

Little Red Book. Five Year Plans. Purges of intellectuals. Sparrows seeking sanctuary in the gardens of the
British Embassy to escape persecution at the hands of
the Health and Pest Ministry. State stability. Westerners and capitalism unwelcome.

Hugh's welcome to The People's Republic had
been doubly assured. The London Import and Export
Company, with whom he had embarked on his business
career, had a long-standing contract to purchase the
annual crop of Kashmir goat wool from the Chinese
State Collective Producers through the Chinese Animal
By-products Corporation to sustain the prestigious
Scottish cashmere woollen knitwear industry, at the
same time representing major British manufacturers
keen to export.

All China's commerce was negotiated through
a plethora of state corporations, one for everything
animate and inanimate, an army of bureaucrats selling
and buying for the whole of that vast complex nation,
and Hugh had once come to the aid of a senior party
official.

The London office had received a disturbing cable
from the commissar of the Chinese National Metal
Import Corporation who had failed in his duty. If
found out by the state, he would at best go to prison,
but more likely just disappear like many before him.
Hugh's name had been passed to him by an interpreter
at the Chinese National Textile Import Corporation
through whom Hugh had previously negotiated a deal
to sell Courtaulds' rayon for use in Chinese tyre manufacture. Could he please help?

The message was coded, its true meaning hidden

amongst a labyrinth of felicitations and Chinese courtesy to avoid the attention of censors and thought police. Hugh, well versed in the tedious, beating-around-the-bush business negotiations in which the Chinese excelled, had deciphered the cable and acted upon it. The country's pineapple crop was about to be harvested and the Chinese National Metals Import Corporation had forgotten to order the raw material to make the tins to put it in. Their usual suppliers in Singapore had sold out. Hugh arranged for ten thousand tons of tin plate from the Steel Company of Wales to be shipped express by Blue Funnel Line. It got there just in time.

Those two prestigious companies no longer existed, the monopoly for excellence held by the Scottish cashmere woollen industry long gone. She put Hugh's wellies outside in the yard to dry. Politicians and commodity brokers had sold Britain cheaply.

Hugh's letters home written fifty years ago had joined those sepia photos of Father in the mildewed trunk from her childhood, the repository and evidence of lives lived over three centuries given a home when Mother went into care.

Julia revisited the trunk occasionally to re-read Hugh's letters, descriptions and observations, small, fragile, yellowed newspaper cuttings saved and carefully placed with his correspondence again seeing the light of day. His comments were out of kilter with current political thinking.

He had taken care choosing the stamps, intending to send her the full set: prints of factory interiors, civil engineering projects, historical buildings, athletes and

174

bold, fearless faces gazing into an imagined future. Julia studied them more closely. Seeing them again, firmly stuck to the fading blue, disintegrating airmail envelopes, she wondered whether they were now valuable.

Hugh had admired the Chinese people, felt empathy with the vastness of their country, understood that a landmass of such diversity and ancient civilisation needed a totalitarian regime to hold it together. Communism, however repressive, was not doing a bad job and the USA should mind its own business. He had been brave enough to say so; he understood why the People's Republic saw capitalism as corrupting and wished to erect barriers to defend itself.

Hugh's first visit to China had attracted the attention of MI6. Would he be willing to be a spy, find out what was going on? He wasn't keen, nor was Julia. Sneaking on others was not within their remit of world understanding and hoped-for trust between nations, but it had been a time of Communist paranoia, inflamed by rhetoric coming from the White House, witch hunts under the spell of McCarthy destroying the remnants of liberal thinking in the States. Hugh agreed to keep his eyes open but had no intention of doing so.

Arriving at his hotel in Peking, reserved for overseas visitors, the first person he bumped into was Graham Greene, thought at the time to have been a fellow traveller, a myth dispelled in his biography. The only other Brit, Peter Townsend, was escaping the media after his failed wooing of Princess Margaret. There was also a cluster of German businessmen hoping to get a foot in the door of the second Five Year Plan that was about to be announced.

At the time Julia had not appreciated Hugh's expertise. His patience and acceptance of the endless, long-drawn-out, fruitless meetings with political overtones, negotiating his way through the Chinese unhurried business protocol of taking their time, discussions interrupted by propaganda, green tea and tirades against America. Negotiations exchanged through a suspect interpreter, wearing down his business acumen, the drip-drip of doubt and indecision cleverly played out. When agreement had been reached and a contract drawn up, a last minute disagreement would be found. The 'thought police', their sinister silent presence held their own countrymen in check. Hugh, arriving back in the UK was drained of patience, his tolerance expended, none left for his family.

There had been further obstacles. The Americans imposed trade embargos on other countries exporting to China. This dog-in-the-manger attitude had rebounded. Hugh found a receptive Russian, happy to become a middle man, through whom he had easy access for British goods into China by the back door. As Chinese political trade barriers started to crumble, Hugh watched as those countries sympathetic to China flooded into the country to benefit from the next five year plan.

Other letters were more personal, light-hearted, when he had had a good day. Missing her and the children, a sentiment rarely spoken, he probably found it easier to say it in a letter. Instructions, what to do about the insurance, car, school fees, garden and what he hoped she wasn't doing, tightening the leash and controlling her from the other side of the world, not allowing her to enjoy four months of freedom.

She laughed again at his description of the Chinese authorities trying to reintroduce bartering into their business transactions. Two tons of dried fleas in payment for British goods. Hugh had tried to accommodate them, contacted Whipsnade, Chester and Edinburgh Zoos to see if they might be interested but their aquarium and reptile houses were already well stocked.

The May Day Parade had impressed Hugh. Tens of thousands of marching soldiers dressed in white tunics without guns, these, together with their uniforms, left in side streets to be reunited later. The Party, anxious that the parade should not be interpreted by the West as a symbol of military strength or aggression. Hugh had been allotted a standing place below Chairman Mao, Chao En Li and Russia's President Voroshilov. A million people: children carrying flowers and red flags, small cloned automatons, an immaculate kaleidoscope of colour and precision; every facet of national life represented, factory workers, farmers, actors, acrobats, puppeteers, dragon dancers, trick cyclists, footballers, club swingers, doctors, nurses, teachers, gymnasts and party officials snaking their way past the Great Leader.

It took six hours for the performing snake to pass through the square, an undulating sea of red, wave upon wave of national pride and political obedience. Hugh had turned to a German from the hotel and remarked what a flawless exhibition. The German commented he had seen it all before in his homeland.

Julia had been denied the opportunity to accompany him on those trips. Wives had not been part of the package and, even if they had been, her sense of duty to the children, particularly with John's ill health, would have prevented her going.

A week later she was in the kitchen, rubbing warmth into an ailing lamb. Hugh turned the radio on. A small item on the midday news brought back another memory. Only half listening, the announcement premised by 'the end of an era'. The male newsreader gave the details. The Ambassadors Hotel in Los Angeles was to be pulled down to make way for new development.

It was a shock, a reminder that she herself was becoming obsolete. The Ambassadors had been their annual base on the West Coast where they were warmly welcomed each year. Julia emerged from the hotel's beauty salon with a makeover camouflaging her real self, ready to play her bit part, a co-opted member of the sales team, before the betrayal.

Although it had all ended in tears Julia looked back with some affection to those heady days of glamour and profligacy, further cementing her discomfort at what she saw as the injustices of the world and a sense of shame that, once upon a time, she had allowed herself to be seduced by it.

At the beginning she had felt like a small child going on an unexpected trip to the pantomime. Everything was unreal, exciting. The private homes in Beverley Hills to which they were invited night after night were stage sets. How did people keep it up? They appeared to go into overdrive at three in the morning when Julia was longing to go to bed, worrying about being on the ball at ten the following morning to join the wives of the industrialists with whom Hugh would have been

178

closeted since seven. She and the MD's wife had been expected to enjoy and fill in their time shopping, visiting film studios, endless coffee and lunch appointments at the swankiest LA restaurants, rubbing shoulders with the celebrities of the day, Fred Astaire, Katherine Hepburn, Spencer Tracy, Lauren Bacall, Humphrey Bogart, lunching at adjacent tables. The incessant trivial bitchy small talk was anathema to Julia. She really had wished she could be part of it but her mind would not leave her alone to enjoy it; it didn't want to know.

One afternoon, returning to The Ambassadors, she felt she needed to meet the people who were making it possible for her to live in a style to which she was unaccustomed. She located a passage leading to the kitchens behind the Empire Room, opened a first door, then a second, to be met by Dante's inferno. A seething mass of black sweating bodies was consumed in steam and smell, the perspiration from their dripping faces caught in coloured neckerchiefs before it could reach food, voices raised, the clash of aluminium against steel, deafening. Her presence receiving a nodding acceptance, she kept walking until she reached the outer door leading onto the street. Dustbin land, where the waste of the wealthy maintained and kept alive the families of the poor in the tinsel city of dreams. Faces of all hues, down and outs, rummaging through the dustbins to find the leftovers, the major part of those two-pound sirloin steaks which had appeared so appetising on the menu. Humanity in all its diversity within three hundred yards, unaware of each other, struggling for survival in their different ways.

The following evening there was an unexpected invitation to a party. They had no idea how they came to be on the guest list. The hotel manager handed Julia an envelope. It was gold-embossed with their names. There was deference in his voice. 'The Musselmans' chauffeur left this for you, Madam.'

Julia had never heard of the Musselmans. The name was not on the copy of Hugh's itinerary. The MD had heard of them. Something to do with casinos, Las Vegas, he thought, probably the Mafia. They too had received an invitation but were not going. Julia got the impression that they felt it was beneath them. She was beginning to suspect that there was a different side to the MD's wife which she was late in recognizing: the woman was a bit of a snob.

The invitation said 'An Arabian Nights Extravaganza Party' and gave a private address in Beverley Hills, no reply necessary. Uncharacteristically, Hugh said, 'Let's go. The others aren't going. It's a chance to get away from them.'

They arrived and introduced themselves. Their host, drawing on his large cigar, reminded Julia of the war profiteer who had usurped her home; overweight, his bald head shiny and sweating. Single-minded in his determination to create his own illusion, he clutched her arm, guiding her through a sea of high-pitched voices and introduced her as Lady Hampton from good old England. Julia had gone along with it; she already knew she was just a character in a play.

A raised stage ran around the interior perimeter of the pleated, pink-chiffon marquee, its overwhelming vulgarity enveloping the extensive gardens and two swimming pools. Brown-skinned belly dancers gyrated at eye level to pseudo-Arabic music. Hugh remarked that they must have hired the entire studio set from the latest Bob Hope/Bing Crosby film, '*Road to Morocco*'. The set was policed by negroes, fine giants of men stripped to the waist. They had pink chiffon pantaloons gathered at the ankles, bejewelled turbans to match gold gondola slippers, scimitars held across their chests, their magnificent, muscled, oiled torsos motionless. Strong faces expressionless, Julia felt their eyes on her. Did she read contempt, a recognition that they were prostituting themselves for some white man's fantasy?

She had left The Ambassadors feeling overdressed. As they approached the house, guests were arriving, gowns jewel encrusted, mink dripping from shoulders, Danny La Rue make-up on midlife faces. Julia instantly felt underdressed, conscious that the string of pearls given to her by her grandmother bore no resemblance to what was expected. She had, on impulse as they were leaving, slipped into her evening bag the twenty-first birthday present from her parents which she never wore but travelled with, just in case. Other than her engagement ring it was the only real piece of jewellery she possessed and now, two decades later, about to come into its own.

It was a pendant designed by Mother and made by a local jeweller from loose, abandoned stones found at the bottom of Grandmother's jewellery box after her death. A spray of graduated diamonds supported on platinum strands, an explosion of stars from a central natural pearl. Why had she never appreciated it before? She made her excuses, passed the eunuchs of the harem, guardians of the powder room, did a quick switch and felt more confident. She spent the night trying to understand what on earth people were talking about, smiling a good deal, enjoying the spectacle, detached.

It had given them a tinge of pleasure over breakfast to report that the party had been quite fun.

With no business dinner scheduled, the following evening the four of them dined at the Coconut Grove, the in-house nightclub. The cabaret included a young Tony Bennett and Petula Clark making a name for herself in the States with 'Down Town' and 'Don't Sleep in the Subway, Darling'.

Judy Garland was one of the diners. Among the sea of faces, Bennett spotted her and invited her onto the stage to join him. She was so drunk she had to be helped to stand. Her glass of red wine upended, pouring down her dress, the large stains visible as she leaned against the piano and started to sing. Immediately, Julia was sitting in the front row of the circle at the local cinema with her brothers, her bare arms and chin resting on the mock velvet balustrade. The voice was still the same, its magic carrying her over the rainbow.

A raucous voice from a far corner of the restaurant shouted, 'Can we launder the dress for you, Judy?'

A party of inebriated sales executives from the American Launderers' Association convention on a freebie had seen an opportunity for cheap publicity. Before her minders understood what was happening, one of the sales reps climbed onto the rostrum, keen to exploit her vulnerability. Bewildered, she turned to

Tony Bennett for assurance, the hush in the room tangible, her humiliation shared by those present. Hugh had risen to his feet in an instinctive act of protection. He never did that for Julia. Perhaps, unbeknown to her, once upon a time, he had walked down his own yellow brick road but hadn't told her.

It was customary to give a farewell party in the Empire Room of The Ambassadors. A 'thank you' to all those whose hospitality they had enjoyed during their four-week stay in the States. Aware that her clothes were becoming over-familiar and a trifle low key for that final gathering, Julia went into one of the hotel boutiques to look for something a little different. An exquisite, jewel-embroidered, lightweight cashmere stole was on a stand by the entrance. She suddenly saw beyond the astronomical price. Rereading Hugh's letters, seeing in her mind those nomad farmers he had described so well. Herding their goats in Western China's arid regions bordering Mongolia, the cashmere wool crop their only meagre income, the fleeces impregnated by wind-blown sand. The children were given a pair of tweezers and the Herculean task of removing every grain of sand manually before the fleeces would be accepted by the Chinese Animal By-Products Corporation for export to the West.

Of course, in the West this would not be allowed, the tabloids screaming child exploitation, but Julia recalled Tattie Week, ten days in October when rural children were given a holiday to help alongside adults to harvest the potato crop. An early frost would make it important to gather them quickly before they froze in the ground, the sense of urgency and being needed, cold, muddy small soft hands working alongside gnarled hardened ones. The pride of achievement when tired, wet and earth splattered, someone patted you on the head and said well done. She had resisted the cashmere stole.

The party went well and hopes were expressed that they would return the following year. Thirty-six hours later they were back home and turned on the TV. Robert Kennedy, the US Attorney General, had been assassinated whilst leaving the Empire room of The Ambassadors Hotel. Gunned down in that familiar passage, leading to the kitchen exit. Leaving the back way to avoid the press.

That had been their last visit to the States. Six weeks later Julia had made her comment about the arms trade and life had changed forever.

Anna shouted, 'One of the heifers is calving.'

CHAPTER EIGHTEEN

The tip of one front foot was peeping out of the vulva. There was no hurry; let nature take its course. But, when two hours had passed and no progress had been made, Hugh helped her bring the two heifers into the barn. That this calf was born alive was not just important to its mother; Julia felt that her own life depended upon it. She knew that if something went wrong, the blame would be hers. Hugh had washed his hands of any possible complications with the comment that she shouldn't have bought them if she didn't know what she was doing.

Father decided human interference was necessary. His frailty was now a barrier to the physical help he hoped to give. Under his instruction, Julia pushed her arm as far as it would go into the birth canal, her fingers exploring, already knowing what they would find, a head turned back, restricting its passage into the birth canal. The harder the mother pushed, the more the head became wedged on the pelvic bones. The heifer had given up, lay moaning. Julia stripped down to her bra and vest, aware that she would need all her unhindered strength to get the calf out alive.

Hugh came to see how things were going and said

he would phone for the vet but they knew that it would be an hour before help could arrive from that quarter. The sense of urgency was now tangible.

In the old days, Thompson and Father would stay up all night with the foaling mares, ready to give assistance at the first sign of trouble; the vet was never sent for. Between them, they must have known what they were doing. Horses were different, the mare's contractions fearsome, quick. If a foal wasn't born within half an hour of a mare throwing herself down to give birth, the prognosis was not good, a head or leg back ominous and a breech birth rarely successful. Cattle and sheep could take their time, hang around for hours, the birth canal accommodating and flexible, but sometimes stockmen could be fooled, make a bad judgement.

Father was holding three pieces of rope; he had made one into a loop and, under the command of his reassuring voice, Julia slipped the loop between her fingers and pushed it and her arm two feet into the heifer. Her fingers carefully felt for a second time, recognising, seeing the head, as a blind person would familiarise themselves with the facial features of a new acquaintance; the eye sockets, nostrils and mouth, gently slipping the lassoed rope behind the ears and under the jaw, sensing its prenatal recoil. Her arm was crushed between contractions. Father said, 'Push the calf as hard as you can back into the mother, until you can straighten the head and manoeuvre its nose into the birth canal.' The heifer tried to expel her arm, its presence adding to her discomfort.

Having secured the rope around the head, Julia

186

attached the other ropes to the two hooves protruding from the vulva and, when she knew that all were in place, asked Hugh to come and help her. They lay side by side on their backs, their feet pushing against the hindquarters of the heifer, pulling with all their strength and making no headway. Hugh suggested the ratchet that he used to tighten strands of wire when putting up a fence. The ropes attached, Hugh slowly put pressure on, mechanically holding any progress that had been made, so that the calf did not slip back into the mother. Julia pulled on the ropes holding the legs, feeling the resistance as again, the calf became wedged at the shoulder. Father instructed, 'Pull on one leg only, as hard as you can, until you hear a click.' When, after superhuman effort, she heard that click as the shoulder was brought forward, allowing it access to its exit route, she knew there was a God. As she had stretched her body to its limits, her mind had been talking, pleading for that extra physical strength from someone and someone had heard.

Pulling on the rope, awaiting the second reassuring click as the other leg straightened, six inches of legs now visible, once again she put her arm in to make certain that the head was going to make it through the pelvic channel. The calf was still alive. She felt its tongue hanging from the side of its mouth, the reflex when touched.

Hugh gradually tightened the ratchet. There was now equal pressure on all three ropes; one ratchet tooth at a time held progress. Concerned for the mother, Julia gently soothed her with her voice, 'Good girl, you're doing well.' Euphoria as the nose came into view. Father's instructions, 'It's a big calf. Keep up the pressure. It may get stuck on the shoulders or the umbilical cord get squeezed and severed before it has a chance to breathe independently.' Brutal minutes for the mother but, when that huge, steaming, slimy, shivering, coffee-coloured bull calf was finally expelled and dragged around to his prostrate mother's head, they knew she would forgive them. Instantly smelling and recognising her own birth fluids, she sat up and licked her first-born son, giving those bonding sounds that animals reserve for their newborn, those unique, soft, gentle murmurings. In horses, Julia knew it was called 'hummering'. Other species probably had a name for it, a guttural sound of pure love.

Julia was violently sick in the corner of the barn, retching from physical exhaustion. Nearing fifty, this was what her inner self had been searching for, affirmation of what she had felt in her teens.

Hugh was uncharacteristically jocular, embraced her, reminded her of the poster they had both seen outside the maternity ward of the hospital where she had given birth to Sarah. 'The first two minutes of life are the most dangerous.' Underneath, some wit had written, 'The last two are pretty dodgy as well.'

The other heifer, having witnessed the trauma of her half-sister's confinement, decided to drop her small heifer calf quietly, on her own, the following night.

At the time, Julia could never have imagined how those two births would affect her life.

Father was making good progress under a supervised new regime. Julia's mother felt confident enough to have him home and he promised that, from then on, it would be a pint of beer at lunch and a double whisky in the evening. He had kept that promise until his death, whereas Julia had become all too aware that she was heading down the same path from which she had successfully diverted father.

She wasn't a competitive person. If there were any competitive genes in her make-up, they were dormant. Acceptance of her place in the order of things had, up to that point, given her peace of mind, so what had made her consider her father's passing remark, 'You should think about showing those two beasts'? Was it pride which made her want to exhibit the two calves, to experience the approbation missing in her marriage? Perhaps she just wanted to please Father or could it be that there was a part of herself of which, until then, she had been unaware?

It seemed a strange pastime to embark upon in middle age. Her knowledge of agricultural shows was confined to childhood, impressions gained when Father had spent many of his summer weekends as president of agricultural societies, making speeches and handing out silver trophies. Those seaside holidays in August had been interrupted by him having to return home to do his duty, the village event as important to him as the long-established, prestigious county and national shows.

Julia had not enjoyed competitions. She participated in the local village show under pressure from Mother. 'You really must enter the gymkhana, dear, to show family presence.'

Julia had been happy riding the five miles to the showground on Betty, clutching her red entrance ticket which said, 'President's Guest Admit One.' As she reluctantly entered the showground, men doffed their caps and said, 'Good morning, Miss Julia, it's nice to have you with us,' and she knew they meant it. She had also known she was about to let everyone down and she suspected Betty knew it also. Betty was a pony of no great show merit. She shared a sanguine approach to life, like her owner. Being asked to jump a man-made, multicoloured pole in front of hundreds of people, for a rosette and ten shillings, didn't come within her remit of enjoyment, nor Julia's.

They blundered over the first obstacle in an uncoor-dinated way but at the second Betty dug in her toes, as Julia knew she would. Her sudden stop dislodged Julia from the saddle. People came rushing up, concerned, helped her remount. Out of the corner of her eye, she saw Father rise to his feet in the grandstand, but he had not left his seat. He understood that it would add to her ignominy to show concern.

In the tradition of her upbringing and, in the spirit of 'try, try, try again' after two further refusals, she and Betty had been disqualified. She was aware of the snig-gers of her peers and fellow competitors sitting on their expensive, well-groomed mounts in the collecting ring, awaiting their turn, and she countered their quips by laughing it off as if it didn't matter and wishing them good luck. But underneath, she would rather not have been feeling as she did. It had been part of the strategy learnt as the only female sibling, trained to accept from the start that life was a bit unfair but it was up to you and you alone how you dealt with it.

She was to be given a second chance.

If she was to succeed in this new world of competitiveness, some spade work was necessary. Life was not just about good or bad luck. It was advisable to know what you were doing. An afternoon at the county show to find out the form had been a good start.

The heat in the cattle tent was soporific, a smell of milk, shit and shampoo. Rows of pampered beasts taking it easy, not a hair out of place on those immaculately groomed, muscled bodies, wallowing in the warmth of two feet of straw, chewing their cud in contentment, their every need a privilege for their owners to satisfy. Trophies and championship rosettes were displayed to impress potential buyers and the general public; proof of their superiority in the animal kingdom for everyone to see. Photos of progeny exported and doing well in far-flung corners of the world. Framed pedigrees giving names of sires and grandsires, dams and grand-dams.

Julia was thrown by the beauty of the animals and the dedication of their handlers and felt that she wasn't quite up to it, but her eye for stock told her that Ferdinand could hold his own amongst such company. The stockmen were male, cattlemen sleeping with their charges. How would they react to a female in their midst? She had better tread warily into this masculine world.

Would Ferdinand need to prove blue blood in his veins to enter? She bought a catalogue, looked up the cattle section and noted that most of the animals had impressive names with prefixes and suffixes, Border Brave Warrior of Eskdalemuir and Ecclefechan Lord Charles.

The naming of their first male calf had been an instant reflex, no thought given to the fact that he might need a title in years to come. He was the reincarnation of Ferdinand the Bull, hero of a much-loved story from her childhood about a gentle bull calf born into a family of fierce Spanish bulls, bred for taking on picadors, toreadors and matadors. So plain Ferdinand it was, Dolly for the heifer. Hugh had already named the mothers Gert and Daisy, after a duo of Cockney comediennes.

The winter months lay ahead. Plenty of time to make plans.

Chapter Nineteen

Unlike the previous five winters, the turn of the year was mild. It enabled them to make headway rebuilding the derelict outbuildings so that, should those freak late April blizzards occur in the future when the ewes started to lamb, there would be shelter for those expected to give birth during the night, safe from predatory foxes and the bitter north-east wind. Respite from searching the fields in the blackness of night with a failing torch, blinded by horizontal snow, the poor beam of light scanning walls to locate the sheep huddled together for warmth. Gloved hands icy, fingers useless, devoid of feeling; the lambs making pale small movements in the darkness on their feet having made it, panic and guilt about the ones who hadn't. Still, white shapes frozen to the earth, lifeless litter, the now-cruel caul, its protective role in the womb reversed, covering the head denying breath; the 'if only' she had got up earlier. Those precious, defining seconds between life or death, months of hope gone in an instant. The mother's despairing vigil, standing guard over her stillborn, taking on the fox, his pungent musty smell overwhelming, stamping her foot, butting him as he moved in to quickly snatch an easy meal to take back to his young.

Euphoria when success overcame disaster. A lamb's head ballooned, three times its normal size, a tongue swollen and black purple, the pressure and struggle of a malpresentation, no guiding legs visible, a dead weight hanging, seemingly lifeless, a quick pull and the gasp of independent life from that monstrous, grotesque, distorted lolling head. Within an hour the swelling abated, licked back to normality by an attentive mother.

Gimmer shearlings, those first-time mothers, unsure of how to react, vulnerable themselves, backing away from the bleating thing to which they had given birth, the maternal instinct late to kick in, rejecting their first-born, butting, butting repeatedly, time and time again, the lamb's instinct overcoming its fear to find the succouring udder until exhausted, it collapsed. Bringing the shearling inside, shackling her, guiding the tiny mouth to the sealed virgin teat whilst the mother railed and kicked against it, reminding Julia of those two teenage, unmarried girls in the village of her youth, who gave birth secretly, in shame, leaving their newborn on the doorstep of the Sunday School, frightened and unsure of whom they could trust, wanting love and understanding but getting police and public condemnation.

Lambing was an exhausting time of year. A time of no sleep, physical exhaustion, flared tempers and blame. But when the weather was good and spring warmth came early, there was nothing in Julia's life to compare with lambing the ewes outside.

The unbreathed, unsullied air of a new dawn filled her lungs. Rising before the sun, its pink glow behind silhouetted mountain, saying it was on its way. Blades of grass wearing their sparkling sheaths of crisp late spring frost, crunched beneath her boots leaving thawing imprints. The utter quiet. At those times, Julia felt she was the only person on earth in that magical stillness, her whole being lifted to a higher plain of consciousness. She could encompass all the beauty and love in the world in her outstretched arms, give the world a new beginning. The silence broken by the bark of the fox to warn her to get a move on before the vixen got to the newborn lambs, that battle of wills and mutual respect ever present.

The new buildings would be a godsend too, if she ever found the time to embark on her showing career.

She tracked down, through the auction mart, the name of the vendor of the two heifers. Their previous owner was an elderly crofter. In reply to her letter asking for information, a grubby envelope arrived, scribbled on the back a note saying what a pleasure it was to know that his two heifers had found such a good home. They were the last two of his life's work. They had been in calf to a bull owned by his landlord, owner of the neighbouring Kallmallick Estate. In the old show catalogue, there was reference to that estate and its pedigree cattle. Ferdinand and Dolly carried a smattering of blue blood in their veins.

In February, she wrote for the schedules of the three adjoining county shows and entered Ferdinand and Dolly in the appropriate classes. She would have to make time to train them, halter and handle them, introduce them to the limelight. It had not been easy in between her other duties.

Ferdinand, twenty-two months old, was almost fully grown. An impressive, strong beast, placid and gentle, weighing nearly a ton, his muscles rippled beneath his skin when he lumbered up to say hello. He and Dolly had been separated to avoid incest and Jack suggested that it would be advisable to have a nose ring to control him. She felt squeamish about it but, in hindsight, she felt more squeamish at the thought of her granddaughter violating her nose and navel with studs.

She didn't enjoy keeping her intentions from Hugh but knew that if she confided he would pooh-pooh them, pour cold water over her enthusiasm and finally persuade her to cancel the whole idea.

She posted the entries: Class 23 Bull, two years old and Class 25 Heifer, two years or under; bought a white overall coat for showing, the stockman's uniform, and felt conspiratorial. Eventually, as the day of the first show approached, she had to ask Hugh if she could have the Land Rover and trailer for two days. He asked why and she had to confess her plans. Without reference to his diary, he replied, 'No, I need it on those days.'

In panic, she phoned Richard the livestock haulier who, on occasions, took their fat lambs to market to see if he could help out. A price was agreed.

She explained to Richard her reluctance to stay the first night in the stockman's quarters, feeling she might cramp the style of those cattlemen whose holidays the agricultural shows were, their one opportunity to get away from their wives. He was more than happy to be with her at three in the morning on the day of the show. All stock must be on the showground before seven.

She tried to sleep. An hour should be sufficient to wash Ferdinand's white bits and the tip of his tail and any dirty patches where he had lain down in his own pat during the night, and to reassure him that this was a first time for both of them. Dolly required little attention other than a quick wash and blow dry, her only white bit a tiny forehead star.

Richard was as good as his word. At two thirty she heard a vehicle making the tortuous ascent to the farm, grinding over the rough track, the strong beams from the wagon's headlights picking up and reflecting the marble eyes of sheep in the adjoining fields. When Richard reversed and put down the ramp, she saw that he had entered into the spirit of the outing. The inside of the wagon was spotless, pressure hosed, with a six-inch layer of pristine wood shavings covering the floor. Had Hugh allowed her to take the old trailer and Land Rover, she would have let down Ferdinand and Dolly.

They arrived on the show field in good time, found the cattle section, offloaded their cargo and bedded them down in the cattle marquee, free straw provided. Ferdinand and Dolly appeared to be enjoying this new experience, hadn't turned a hair, had been greeted by a deal of bovine chat, others mooing to establish any possible recognition.

The secretary's tent opened at seven. She collected her two showing numbers, bought a catalogue and a couple of bacon butties and, with Richard, sat on a bale of straw, reading the names of other exhibitors in the catalogue and summing up the competition, warming to the ribaldry and bonhomie of other exhibitors. As newcomers to the game they were seen as no threat.

There were eleven entered in Class 23 and fifteen in Dolly's. When she read the stark name 'Ferdinand' among those triple-barrelled names, she felt out of her league and suggested to Richard that he show Ferdinand. He was having none of it but said he would be at the side of the ring if Ferdinand turned stroppy.

Ferdinand's class was called over the tannoy and Julia fell in behind someone who appeared to know what they were doing. After two circuits of the ring, the judge asked the bowler-hatted steward to bring the first two that had caught his eye in to the centre of the ring. Julia had a quick word with God, 'Please don't let us be pulled in last,' allowed her concentration to lapse for a moment and got too close to the bull in front. Ferdinand, who must have thought something was expected of him, mounted his nearest rival, his stirrings of sexuality having got the better of him. Just as she had seen her father, out of the corner of her eye, rise to his feet when she had fallen off Betty, she was conscious of the steward calling, doffing his bowler; it was to be ignominy all over again. The handler of the bull which Ferdinand had attempted to seduce was muttering something uncomplimentary under his breath. The steward was gesticulating, waving his bowler, coming towards her. She was going to be expelled from the ring. But no, he was smiling and said, 'Would you come in third, please?' She found it unreal, she hadn't been brought up to believe or accept that she might be a winner. At the ringside, Richard gave the thumbs up.

The young bulls were lined up. The real judging was still to come. It took almost an hour for the hands-on examination of all eleven beasts. Much time was spent on Ferdinand's balls. (Richard told her later that the judge was looking for split cod, an incorrect division of the scrotum associated with irregular testicles, not good news for potential breeding bulls.) There were a few things Father hadn't mentioned. During that inspection Ferdinand closed his eyes and licked her hands with that gentle, reassuring, rough-sandpaper tongue and never moved. Julia could see others were playing up and down the line and, when the bull which had been pulled in last had been duly assessed, the judge had a quick word with the steward, who approached Julia and asked her to go into first place.

She felt faint, in a haze of disbelief. She led Ferdinand off in the wrong direction until checked by the steward. She was vaguely aware of dissatisfied mutterings from the two she had displaced, but her first thought was Father. She would find it difficult to wait until evening to find a call box, to phone him and tell him the news.

The judge handed her the red rosette and said nothing; there were still the championships to come, he had six more classes to judge. As Julia left the ring, Richard was there to congratulate her. She could see that he was proud of being part of the team, chatting to bystanders, basking in her success, and now anxious to be the one to show Dolly. Out of a class of fifteen, he was awarded a third. So was born a showing partnership which lasted thirty years. Julia wished it could have been with Hugh, but Hugh would have found it difficult to cope with her success.

Ferdinand went on to win the junior championship and a trophy for the best male bred by the owner.

Immediately on her return home, she phoned Father. He was over the moon, had probably expected it. From his voice, Julia knew he was longing to have a celebratory drink but she knew he wouldn't.

When she told Hugh his response was, 'Can't have been many in the class.'

The following day there were three telephone enquiries from people wanting to buy Ferdinand.

CHAPTER TWENTY

The invitation came out of the blue. Bill, a fellow officer from HMS *Vanguard* days who had married the Cape Town heiress, hoped to renew past friendship. The battleship herself, the last to be built on the Clyde, was long since gone, sent to the scrapyard. Her final duty had been to carry the Royal Family on that journey to South Africa, the start of which Julia remembered for different reasons at Waterloo Station.

The dovetailing of disconnected episodes in people's lives fascinated Julia, coincidences thrown up against all the odds, points changed, diverting lives down branch lines.

The invitation was a spin-off from a Ships' Association annual reunion to which she dutifully went to support Hugh. She couldn't really get out of it. He was the president; it was expected. An all-ranks, annual gathering, wives included, veterans who had served together aboard an Illustrious class aircraft carrier with the British Pacific Fleet attached to the US Third Fleet, who had endured youth and hardship together in a forgotten war.

Hugh's remarkable memory made him a worthy president. He recalled the names of everyone, from the lowliest stoker upwards, and they all loved him for it. His ad lib after-dinner speeches were full of anecdotes. The time a visiting American admiral, anxious to find fault with the British Navy's fire drill had, on being piped aboard, thrown his gold-braided cap on deck and shouted at the welcoming party standing to attention, 'That's an incendiary bomb. How would you deal with it?' An enterprising AB had stepped forward and kicked it overboard. There had been much banging of spoons on tables; most of the jokes were at the expense of their American allies.

Julia understood how essential get-togethers were for those ex-servicemen and their families. Ordinary people, thrown together by war, needing to remind themselves of a comradeship growing thinner in number each passing year. They gathered in a smart hotel in the Midlands for a long weekend, from all over the UK, Australia and Canada, joining the congregation of the local church for Sunday Matins and parading the Association's standard through the town.

It was a part of Hugh's life of which Julia knew little. She knew where the war had taken him but was ignorant of the high esteem in which he had been held. She found it difficult to equate his concern for the men under his command with his lack of awareness for the emotional needs of his family. He could not see the hurt in the eyes of his children when his temper flared and they were unjustly accused. Yet these old salts were telling her stories of her husband's magnanimity, his understanding when members of the ship's crew were brought before him at 'defaulters', kangaroo courts of naval discipline. They told her of her Hugh's decency, his fairness to those hardened by a criminal past, whose prison records caught up with them, their names to the fore when anything was reported stolen on board.

The old lag who had spent more of his life in prison than out of it until released to serve king and country, gave her a drunken hug. 'Your husband was the first person to believe in me.'

Julia was aware that there was this other side to Hugh but it was in a different compartment to the life they were trying to live together, isolated in both their minds, unable to make contact or cross imaginary boundaries of earlier experiences. She felt she should try harder to understand him, but that would not be easy. He lacked awareness of her and the good job she felt she was doing on his behalf: remembering people's names, where they lived, how many grandchildren and great-grandchildren, the state of their health. She could tell by their response, the kisses and hugs of yearly recognition, that she had been oiling the wheels. Of this, he was totally unaware – or refused to accept it.

As the two busloads of veterans left the hotel for the traditional pre-booked Saturday morning visit to a local stately home, she was looking forward to it. Just as they were about to board the bus, a man wearing a Burma Star and Pacific ribbon felt unwell and Julia stayed behind with him. Hugh was not aware that she was not in her allotted seat on the bus. For something to say, over lunch, he had asked whether she had enjoyed the outing.

They were asked to Bill and Jane's summer home in Italy. The rest of the party were three other naval couples, two of whom she knew vaguely; they were on Hugh's Christmas card list. Hugh immediately said no. She tried to work on him, to no avail. She remembered those Italian prisoners of war from childhood; she needed to see where they came from and what they had been made to sacrifice in the name of patriotism.

Hugh was generous in saying, 'Go on your own.' He could cope with the livestock and there was Anna to help. Late August, early September she would be home. Julia phoned impulsively. Jane answered; there had been no hesitation.

Julia was beginning to realise that her impulses usually turned out well. Gert and Daisy, their extended family, and the land on which they flourished, were proof. It was when she started thinking hard about something, weighing up the pros and cons that things went wrong.

Julia had never travelled for pleasure before. There had been numerous business trips abroad in that other life, those artificial excursions into people's domains, restricted in their understanding of others by contracts, balance sheets, profits, company loyalty and corporate entertaining. She had never experienced the freedom of meeting real people, other than that sprint through the kitchens at The Ambassadors in Los Angeles and a stopover in Boston en route to LA. Whilst Hugh had given talks to students at the Harvard Business School and the Massachusetts Institute of Technology, she had been taken under the wing of an elderly professor and his wife, delightful New Englanders, intellectuals. Been welcomed into their understated and tasteful home, an antidote to the brashness awaiting on the West Coast.

They had been more English than the English, their manners and voices gentle, the leather patches on the elbows of the professor's jacket endearingly familiar.

She could understand Hugh's reluctance to go to Italy. He had seen the world under different circumstances. Places were fixed in his mind, he had convinced himself that nothing had changed for the better and lacked the imagination and optimism to believe that anything could.

But she was remembering *'bella, bella'*, half-forgotten words of appreciation, an awakening as she sat unsure of herself on a wall.

Leaving Pisa airport, every fibre of her being was attuned to the sights, smells and sounds. Armed with a train timetable and instructions from Jane, she caught the train to Sienna and changed on to the branch line to Montepulciano, where someone would meet her.

As the train passed through the southern Tuscan countryside, she was farming every inch of it, her love affair with the soil feeling a new warmer earth. The great expanses of rolling, creamed-coffee land were already under the plough as autumn approached, turning up clay blocks of impacted soil. How could seeds be expected to germinate in those heavy, lumpen, angular sods baked hard by the sun, she wondered? The plough reached higher and higher as edicts and cash from Brussels took their toll, acres of olive trees ripped out, bonfired because some EU bureaucrat had persuaded Italian farmers, against their better judgement, that there was more money to be made from growing pasta maize. The same cash inducements given to British farmers by bureaucrats to strip out hedgerows to make way for greater productivity.

As the train reduced speed near small rural stations, she caught glimpses of sheep still grazing on the stubble. She opened the carriage window and heard the faint, muffled chimes of the belled flocks, the large white Maremma dogs, a cross between a Great Dane and a Labrador. They were marshalling their wards on the unfenced plateau, aware of every would-be predator, on duty twenty-four hours a day, guardians of their masters' livelihood as that breed had done since the thirteenth century, their images sketched into pastoral scenes, cameos in the backgrounds of paintings by old masters.

Bill was there to meet her in a clapped-out Morris Traveller. They kept two bangers permanently in Italy for their five-month summer visits; the village joiner used them during the winter. Bill was wearing those familiar khaki, tropical-issue naval shorts, a grey beard and digger hat. Within a minute, there was a marriage of minds. By the time they arrived at the old Tuscan farmhouse, a half-hour drive, they felt they had known each other for ever.

The approach to the farm, perched on the crest of a hill, had superb, uninterrupted views in all directions, hectares of fig and olive trees, poplars replacing the oaks of home. The evening light bathed the large square stone building in a ripe cantaloupe, melon softness, dark green shutters open and smiling, the track stony and narrow, dusty.

Jane greeted her warmly. Others had already arrived, having spent most of the summer motoring through Europe.

They were sitting in a small cobbled courtyard in a bower of mellowing vines, the leaves beginning to turn yellow, the fruit awaiting that late opaque bloom to appear before harvesting could begin, having a drink, enjoying the last rays of the quickly setting Italian sun. They rose to greet her. Julia quickly realised her good fortune. She was to spend the next three weeks among a group of people whose outlook on life reflected her own; an outlook which had been pushed to one side, bogged down in trying to keep her family show on the road. She had been catapulted into a cultural oasis of like minds, a replay of those exeats from school when Prue's father had opened other windows for her.

It came as no surprise that Jane had spent four weeks in a Cape Town jail, a member of the Black Sash movement, fighting against apartheid and Mandela's imprisonment. Her family had, for generations, held out the hand of friendship; now suspicion and resentment were insidiously getting a new grip, all the goodwill again viewed with mistrust. Which sage wrote, 'Those who try to change history are bound for disappointment'?

Jane's voice could be heard answering the phone: 'Come and have something to eat. We've a few friends staying.' Two Land Rovers, roofs laden with camera equipment and sprouting antennae, arrived, friends of her children, on their way to Rimini to catch a boat across the Adriatic to report on the turmoil and ethnic slaughter going on in Bosnia. Jane's home was a watering hole for a new generation trying to make sense of the mess the world was in.

A lovely girl, slender, immaculately clothed, arrived

just as they were finishing lunch in the garden, grace-
fully detaching herself from the driver's seat of the
Bugatti, her blonde hair moving like a shampoo ad,
red stilettos uncertain of the cobbles, hugging Bill and
Jane. Julia thought she must be an Italian film star. The
visitor and Bill strolled out of hearing and were in ani-
mated conversation.

Julia remarked, 'What a beautiful woman,' and
Jane replied, 'Yes, with a razor-sharp mind. She's
come to pick Bill's brains. She's a high-powered lawyer
representing the Vatican, taking on the sleaze and corruption endemic in Italian politics.'

Julia felt a great event briefly touching her; a new
history in the making had brushed momentarily against
her. It made her feel strangely insecure, inadequate,
out of her depth.

Bill and Jane were not out of their depth, inte-
grated into the small community in which they lived
from May to September. They spoke Italian fluently,
had taken the trouble to acquaint themselves with the
customs of the area, and were accepted as villagers.
When the butcher died during Julia's visit, it was expected that they all join the funeral cortège, walking
behind the young blades of the village who carried the
coffin, following the priest from house to house, the
sweet smell of incense pervading the small dark homes,
to say goodbye to all he had served so well and receive
their thanks and blessings in return.

Bill and Jane's house was beautiful in its simplicity.
The main building was as it had always been, the wide,
spiral, rough-stoned staircase a reminder of her own
home in a colder climate. The bedrooms were huge

and shuttered, menthol candles on the window sills to light at nightfall to discourage mosquitoes; a bed, a rug, an old chest of drawers, the views the only permanent fixture necessary.

The communal bathroom and loo were un-trustworthy, unable to cope with the extra strain put on them by a household of nine. Julia had been well-schooled in bathroom deprivation. The huge enamelled white bath was too big for the water supply. Four large sofas and four large lamps and a scattering of oriental rugs covered the stone floors in the living area; tea chests full of books, their foil lining still intact, smelling of Ceylon tea and plywood, escapee leaves clinging to the covers of books, bran tubs of other people's thoughts to be delved into when the log fire was lit on chilly September evenings.

The kitchen was cool, slabs of stone built into the walls of the old dairy on which pigs were once salted, the only surfaces available on which to prepare food and pile crockery and utensils. The antiquated Calor gas stove guaranteed that hot meals were a rarity.

But it didn't matter. Jane cooked Italian, effortlessly producing easy meals: *insalata caprese, insalata di rucola, parmigiano e pera*. Bundling everyone into the two decrepit Morris Travellers, their shock absorbers stretched to the limit, they crossed into Umbria in search of the best black truffles for *tagliatelle al tartufo nero*.

At breakfast everyone was left to their own devices. Julia, always an early riser, up before the others, gathered the ripened figs. Bill joined her to watch the sun rise, checking the nets placed under the olive trees to collect the nightly fall of fruit. Together they talked and put the world to rights.

The simplicity appealed to Julia's quasi-Quaker upbringing. The philosophy of 'only possess that which thou needest but let that be a thing of beauty'.

On the obligatory day trip to Florence, she found it hard to like the gilded, over-cherubed, cold, oppressive cathedrals on the tourist trail. There was a limit to how much history she could absorb in that heat. Late in the day, when feet were swollen and an earlier return train mooted, they discovered the Museo Di San Marco Dell'Angelico.

Julia was bewitched by the simplicity, beauty and softness of those early fifteenth-century frescoes: their colours; golds, reds, terracottas, blues, with their message faded, muted by time. Friars finding inner peace in their monastic cells. In how many different ways people tried to reach God. It was knowing He was there for the finding that was important, and she was beginning to understand and appreciate with what passion and belief those craftsmen built those over-the-top edifices as manifestations of their faith. Ornate, awesome, gilded symbols to the glorification of God. She could only admire and marvel at their dedication and belief as they watched them grow. A half-remembered line from a poem her father had read to her as a child came into her head: 'They climbed on sketchy ladders towards God.'

Father wasn't into poetry and that is probably why it had stuck. She remembered him saying, 'This poem was written recently by a Welshman.' When she got home, and if she remembered, she would look him up.

During acts of worship in these places there could be no fear of the mind wandering; there was too much to see and be overawed by, on which to feast the eye, to focus. The smoke from the swinging incense caught in the rays of the sun, drifting heavenwards. A drifting mind wouldn't stand a chance amid such splendour. Unlike the isolated quietness of Quaker meetings which Mother insisted she attend occasionally. Nothing to distract, higher thoughts overridden within the first five minutes, Mother whispering that she had forgotten to tell Nellie which vegetables to prepare for lunch, minds floundering on their own, nothing to guide or distract their descent into the mundane.

As the time arrived to return home, Julia was relieved, tinged with a sense of disloyalty that Hugh had not been with her. His right-wing comments would have jarred, been out of place, garrulous amongst enlightened reasoned debate. She had been given freedom to express herself without the hindrance of ridicule. It had surprised her that there was so much stored in her mind waiting to get out, and people who actually wanted to listen and were interested in what she could contribute.

Goodbyes were said with an eye to the future, the casual, 'See you all again next year,' meant. Julia returned home rejoicing, to her northern hills. Her mind had its next year's holiday booked.

The week after her return home, she found time to go to the library and ask the librarian whether she could locate the author of that remembered line, the only clues that he was Welsh and contemporary. And there he was: John Ormond 1923–1990. She read his

poem 'The Cathedral' again, delighting in that powerful description of the mason's lot − and the final line
that put everything into perspective: *Cocked up a squint
eye and said, 'I bloody did that.'*

CHAPTER TWENTY-ONE

On her return home, Hugh was genuinely pleased to see her. His three weeks of enforced bachelorhood had made him aware that cooking, keeping the house moderately tidy, answering the telephone, watering the garden, looking after the livestock and dealing with the mandatory instructions of official gobbledegook emanating from the Ministry of Agriculture Fisheries and Food, plus dealing with his offsprings' imagined disasters, wasn't something he would like to take on board on a permanent basis.

The home-cooked food Julia had carefully planned for her three weeks absence and put in the ageing, rusty freezer in one of the outbuildings had remained untouched. Remembering to thaw out the following day's meals the previous evening had required too much domestic forward planning. Hugh had found it easier to drive to the nearest pub four miles away or accept hospitality from neighbours who, on hearing that his wife was gadding about in foreign parts, had taken pity on him.

A farmer's wife holidaying on her own, especially abroad, had been viewed with suspicion. The mores of half a century ago were still in place, the old ways dying hard. Vera still used heavy irons reheated every ten minutes on the red-hot open fire as she thumped her way through huge piles of sheets, shirts and cross-stitched, home-embroidered tablecloths. She never had holidays; there wasn't time between lambing, hay-making, calf weaning, clipping, dipping, preserving the surplus of spring eggs, sealing them in sodium silicate for future cake making. Farmers chose their wives with care, with the same discernment and thought with which they would purchase a brood mare, and if there was an acre or two of land as dowry all the better.

Farmers now, Julia thought, found it difficult to find wives, they advertised on the internet or entered TV competitions and in desperation, married pretty hairdressers who divorced them within a couple of years for unreasonable behaviour and claimed half the proceeds from the enforced sale of the farm.

Gert and Daisy were in calf again, having suffered the ignominy of artificial insemination with the con-nivance of the vet. Two straws of semen, one contain-ing the wherewithal to produce another Ferdinand and the other from a totally unrelated bull in the hope that a line of females would be produced to create Ferdinand's planned harem.

Neither she nor Hugh enjoyed inflicting that kind of sex on the cows. They were as entitled to their bit of pleasure as anyone. Julia felt that humanity was already being taken over by scientists and, if mankind wished to conceive by joyless means, we had no right to inflict such unnatural forms of procreation on the animal kingdom.

Now, standing at the sink, using an old newspaper

214

to wrap the bleached, soft bones from the stockpot before consigning them to the dustbin, the headlines of a small paragraph caught her eye. A report of an Easter message from an Archbishop Comastri of whom Julia had never heard but, in her opinion, hit the nail on the head: 'Lord, we have lost our sense of sin. Today a slick campaign of propaganda is spreading an inane apologia of evil, a senseless cult of Satan, a mindless desire for transgression, a dishonest and frivolous freedom, exalting impulsiveness, immorality and selfishness as if they were new heights of sophistication.'

She investigated further the soggy torn paper and found above it a less verbose message from the Pope: 'Lord Jesus, our affluence is making us less human, our entertainment has become a drug, a source of alienation and our society's incessant message is an invitation to selfishness.' She cut the quotes from the paper and put them on the range to dry, grateful that out there was someone fighting her corner. The poor old Ten Commandments, that blueprint for mankind's contentment and harmony, those concise fifty words of dos and don'ts, had been silenced, rejected and given less credence than a ninety-thousand word edict coming from Brussels on the transportation of duck eggs.

Julia kept trying to reign in her mind, stop it jumping backwards and forwards between decades and events but it didn't want to listen. It was having a rare old time with her memory and she was having difficulty keeping them both under control. She was becoming like their four-year-old hyperactive grandson whose imagination took flight when he came for a sleep-over and she forgot about those ominous E numbers listed on the back of a tube of Smarties and gave in to his pleadings.

Within eight years they had built up a fifty-strong pedigree herd of suckler beef cattle. Ferdinand may have been laid back but he knew where his duties lay and his lady friends now queued up for his favours. Julia and Richard continued their successes in the show ring. Ferdinand's progeny now won the honours. There was a trickle of enquiries from abroad for Ferdinand bloodlines, competing with an already flourishing home demand and Julia, much to her surprise, was invited to join the official panel of judges of the breed.

Things were easing financially and all was set fair. That they had planted their latter-day roots in that idyllic place more by desperation than design, added to their overwhelming feeling of good fortune. Father was still alive. Her success gave him immense joy. He knew the pedigrees of all the cattle and continued to advise on blood lines.

He and Mother, now living for most of the year in the south with David, came north annually for two or three months, arriving with the spring, the return of the swallows and Hugh's resentment. Those weeks of verdant renewal, the countryside a mosaic of yellow, limes, green and red copper budding trees. The oaks, planted against local advice, were thriving. The skylarks, soaring specks almost invisible to the naked eye, the purity of their song confirming their presence.

Halcyon days had lasted not just their legendary seven days before and after the winter solstice, but for the next eight years.

Even the unpleasant jobs which come with custodianship of animals gave Julia pleasure. Unclogging the bottoms of the week-old lambs when the richness and plenty of the ewes milk created an outflow of bright yellow, double cream shit which became hardened when exposed to the air, cementing tails to backsides. Without human help, the lamb would explode, its anus blocked by a hard core of yellow larva. The crustaceans were so hard that a knife was necessary, followed by that satisfying expulsion of gas. The pungent smell of rich digested milk engrained under her fingernails lasted for days. Julia enjoyed every moment.

She vividly remembered what she was doing, planting out geraniums, when she received that stab of awareness, suddenly thinking, 'This is too good to last.' A physical pain of acute unease; something was about to happen, a reawakening of the Gaelic Taisch, that second sight of foreboding. And it had...

One morning she noticed that whereas normally Jack's cows and calves would be grazing the fields adjoining theirs, there was no sign of them. His friendly visits were rare that spring. It was already mid-summer; her parents had migrated south. Julia wandered down to his farm with a mixture of concern, not wanting to interfere. Like all dog-and-stick farmers, true men of the soil, problems among their stock were private disasters. Admitting that you had lost a calf or cow was a sign of failure best kept from neighbours.

She knocked on the door. It wasn't the usual Jack who answered. He was unshaven, his usually bright eyes dulled. He was pleased to see her, said come in, his wife silent and suspicious in the background, unwelcoming.

All but one of his cows had aborted. In his sixty years of farming he had never experienced anything like this. Julia suggested the vet, but knew he would resist. Cattlemen are a proud breed. To admit failure to someone with only paper qualifications was not within their reasoning. She suggested that perhaps others were having similar problems and it was important that experiences were shared. In the end he gave in and the vet was called.

The media picked it up – 'Mad Cow Disease' – and insisted on showing night after night the horrendous picture of a wretched, staggering, stricken black and white cow. It was regurgitated decades later, whenever anyone mentioned CJD.

Rumours were rife; something nasty in the cattle cake produced by the giant multinational animal food-stuffs industry. Hugh immediately wrote to the producers, demanding to know what exactly went into those animal feeds. What did the label stating seventeen per cent protein consist of? Until that moment most country people had trusted those companies, the good relationship with the reps who called once a month for the order, taking their time over home-made cakes and tea, passing on the chat and gossip from along the fell side. Protein was assumed to be what it had always been: soya or flaked maize.

The answer to Hugh's letter was revealing. The source of protein content in their feeds was a commercial secret which they were unable to divulge. Hugh did not give up. He demanded an assurance that no animal offal or remains of animals went into the cake fed to herbivores. The company refused to give that assurance and the whole ghastly story unfolded.

Tragedy was only a week away. Harry, the elder son

of their good neighbours Sid and Vera, that welcoming, hardworking family who had held them together during that first harsh winter, was the unsuspecting conduit by which misfortune had befallen others. Brought up to be thrifty, Harry had sourced a cheap supply of cattle cake and shared his good fortune with neighbours and farming friends within the area. When it became common knowledge that BSE and CJD were caused by the obscenity of big business seeking higher and higher profits, conning farmers into using the ground-up remains of deceased animals in cattle cake, he was unable to live with himself and the misfortunes he felt he had inflicted on his friends.

He was found by Vera, hanging from a beam in the barn, all that love, trust, kindness and innocent humanity choked from him, his rosy-red, fresh-air, happy face turned to ballooning blue.

Julia looked up the share price of the company which had killed him. It was doing well, being taken over by another multinational, making a different kind of killing for the financial whiz kids in the City.

Harry's funeral reminded Julia of that funeral in Italy, an outpouring of grief for a decent, humble, human being, the crowds attending overflowing into the fields surrounding the tiny isolated Norman church. A good person of no national nor media significance. His memory, however, would not be as easily erased as that of those who held themselves in greater esteem.

The growl of her old adversary awakened Julia the following morning. All it had needed was that push in the wrong direction, from being in control, on a high a week ago. Her subconscious must have been absorbing

219

and retaining all the man-made misery and unhappiness of the world like a sponge. Many times she had told herself not to watch news programmes, but she had needed to know what was going on.

It was 'pull yourself together' time again and she tried hard not to let that insidious, grey cloud engulf her, separating her from what was happening around her in order to have her thoughts to itself. She tried to be rational but then something else happened, which gave her mind that final push over the edge.

Father rang one evening. She reassured him that they had no problems with the cattle. That was the last time she spoke with him. He died that night from a stroke. It wasn't his death that tipped the balance. At eighty-five it was to be expected and with his history of drinking he had lasted pretty well. It was the fact that Mother had taken him at his word. His funeral instructions to be wherever and however it would give those he loved the least trouble, his thoughtfulness for others constant to the end. Mother plumped for cremation. Julia motored south for the funeral, her lack of concentration a danger to other motorists, the black dog of depression her back-seat driver.

Afterwards she blamed herself for not discussing the funeral arrangements with her brothers. She had taken it for granted that guardianship of his ashes would return with her, to be blown to the winds in the solitude of his trusted northern hills. Instead, before she could stop it happening, they had been quickly dispatched in an overcrowded cemetery adjoining the Somerset Levels. She had prayed that a southerly gale would get up and blow the odd particle northwards.

She had let him down. He was still not at rest. The sense that she had betrayed him in that final act pushed her again into the steep-sided, slippery pit.

CHAPTER TWENTY-TWO

How could a mind surrounded by so much beauty descend into such despair?

When sleep allowed, the commonplace anxiety dreams, the need to be at an important meeting half an hour ago and she still had a three-hundred-mile car journey and couldn't find her shoes, had been replaced by a macabre form from which she struggled and fought to awake. Forces bent on doing harm to those she loved and powerless, night after night, to prevent them, her heart racing, thumping with such force that it awoke her, her body bathed in sweat.

But it was not reality to which she awoke. Asleep, she was vaguely aware that the nightmares and uneasy dreams might end. Awake, there was no such escape. A curtain descended through which everyday things became distorted, indistinct, hostile. She no longer trusted herself or others. Despair engulfed her, took hold. Previous invasions had been repelled but this one became her master. Nothing was important any more.

Going through the motions of caring for the live-stock, an automaton, her deadened eyes saw nothing; her reflexes were programmed, the muffled sounds of life going on beyond the sea of isolation in which she was drowning.

She wondered whether Ferdinand sensed the change in her. His affection was undimmed, licking her hand for the last vestige of the proffered apple, his snuffling, wet, hard, shiny nose exploring her face as those cattle from her youth had done. But she was no longer sitting on her special flat, yellow lichen-covered stone, warmed by the sun, on top of that secure enchanted kitchen garden wall, that gateway between childhood and adolescence with its long views of the promised land beckoning, stretching out to her from outside the protection of family.

Now her face was cold. Ferdinand was licking her salt-laden tears with his gentle, nutmeg-grater tongue.

The dreams and hopes conjured up from that high vantage point had been temporarily dashed. Irrationality took over and her normally sound instincts went off the rails. Now impulse led her down wrong paths to do things which, had she been of sound mind, she would not have contemplated. Driving off in the middle of the night, not telling Hugh where she was going, unsure herself, waking up her GP, that purveyor of Valium, taken in, weeping.

Then there was the letter from Bill. Sorry that Julia had not managed to get over to Italy that year for their annual get together. He was in the UK on business, staying at the Savoy; any chance of meeting up for a meal?

Julia's off-balance mind read into the letter a panacea for all her ills and, without a moment's thought, she bought a railway ticket, told Hugh she would be spending a few days with Sarah in Cambridge and left home, leaving Hugh to cope as best he could.

She did not recognise the dapper-suited, clean-shaven man carefully avoiding the puddles on the rain-drenched station platform, shorn of his carefree Italian stubble. It was an awkward meeting of strangers. He was surprised by her appearance.

'You're not looking well.'

After dinner they went up to his room. She knew now that neither of them wanted it. She suspected that, from a lifetime of sending out the wrong signals, she had been misunderstood. Bill was possibly being chivalrous. After all, she was in her fifties. Though her childhood perception that she was an ugly duckling had abated over the years, the thin, mousey, straight hair had somehow thickened and looked better grey and she had acquired a simple elegance, she still remained unsure of herself.

Julia had not known that Bill carried his own adversity, well-hidden, camouflaged from the world and his family and, like her, he may have mistakenly believed that the clandestine warmth of intimacy could lay ghosts. They had hoped for a cerebral reunion. Instead it became a joyless, physical joining born out of despair, as though happening to another couple. Their sense of wrongdoing was a further burden to be carried, a betrayal of Hugh and Jane. When they met in future, they avoided each other's eyes. Something precious had been lost.

How fortunate, Julia thought, are the young with their off-the-shelf, one-night stands, immunised against guilt.

As they lay on the bed afterwards, holding hands,

Bill started talking about a tragedy from his childhood.

It had happened one summer when he was eight. On holiday at the seaside, he and his only sibling Joannie, two years his junior, had gone to the sands to dig and paddle. They were in the charge of nanny who, anxious to finish reading the final chapter of her 'who done it', had settled herself down in a hired deckchair and instructed Bill to keep an eye on his sister as they raced towards the incoming tide.

It was over in less than half a minute. Joannie had slipped under the water, sucked down by powerful undercurrents, so an inquest was told. But Bill had been told nothing, deemed too young to understand. Joannie's name was never mentioned in the house again, as though she had never existed, and he had been sent back, three days early, to his preparatory boarding school, ignorant of everything except his own sense of responsibility. No one hugged or comforted him, attempted to explain. His parents had abandoned him in order to deal with their own grief, and he had reached manhood carrying that guilt.

As he wept, Julia gently kissed the forehead of the tortured small boy, still imprisoned within that hardened, decorated, naval war hero, who had witnessed other unimaginable horrors but was unable any longer to keep the lid down on that particular one.

Looking back, Julia wondered what Freud would have made of that sad encounter. No doubt he would have convinced them that it had been therapeutic, but she now knew that comfort was more easily found amongst the familiarity of a long relationship, however difficult, in the satisfying knowledge that eventually she would learn in which order to take things for the best result. To change might be too much hassle, like installing a new bathroom or moving house.

How many marriages got everything right? Probably very few. When she couldn't sleep, she imagined what was going on in the marriages of their friends, her mind arranging wife swaps. Once Hugh had asked what she was chuckling about. She couldn't explain that her mind was somewhere else, trying to maintain its sanity. He would not have understood, not seen the funny side.

She didn't hear the jailor's key in the lock. Suddenly she was outside the door of her prison, emerging from solitary confinement, no longer contagious. At the end of the passage she saw her old enthusiasm for life beckon. She quickened her step and emerged into a blinding light. The world welcomed her back.

That sea of darkness, her constant companion for more than two years, had taken itself off, washed up on someone else's shore, an unseen vapour ready to invade another's peace of mind, cause havoc elsewhere.

She felt the invasion and occupation of her mind as a malicious spirit. Now its modus operandi was known and understood, an imbalance of chemicals in the brain, a lack of trace elements. If she had bothered to read the contents of the mineral licks to which the cattle had free access, she would have known this.

Hugh's reaction to those lost two years had been to bury his head in the sand and make comments about her instability and drinking. Unable to crack hers, he had retreated into his own personal shell. His out-of-bounds study was piled high with dust, books and newspaper cuttings to indulge his passion for military and naval history, of which he was a true scholar. His knowledge and memory of events was awesome, his absorption and retention of facts phenomenal, which made watching an historical drama on TV in his company a restless affair of criticism, the plot lost in the barrage of fault finding: the railway gauge is the wrong size; the number of buttons on that uniform incorrect.

In his latter years, he had turned this expertise into a thriving antiquarian and second-hand book business, but not before his whole persona had had a complete makeover. When he was a leader of industry he had insisted on the correct cufflinks to go with the Savile Row suit, the pure-silk, Jermyn Street tie and matching handkerchief folded into the breast pocket to complement the carefully chosen shirt, his appearance meticulous. Now his adult children were making remarks about his unkempt appearance. The unruly abundance of white hair, sideburns and undesigner stubble when he couldn't be bothered to shave. He had long ago given up going to the barber as a waste of time and money and Julia persuaded him two or three times a year to allow her to give his hair a trim with the kitchen scissors. This, coupled with his predilection for second-hand army-surplus clothing, solicited such comments as, 'Gosh, Dad looks like a down-and-out. Can't you take him in hand, Mum?' But of course, he was following her lead, expunging all trappings of worldly success.

He became obsessive about the sanctity of his study, the old cooling parlour, chilly in winter. Nailed to the door was a board on which were written some Japanese symbols. It had been a keepsake from a repatriated prisoner of war and was meant to keep the family out. They suspected it said 'latrine'. Hugh convinced them it said 'Captain's Office'. One day, one day, one day, she would find the time to have it translated, together with 'HEB DDUW HEB DDIM DUW A DIGON'.

Hugh now possessed a computer. Forbidden access to his study, Julia had no way of bringing her long-forgotten office skills up to date or becoming computer literate. She suggested buying her own and taking lessons, but this was forbidden on the grounds that another computer would overload the system. What this meant she had no idea, but she had accepted it, for Hugh knew about these things and she did not.

On occasion she was allowed to borrow his old Imperial typewriter, one of his many treasured possessions, in order to write letters of concern to Members of Parliament, her efforts being given short shrift when they arrived on the desks of Permanent Secretaries, the *t* missing and the centres of the *o* and *b* solid with ink.

Then, unexpectedly, on her seventieth birthday, Hugh gave her a Sharp's word processor.

CHAPTER TWENTY-THREE

Hugh was to be congratulated. He had given her something practical, had taken on board that she was not a jewellery person. Her only jewellery was the string of pearls bequeathed to her by her grandmother, her engagement ring, a diamond eternity ring which had belonged to her deceased mother-in-law, and the diamond pendant, the twenty-first present from her parents. The only adornment which gave her delight in its wearing and never left her wrist was a heavy band of oriental silver, thought to be of little value, said to be the anklet of a Sudanese slave girl and given to her by her father-in-law because his wife hadn't liked it, thought it ugly and cumbersome.

Once or twice the pendant was given an airing. Hugh's name remained on the list of influential businessmen imagined to be worth a bob or two, approached by charity event organisers who didn't realise their now impecunious state. The odd invitations to provincial charity 'dos' still arrived, their names having slipped through the net of researchers. If they were within striking distance and the old army Land Rover was considered fit to make the journey, they bought tickets in a good cause, pressure-washed their means of transport so that it wasn't too conspicuous amongst the Jags and BMWs, got their glad rags out of mothballs and ventured forth.

In order to make the most of those forays back into the lifestyle which they had abandoned, they usually reserved a room for the night in a nearby hotel.

One hostelry Julia remembered from her youth, a drab station hotel whose bar her father had frequented and from which Julia had rescued him more than once. Then it had smelt of beer, cigarettes and drains, but in the intervening years it had had a makeover. Its new décor was rabid rococo, buttons and bows and gilt everywhere, the public rooms over-cherubed, beds cushioned and teddy-beared and every space in the bathroom taken up by bottles and jars of highly scented unctions for every orifice of the body. The Gideon Bible was even more alien. Other values had taken over in the universal panic rush towards materialism. They had been relieved to get back to their flagstone floors.

Occasionally they bumped into half-remembered business ghosts from the past, the wives still playing their bit parts, jaded, bored and disillusioned, their stressed-out husbands not having made it to the top, still living frenetic lives, pitting their designer labels against one another. Julia had never regretted their decision for a moment. To have been given that, at the time, unwelcome push before greater promises of success and money sucked them in, leaving them no escape route.

The old Land Rover had failed its MOT and, as Julia waited for the prognosis, she correctly surmised that a courtesy car was not on offer. Eligibility for such perks was dependent on whether you looked as if you were in the running for a new car. Just as Julia knew she was a good judge of cattle, the slick, over-perfumed salesman could tell at a glance from which direction his fat commission would be coming and it wasn't going to be from her, however much interest she pretended to take in the glossy car brochures.

The customer lounge was warm and comfortable, a space set aside in the smart car showroom with its highly-polished composite floors from where persuasions and deals could be heard being negotiated.

Knowing that the Land Rover might be suffering from a terminal illness, she should have brought a book to read. Others were approaching the sophisticated coffee machine, its message 'For our customers' comfort'. There may be three or four hours ahead without sustenance; a cup of tea or coffee would be welcome. Facing the machine, she had a sense of foreboding, her inadequacy when dealing with anything mechanical the reason why the word processor which Hugh had so kindly given her was still in its box.

As she stood in front of the coffee machine, a female voice with a foreign accent said, 'Are you having trouble? May I help you?'

Julia's mind registered the word 'may', an educated usage. She had become used to 'can'.

Suddenly the machine was forgotten and the voice said excitedly, 'Where did you get that bracelet?'

Julia turned round and said, 'Well, I think it came from the Suez Canal. My father-in-law bought it from an Arab trader on his way to India in the 1920s. It belonged to my late mother-in-law.'

The woman was attractive, dark haired, late forties, confident and sure enough of her immigrant value to her adopted country to announce that she was Latvian, married to a consultant at the county hospital. They had come to buy a new car; her husband was deep in conversation with the salesman

'When I've got you your coffee, may I have a closer look?'

They sat down together, the grey liquid in paper cups burning their hands. Julia removed the bracelet from her wrist and placed it on the brochure for the latest turbo-powered, four-wheel-drive, 'must-have' means of transport, on which her coffee cup had already left a guilty stain. Her new friend became more excited, drawing attention in a foreign language. People were staring in that embarrassed 'I don't want to get involved' British way.

Her new acquaintance appeared to be trying to pull apart the three thick bands of silver twisted into a braid which Julia had always assumed were welded together. Now, under the powerful fingers, she saw they were separate.

Just at that moment a voice called, 'Who's the owner of the clapped-out old military Land Rover?' Julia raised her hand as if admitting to a misdemeanour at school.

The voice had bypassed the two girls with intimidating, long, manicured fingernails clacking at their keyboards at reception and was standing in heavy-duty shoes on the sales floor, wiping his hands on a blackened oily piece of cloth. She could smell the oil which overrode the powerful aftershave. Reluctant to tread further, he called out, 'That's a splendid vehicle you've got. I shouldn't trade it in if I were you.'

Julia felt she should somehow be apologising for her presence.

Her Latvian friend said, 'Go and have a word with him. I shall write down what I know about your brace-let. It is certainly a Namejs.'

Leaving the bracelet in her care, Julia walked over to the mechanic. The name 'Kevin' was embroidered on to dirty overalls in grubby white. He was smiling. He talked animatedly, 'Whoever put the Perkins diesel engine in that vehicle knew what they were doing.' (Hugh really would be pleased to hear that.) He then added, 'You know it's illegal?'

Julia had suspected it might be, but felt Kevin was on her side. She said, putting on her innocent voice, 'Goodness me, I know nothing about engines. All I know is that it's a jolly good farm vehicle,' and smiled.

He replied, 'Don't worry. I'll slip it through its MOT but don't mention it to anyone. Give me thirty minutes.'

She felt slightly uncomfortable. This was minor corruption but she trusted Kevin more than she would the salesman and rummaged in her handbag to find a ten pound note which she would give him when no one was looking.

If she had taken a book to read she might have spent two hours with her head buried in someone else's thoughts. Now she knew that her bracelet was Namejs, a symbolic piece of jewellery many centuries old, the silver bands representing Vidzeme, Kurzeme and Latgale, the three ancient tribal regions of present-day Latvia, a symbol of identity rather than an item of faith, unlike the Sikh Kara bracelet. She had to abandon the romantic myth that it had once embraced the ankle of a Sudanese slave girl.

She exchanged names and addresses with the woman, her friend leaving in the new car driven by her husband, calling out as she left, 'It should be in a museum, you know.'

In hindsight, she could have flogged it, made a fortune, and solved their monetary problems, but she loved it, though she had been brought up to believe that you couldn't love something inanimate. Love could only apply to humans, dogs and ponies. Love needed to be responded to, reciprocated or rejected in some way. You couldn't love a thing, you could only take pleasure in it ... but now you were allowed to love your handbag as much as God.

The boxed word processor remained unopened for a further six months, adding to her sense of failure in Hugh's eyes. She took his advice and read the manual with alarm. His words of help and tuition were, 'Any idiot can do it,' but the language in the book of instructions appeared to be written using words that were not in her Oxford Dictionary and open to misinterpretation: floppy discs, merge codes, creating headers and footers, making multiple attribute settings. A mist appeared in front of her eyes.

Then fate came to her rescue. An old friend of Hugh's dropped in to see him; it was close to lunchtime, Julia offered him scrambled egg and the conversation turned to computers. Hugh mentioned how generous he had been in giving her a font writer and how unap-preciative she was.

Dick's reaction had been positive; he was in no hurry, happy to show her the ropes. The afternoon was spent getting to know Julia's font writer and within a couple of hours she had mastered the essentials.

That an inanimate object could become part of her being was a revelation, its acceptance rather like her belief in God; both would eventually free her from a lifetime's conditioning. All that was needed was the knowledge of how to work one and to acknowledge that the other existed. She knew that if you didn't ask too much of either they would come up trumps. It was unfair to ask God for anything, giving was no longer within His terms of reference. He had already given everything He had on that BC/AD date way back, but her acknowledgement of a concept of Him, in what-ever form, helped get her through the day.

Now she could put her feelings down, give them an existence. She had this machine into which she could pour all thoughts in her head, reservoirs of them breaching her mind's dam, overflowing onto a floppy disc. Her fingers regained the speed of their youth, almost keeping up with the ideas bursting from her brain, stacked aircraft awaiting the word from traffic control to take flight. Every morning became a renewed celebration of life.

Initially, when she felt the urge to write, she carried the machine from the dining room to the kitchen table, by which time her thoughts had vanished, never to be recovered. So she reversed the procedure. She took over the dining room – a misnomer, for it had never been used as such. There was no time for formality; all meals had become kitchen meals, but the beautiful Georgian dining room table, worth a small fortune, at which she had entertained those tedious businessmen and their wives in that distant, false life, became her desk, strewn with papers, reference books and cuttings from newspapers.

In deference to Hugh's obsession with possessions, she placed her machine on a folded blanket, bedded it down, a permanent welcome guest at her table. Not a word was said. She thought of all those wasted years when she had been too dutiful, too afraid to have a mind of her own; perhaps freedom of mind is one of the great gifts bestowed upon the elderly but seldom taken up. Julia thought of those depressing rows of octogenarians living enforced second childhoods in homes for the elderly, being called 'love', 'duck' or 'dearie' and made to sing World War Two songs and catch balls, all dignity squashed by the single-minded aim of preserving their bodies. It wouldn't happen to her; she was hoarding the paracetamol.

Her metaphysical trinity became a foursome, joined forces with an all-too solid accomplice. Her mind, memory and thoughts were in league with her word processor; they wouldn't leave her alone, got together to save her from the old age she had been dreading. The rebirth of her mind was totally unexpected. Over the years she had watched her body deteriorate. The Grim Reaper lay ahead to claim his four score years and ten, then this amazing transformation by the part of her which had caused her so much trouble in the past. Mushroom spores lain dormant in the soil for decades, bursting forth in abundance when disturbed.

Why did she feel the need to put these thoughts down on paper? It was becoming an obsession, an addiction, an arrogance. She remembered again that last interview with Arthur Miller, his reason for writing: 'To leave behind a trail of my presence.'

Her great-great-grandchildren would know that she had existed, that their genes had been there before them, delighting and revelling in the joys and challenges of life, weeping for its tragedies and perhaps helping them cope with its downsides and disappointments.

But Julia suspected that on her death, amidst the chaotic untidiness of her home, her notes would be overlooked, destined for the skip.

CHAPTER TWENTY-FOUR

Obsession with her new toy caused additional friction. Hugh complained that she was spending too much time playing with it; meals were late or forgotten altogether on the days when her thoughts took over completely, pieces of shrapnel exploding in her mind until she could get them down on paper.

His complaints were valid and he was beginning to see that his gift to her was the cause of his own discomfort. He was of that generation who had never boiled an egg and been too lazy to learn. Julia had shown him how to wash a potato, prick it with a fork and put it in the oven for an hour then fill it with whatever was to hand, but even that proved too irksome for him.

She rose at six, did a speedy check of the livestock, cooked a hearty British breakfast for Hugh and then settled down with her new love. Around ten thirty, she was in the habit of pouring herself a large whisky to keep her going through the day and this ritual continued until something catastrophic broke the routine.

There was no Taisch to forewarn of impending disaster. Her mind was too busy engaged elsewhere to receive messages, and the first intimation that the countryside was about to implode had been a phone call from Sarah. 'Have you seen the news?'

They hadn't. A suspected case of foot and mouth; the pictures shown on TV, Swaledales, hardy northern sheep.

Alarm bells had rung in their daughter's head. She was picturing again the lime pits and pyres of burning cattle surrounding her boarding school on the Welsh Borders in the 1960s, those magnificent, pedigree dairy herds of Shropshire and Cheshire wiped out.

Forty years on, something apocalyptic was about to happen, besides which those events would pale into insignificance.

When the news hit the farming community, it had been presumed that lessons had been learnt from previous outbreaks. But recommendations had been ignored, filed away and forgotten, gathered dust. The last outbreak had occurred at a time when the Ministry of Agriculture Fisheries and Food was staffed by people with some understanding of livestock. Many had agricultural degrees or diplomas from local agricultural colleges. They knew the difference between a gimmer shearling and a wether.

In 2001 those manning MAFF were more likely to be straight from university with a degree in Environmental Studies, Economics and Politics; book experts with no hands-on knowledge or understanding of animal husbandry, nor the logistics and planning which would be needed if the situation got out of hand. Which it did, with alarming speed.

Their only solution was to slaughter everything, with no plans to deal with the thousands upon thousands of bloated animal corpses stinking, swelling and exploding in farmyards. The desecration was witnessed by their erstwhile custodians, hardy men, unable to watch as the petrol was poured on and the pyres lit, the smoke rising from those bonfires of death so dense that the sun was eclipsed and people within a five-mile radius became ill from toxic fumes.

As farm after farm went down it came closer, a forest fire over which there was no control. They could smell the stench of burning, tumid, rotten flesh on the wind. Life took on a surreal quality and there was no one in Westminster who seemed the slightest bit interested in anything that was happening outside London.

Hugh and Julia made contingency plans. It was one of those rare occasions during their long marriage when they felt they were pulling in the same direction, though probably not for the same reasons. Hugh enjoyed any chance to take on officialdom whatever the cause, right or wrong. Julia's concern was for the cattle. There was no way they would allow a faulty bureaucratic system to destroy their life's work, to slaughter healthy animals unless they actually became infected.

It was March; the cattle were still inside, six precious generations of Ferdinand genes. Ferdinand had died three years previously, gone off his legs which had been unable to carry his impressive weight. He was laid to rest amongst the daffodils, his headstone bearing his name and the gratitude of his human family.

Because of the shambles at MAFF and the fact that few hill farmers were on the Internet, information was scant. Their lifeline was the local radio station, a special unit set up and run by the daughter of a farmer whose stock had already been taken out in the initial cull, who understood the heartbreak and trauma farming families were going through. A phone-in line open twenty-four hours a day, a rural Samaritans through which strong, independent, self-reliant men could be allowed to weep on air without censure, unable to understand their enforced isolation, something over which, for the first time in their lives, they had no control.

Hugh and Julia barricaded themselves in, laid siege. No one would be allowed to come within a mile of the farm. The smell of disinfectant replaced the magical smells of spring. Every crow, starling, blackbird, thrush, robin, curlew and skylark looking for a place to nest was now a potential enemy, a carrier of death.

Some distant neighbours cowered under the officialdom, honest men who respected authority. It was the fabric which held a nation together in times of trouble and, until that moment, had been trusted implicitly. But they were betrayed, overwhelmed by the incompetence and uncertainty coming out of Whitehall. They cooperated when the hit squads arrived to slaughter their cows, believing what they had been told, that it was for the general good. Julia and Hugh would have none of it.

The Ministry announced that all non-infected cattle, even those protected by being inside, as well as all sheep within the three-kilometre contiguous zone must be destroyed. Julia rang their vet and he said, 'Don't let them on the land. They have no legal right to destroy healthy animals in non-contact zones.' They stood their ground and just as well for, within twenty-four hours, that ruling was rescinded, an apology extracted from Whitehall.

But it had come too late for many. They had obeyed when officialdom arrived on their doorsteps accompanied, not by a local bobby, but a seconded urban policeman and a foreign vet. The latter was one of the two hundred from twenty different nations brought in to fill the gap which Maggie Thatcher's policy of running down the State Veterinary Service had created. Sensitive men and women who were unable to communicate their distress at what they were about to sanction and be understood in their mother tongue, expressed compassion and understanding in their eyes and friendly gestures. They held out maps on which the farms to be culled had been circled in red ink, and within those treacherous twenty-four hours many of the finest suckler herds in the county had been massacred, wiped out unnecessarily.

Hugh had read somewhere that during the 1960s' outbreak a farmer, who was still free of the disease but whose neighbours had already succumbed, decided to try a method of protection, an old wives' tale handed down from father to son. The foot-and-mouth virus could be absorbed by raw onions and, in desperation, he festooned his farm buildings. His animals escaped the disease. It was certainly worth a try.

They found an ally in the local Tesco supermarket which, realising that their rural customers had deserted them, speedily introduced a phone and delivery service within a forty-mile radius, leaving groceries at the bottom of lanes and outside farm gates. They did not query it when Julia ordered six sacks of onions. Hugh collected them from the bottom of the lane on the tractor and, throughout the night, they peeled and threaded them onto pink baler twine, their eyes smarting, the tears streaming down their faces. By dawn they had made raw onion bunting four hundred yards long and hung it around the cattle sheds.

But suddenly things had moved into a higher gear. The following day Jon Snow, the TV journalist, came north to see for himself what was happening. He was so shocked by what he found that he stayed in Carlisle to broadcast the following day's Channel 4 news bulletin. It was now accepted that his reporting was seen by Blair and triggered the PM's commitment to bring in the army.

Later on Snow said that that experience still seared in his soul. Air crashes, road accidents, riots, murder, nothing in twenty-five years of reporting domestic news had ever prepared him for the scale of human trauma he experienced in that mad March weekend in 2001. It was utterly brutal.

How prophetic those words had been. Since they were spoken more than seventy farmers and seven vets had taken their own lives; none had received any proper investigation by the press.

The modus operandi changed. Animals were no longer to be slaughtered at home within sight of their owners; they were to be loaded live into trucks and transported to the death camps, the Belsens of the animal kingdom, off-loaded, shot and dumped in vast trenches. It was even more traumatic and distressing than the home slaughter.

Pregnant ewes, driven into wagons, were trampled on as they gave birth, the pressure of those behind pushing them forward, unable to attend to their newborn, the lamb's minute of life crushed out of them by the mad rush up the ramps of a thousand hoofed feet. The distressed maternal bleatings of those whose day-old lambs were taken from them and given a quick lethal injection by the attendant vet. Nightly, the local newsreels showed the tipping wagons disembowelling their cargos into the vast deep pits. It was government-sanctioned animal cruelty on a vast scale.

Julia was so appalled that she phoned the London headquarters of the foremost animal protection organisation to ask if they knew what was going on. They appeared disinterested, too engaged in the myopic campaign against hunting, their political duplicity clouding their judgement.

'Cruelty,' Julia remembered saying. 'It appears you are selective in what you consider to be cruelty.' They didn't like that, perhaps a bit too near the knuckle, but Julia had not been far wrong. Her anger and suspicions were vindicated when, the following day, the major newspapers carried full-page anti-hunting advertisements costing hundreds of thousands of pounds. Did those caring and generous old ladies who contributed to the society's coffers and left bequests in their wills really know how their money would be spent?

Julia had no quarrel with the inspectors on the ground; they were knowledgeable, courteous and well able to differentiate between ignorant calls and the genuine thing. One veteran inspector had, some years earlier, confided that fifty per cent of call-outs were found to be the former. A well-meaning rambler reporting cruelty to a lamb with a condition called sway-back caused by a copper deficiency, similar to spina bifida in humans. When those rare cases occurred and the lamb could suckle, Julia and Hugh had in the past given it a chance, but the hassle to which they had been subjected by do-gooders had made them revise their policy. It was less stressful to both man and beast to despatch the lamb at birth.

When the time came to sacrifice their three-hundred-strong flock, as Hugh and Julia had known they inevitably would, when they were finally sucked into the three-kilometre dangerous contact zone, they were overwhelmed by their sense of betrayal of those animals they had nurtured and loved. As the sheep were loaded, some hesitated, stopping halfway up the ramp, their beautiful marble trusting eyes hoping for a ewe nut. Hilda, Gladys, Sophie, Mabel, Kay, Boss Girl's granddaughters and One Eye, whom Hugh had nursed with such loving care when she almost succumbed, found cast in a treacherous peat bog half submerged, her exposed eye pecked out by crows.

Did animals have a sense of foreboding? Thankfully, both Julia and Hugh resisted the temptation to inflict animals with human sensibilities and were pretty certain they did not. They had good memories and strong survival instincts but, having worked closely with them for many decades, the certainty that they were unable to reason lessened the guilt which they both felt.

The land took on an eerie silence. The fields should have been full of rebirth; it was in the evening that they felt it most, when the fields would normally be a cacophony of bleating ewes and lambs calling to find each other before the sun went down and foxes made separation a dangerous game. The swallows failed to return, the stink of disinfectant warning them that mankind was having problems. It would be another three years before they would regain their trust.

But Julia's cattle were still secure, safe in their allium fortress. It was the only herd surviving within a twenty-mile radius and was viewed with great suspicion by MAFF.

Kerstin, a vivacious Swedish vet whose home was in the small town of Alingsås, north east of Gothenburg, had been given the daily task of checking their cattle. She arrived promptly at eight thirty each morning, having left her vehicle a mile down the lane and disinfected her wellies in the buckets standing sentinel at the farthest gate. The only part of her visible from within the white protective clothing was her smiling blue eyes.

There was an instant rapport between her and Hugh, a great deal of flirtatious giggling when they disappeared into the byre together to take the blood samples which would establish the cattle's fate. Their relationship lightened everyone's load and Julia thought what a good thing flirting was, a letting-off of emotional steam, a tentative exploration of another's feeling without commitment, an interaction of mutual warmth with a hint of sexuality without points of no return being crossed. One morning, three weeks into the nerve-wracking tests, when a positive result would destroy thirty years work, Kerstin broke MAFF rules, threw caution to the wind, took off her white-hooded, protective boiler suit, gloves, mask and welly boots and came in for a quick cup of coffee, her real self exposed.

Julia could see why Hugh had taken to her. She was lovely. Not only was she beautiful to look at, she had a rare inner quality. She radiated happiness and Julia wondered why, at the age of twenty-eight, she hadn't been snapped up by some Swedish male.

Kerstin confided in perfect English. Julia, who, because she had always felt no one wanted to listen to her, was a practised listener, one of the good traits, probably the only one, inherited from her mother. Mother had had the ability to make total strangers feel at ease, to allow them to pour out the most intimate details of their lives in bus queues and supermarket car parks. They hove to her like moths to a flame. Julia had inherited a similar empathy; ten-minute intimacies with men and women whose paths were unlikely to cross again, momentary exposure to the thoughts and worries of strangers, cameos of lives freely given, confirming what she already knew – that happiness is not some attainable goal but the by-product of an acceptance of how life turns out.

Even Jack, now in his eighties and after too many whiskies, had admitted that he made a mistake sixty years previously in marrying his dour wife. He had loved someone else who lived a distance away but he had, because of convenience and family pressure, married the girl next door. Their fathers' farms adjoined and there was land to be had. Julia sensed he had never come to terms with his betrayal, for he added, 'She never married.'

To break the ice Julia asked, 'Are you looking forward to going home to Sweden?'

Kerstin put her head in her hands: long-fingered, sinewy strong hands, weathered brown, working hands.

'I don't know what to do. If I go home, there is this

man everyone is expecting me to marry. My parents adore him. The kind of ambitious son-in-law they hope for.'

But since being seconded to the UK, Kerstin had glimpsed, through the anonymity of her protective clothing, a different type of male; rural lads with no education other than the discipline of work. She had witnessed their kindness, tolerance and support as they stood behind their fathers, watching their future being massacred and burnt with that sad look of acceptance.

Kerstin added, 'Torsten never laughs. He's always talking about money.'

Alarm bells started ringing in Julia's head. Her memory was awakened by mention of money, resurrecting words which had been forced into her brain at school. Understudying the part of Goods (riches and possessions) in the Medieval morality play *Everyman*, she had learned: 'A season thou hast had me in prosperity. My condition is man's soul to kill.'

Her memory threw up images: Tessie O'Shea, Two-Ton Tessie, that enormously fat, peroxide-blonde, music-hall comedienne of the forties and fifties, dressed in bright yellow, belting out, 'Money is the root of all evil, Money is the root of all evil. Don't contaminate yourself with it. Take it away, Take it away, Take it away.'

Kerstin must be saved.

Frank, yes, Frank was the answer. Since the tragic death of his brother Harry, he had become withdrawn, a double burden of work having fallen upon his shoulders, together with the responsibility of dealing with the inconsolable grief of his parents. Frank and Kerstin must be brought together. She mentioned her thoughts to Hugh, who responded, 'Interfering will only bring heartache,' but her intuition advised her otherwise.

She suggested to Kerstin that, when the nightmare was over and before returning to Sweden, she must come and have supper with them.

The 'all clear' finally sounded on the stroke of midnight on New Year's Eve. The nation was declared free of foot and mouth and 2002 a new beginning. The inevitable blame and counter-blame reared its ugly head. There were stories of inflated compensation claims and prize rams being hidden in attics.

Frank arrived early, wearing the same ill-fitting suit which had hung off him when he had been a bearer at his brother's funeral, probably unused since. Now too small for him, the fly zip strained to make it to the top. Julia suspected that his mother had insisted upon the suit, thought it was the done thing. Hugh, upstairs putting on a clean sweater, had seen him from the bedroom window crossing the yard and shouted out, 'He's misunderstood casual,' and responded positively by putting on a tie to lessen any embarrassment which he thought Frank might feel, at the same time mumbling, 'I don't know why we are doing this.'

Socially there had been little mingling but as neighbours, contact had been on a daily basis. A stopping of tractors to pass the time of day, help at hay time and clipping, and once Vera had proudly shown Julia Frank's final school report. He had left school just short of his fifteenth birthday and his teachers had told his parents that, had they allowed him to stay on into the sixth form, he had had the potential to choose whatever career he wished. What might he have achieved had he been allowed to explore wider horizons? But the lessons he had learnt at his mother's knee, of chivalry, kindness, humour, hard work and good manners, were about to stand him in good stead.

He stood at the door, uncertain of himself in those alien clothes. When Kerstin finally arrived late, kicked off her wellies in the yard, came barefoot into the kitchen, she immediately saw beyond the black mourning suit. On being introduced she felt she had seen him before, standing in the background whilst she had overseen the slaughter of his father's livestock. She had been unrecognisable to him, encased as she was in her sanitised spaceman's clothing.

In the isolation of his tractor cab, hour after hour, ploughing his lonely furrow, Frank may have dreamt of such a person, fantasising to make the daily grind bearable.

During the meal, he was humorous, self-deprecating, trying to make light of the tragedies which had befallen his family. Kerstin coaxed from him his knowledge and love of the land and the pride he displayed in its custodianship, encouraging his confidence with her interest.

Even Hugh, normally dead to the feelings of others, felt the fusion.

They married at the end of that spring, on one of those days when the early sky promises much; clouds present the previous day hanging now above the fells to the east, the deep purple of the foothills still in shade, crowned by a pinkish ribbon of early light from the rising sun, creating a strata of hill and cloud, the reds merging into the wash of grey, silver and blue.

The vicar, mindful of his ever-depleting congregation and church coffers, was accommodating when asked to adjust the marriage service; nothing about worldly goods or for richer or poorer. A quiet plighting of troth, no hymns to embarrass the harmonium with its missing notes.

Vera got up early to bedeck the church with any wild flowers to hand; it was too early for the wild geraniums, campions and ragged robin but she had found some late daffodils and bluebells and branches of pussy willow, the soft cotton-wool buds sprouting again through shell-hard husks shouting faith.

No invitations were sent out. Kerstin and Frank let it be known that all were welcome and the date and time were circulated by word of mouth. Neighbours left cars down the lane to walk the final three hundred yards across open fields to the isolated small Norman church, through the gravestones which bore the familiar names of the living. The lambs and sheep which normally would have been grazing and dozing in the warmth, their heads stretched upwards towards the sun, were now consigned to the earth, having prayers said over their mass graves by the Buddhist monks of Eskdalemuir.

Kerstin, caught in a shaft of dusty sunlight which shone through the plain east window, her loose hair, simple chiffon dress and nosegay of wild flowers, reminded Julia of Millais' painting of Ophelia now raised from a watery grave. As the couple left the church, they laid Kerstin's posy on Harry's grave.

Kerstin's parents had not made the journey from

Sweden. Kerstin confided to Julia that it had been a relief. They would have brought with them the ghost of Torsten.

There was no honeymoon. Kerstin filled Harry's place in the farmhouse and immediately got down to the task of giving help and advice on restocking the land and sorting out the mountain of paperwork now being invented by bureaucrats to make the lives of those farmers brave enough to start again an even greater challenge.

Hugh and Julia had already decided not to restock with sheep and to reduce the number of cattle. They were both getting on a bit. Hugh was almost eighty but still agile and strong.

Within a year Frank and Kerstin produced a blue-eyed son whom they christened Harry. Nature was realigning herself, getting back into her rhythm, settling down again.

CHAPTER TWENTY-FIVE

Julia's decision to go on the London Countryside Liberty and Livelihood March was a last-minute one. The event had been postponed for eighteen months because of foot and mouth and she had told herself that her old body was not up to it, though her mind was raring to go. Father was egging her on. Her most pressing concern had been, would there be loos along the route? She phoned the organisers to see if there was still a place on the bus, asked about the loos, received a confident and enthusiastic response and an, 'All welcome, so long as you don't mind being a bit cramped in the bus for five hours.'

Hugh, concerned about the dictatorial mindset of urban politicians being inflicted upon a subordinate countryside, offered to drive her to Carlisle, the final pick-up point for two buses starting south of Glasgow. He had, however, been unable to resist the temptation of saying how stupid was her decision to go.

She clambered aboard the bus with her stick, clutching the handrail tightly, exposing her prominent veins. Someone said, 'It's a bit of a squash. Go to the back row and ask old Clive to move up a bit, there's not much of him.'

Other marchers were already dozing as Julia made her way between the seats, trying not to disturb them, their snores staccato as they awoke, startled by her presence, trying to remember where they were. Julia's legs were unsteady and the plastic Liberty's carrier bag with the William Morris design cumbersome, the bottles of water, which Hugh had insisted she took, taking control, swaying, ricocheting from side to side as she tried to hold her stick and keep her feet. In the dimmed lights of the bus she stumbled over an outstretched, heavy booted foot, its owner's face snoring beneath a copy of *The Sun*, his exposed arms a confusion of tattoos. She apologised for waking him. He removed the newspaper from his head and immediately recognised her. She didn't recognise him, his presence out of context, until he said, 'Hello, pet. How's the old Land Rover? See you later,' as though he were an old friend.

People shuffled to make room and, as she sat down, her thigh touched the thigh of a wiry, weather-beaten octogenarian who smelt of her father. Suddenly, so unexpectedly that it alarmed her, she got a sensation which, after thirty years in the sexual wilderness, was just another memory.

The realisation that she would have to endure these reawakened surges for the next two hundred and ninety miles, Julia found disconcerting. It never occurred to her that he too may have been feeling uneasy. Christian names were exchanged, the divisiveness and vindictiveness of the anti-hunting bill now before Parliament discussed. Their shared experiences of the devastation that foot and mouth had caused, and was still causing to the countryside and its people, sealed their common experiences. They chatted easily, but it was a relief when, in the early hours, their attention was requested by the organisers, instructions given for where and when. Others, better prepared than she, had maps. As part of the Liberty contingent they would be disembarking at South Carriage Drive, near to Hyde Park Corner. The Livelihood Route was starting on the Embankment at Blackfriars and the two groups merging at the top of Whitehall to march to Parliament Square.

As they were disembarking Julia, in an unguarded moment, confided to this stranger the problems with her bladder. Clive took her elbow and said, 'Stay close to me and, when the need arises, I'll wait with you and we can catch up with the others together.'

In fifty-four years of married life Julia had rarely experienced that kind of concern for her well-being and comfort.

She need not have worried; the organisation was superb, portaloos clearly marked on the map.

Clive said, 'I'm certain I know you from somewhere,' but before Julia could respond they were being shepherded. Official banners were handed out and those who had made their own applauded for their originality and humour, rural Britain showing off its native wit. 'Eat British lamb. Three million foxes can't be wrong,' 'Save a cow; eat a vegetarian,' 'My sitting room carpet has seen more wildlife than most Labour MPs have seen in a lifetime,' 'Blair, you wanted a war; now you've got one,' 'Bomb the Ban.'

Clive said, 'If we get split up, first back to the bus bags a couple of seats on the back row.' They giggled like conspiratorial teenagers.

They took up their places on the outside, her dodgy knees and stick uncertain of the maelstrom that might be encountered at the centre of the cavalcade and, in a wave of good humour, they set off. There was an autumnal feel in the air; leaves were on the turn, the early sun catching splashes of gold on the trees in Green Park as they walked down Piccadilly, turning right into St James's, getting into their stride, enjoying themselves. Down Pall Mall, past the Media Centre and additional loos.

A voice from the pavement shouted, 'F*****g animal murderers.' Julia turned to face the voice and smiled; their eyes met. 'Filthy scum. Tory bitch.' Well, he was wrong about the Tory.

Clive slipped his arm through hers and pressed their elbows together. She wondered why it was that the French so zealously defended and protected their rural way of life whilst the British, over the past two decades, had put so much effort into destroying theirs.

Cockspur Street, Trafalgar Square, a quick glance towards Northumberland Avenue, smelling again the musty leather and cigar smoke of the old Constitutional Club and felt Father's ghost.

She was becoming light-headed.

Then waters met, as the two great rivers of people joined together under the entry arch into Whitehall, into the counting zone and out again, four hundred and seven thousand, seven hundred and ninety-one. Waving to the television cameras before crossing Westminster Bridge to the Exit Point.

People were already in party mood as they climbed onto the bus for the long journey north. Someone had made sure that a plentiful supply of whisky and beer was aboard, weary legs rejuvenated by laughter, bodies sweating in Barbours. Red faces and flat caps and the smell of tweed. Clive produced a bottle of whisky and passed it round; she was on familiar territory. High-pitched, upper-crusty voices now uninhibited, mellowing alongside Geordie and Scots.

Songs were sung, 'De yer ken John Peel', that well-loved marching song of the now disbanded Border Regiment, latterly the King's Own Scottish Borderers. Even John Peel, that revered foot huntsman of the high fells had not been allowed to rest in peace. His grave in the small village of Caldbeck in the Lake District had been desecrated in 1977 by animal rights fanatics.

Two hunting horns were competing for attention. A voice from the front of the bus called out, 'What about a song from his lordship?' and that now familiar and pleasurable thigh became detached from Julia's as its owner rose to his feet, slightly the worse for wear.

He did not sing a song. He recited a poem about the hounds, 'Running On' by W.H. Ogilvie which she had learned at her father's knee. His voice gathered force as he said: 'The count of the years is slowly growing / The Old give way to the eager Young,' and dropped almost to a whisper at the final lines: 'Good men follow the good men gone / And hark! They're running! / They're running on!'

A quietness descended upon the bus, marchers aware of why they were there, what was about to be lost, those tenuous physical strands which bind man to nature. In the older men's eyes, Julia imagined she saw again the tears of her father in a London theatre.

It took a couple of minutes for people to regain their composure, to re-enter the world and applaud. Clive sat down amidst murmurs of approval. People became serious again; tiredness and alcohol were taking control, eyes were closing. He said, 'You're that woman who judges cattle,' and fell asleep on her shoulder.

She saw Kevin get up from his seat and come towards her. Squatting on his haunches, balancing his frame against the movement of the bus, he placed a large hand on her knee with filial concern, a hand like Jack's, but oil rather than sheep shit beneath its fingernails. He asked after the Land Rover as he would a person. She now saw in detail his arm tattoos: on his right bicep St George rippled, a cross on the armour picked out in red and the lance thrusting down the length of his arm into the body of a dragon encircling his wrist. Although Julia abhorred tattoos, this one was impressive. With his other hand he drew from his pocket a scruffy receipt with his name, address and telephone number on, handed it to her and said, 'If ever you need someone to help with anything, give me a buzz,' and returned to his seat to fall asleep with others.

Clive awoke as they were nearing Carlisle and the Border. He rose to let Julia stand, her joints stiff from sitting and her varicose veins hot and tingling. He gently kissed the grey hair on the crown of her head; she sensed the affection in the tenderness of the action. There was just time to exchange names and addresses before the bus put her down.

Hugh wasn't there to meet her; the bus had arrived in Carlisle shortly after midnight ahead of time and he had assumed it would be late. Julia sat alone in the raw cold of the unlit bus shelter, the muffled vibrations of the sleeping city embracing her, the only discernible sounds the distant wailing of a police siren and the rustling of half empty, non-biodegradable polystyrene fast-food containers and plastic bottles caught and tossed in the sudden gusts of mini whirlwinds. In the light of the moon she could see her other companions, cigarette butts, syringes and used condoms.

A red condom. There hadn't been that choice in her day. Too much choice could lead to uncertainty and dissatisfaction. She wondered whether its user had found satisfaction.

Whatever her weary body was trying to tell her, her mind was contradicting it. A feeling of joy overwhelmed her and with it, the absolute certainty that, a bit late in the day, life was just beginning.

CHAPTER TWENTY-SIX

The relationship slotted gently into the progression of their lives. There were no demands made on either side, just the comfortable knowledge of the other's presence, the Taisch between them tangible, a reading of another's mind, thoughts expressed without a word being said.

There were boundaries, for they both understood that happiness could not be bought at the expense of others. Julia was totally open with Hugh. He didn't believe her, said she was making it up to annoy him. Because he found her ageing body physically unattractive, he could not understand why anyone could think otherwise and he had never been in love with her mind. That part of their marriage had been annulled within weeks of the ceremony, unconsummated decades ago.

To Hugh it was all a bit of a joke; when the phone rang he would call out, 'Probably your boyfriend,' and disappear into his study to renew his love affair with his books and the past.

Clive's wife had been in a nursing home suffering from dementia for three years, no longer recognising him, which mildly assuaged Julia's guilt. Her conscience, however, reminded her that whereas men rarely pass that physical milestone of procreation women do, which makes sex after a certain age morally questionable. When, she asked herself, does it switch from being a pleasurable means of keeping homo sapiens going and become physical gratification? She knew she might be about to break one of the Ten Commandments but it was the one which she had always felt was of lesser significance than 'love thy neighbour'; her possible breaking of it reminded her of those teetotal Methodists who bought brandy at the village store for strictly medicinal purposes. She hoped God, with whom she had always credited a sense of humour, might see the fun in one of His flock being taken on as someone's mistress at such an age.

They met whenever other duties allowed. Neither of them liked driving in the dark; their old eyes reacted dangerously to the lights of oncoming traffic, sending uncertain messages to tightly-clasped hands on steering wheels, their eyes strained, leaning forwards to peer and pick up those reassuring cats' eyes. Initially, throughout those first winter months of friendship, they met infrequently for lunch at various hostelries along the border, pub lunches in traditional old inns with open fires, good chat and no piped music, but these establishments were difficult to find, becoming obsolete like themselves, taken over by money-orientated big business and turned into soulless, chromium, cash machines.

He always arrived ahead of her; she could feel and see him before she saw his car, that slight, wiry, weather-beaten frame. He was only a little taller than herself, but had a presence which she noted others respected.

His manners were impeccable, the same in private as in public. Hugh, on the other hand, kept his manners for show, to be seen by others.

He always greeted her in the same way. Rising from a seat by the fire, pipe in hand, he would say, 'Ah,' put down his pipe and come to greet her, give her a long hug and order drinks. They would sit enjoying looking at the menu, giggling when glancing at the huge platefuls being offered to other customers, their almost octogenarian stomachs not up to the challenge, as laughingly they asked for children's portions.

They never talked about the past or their marriages, just their immediate news, enjoying the moment, living in the present. Julia had no idea what Clive had once been or done with his life and didn't ask. He had the advantage of seeing her before in the distance and called her his 'cattle lady'.

He had recently inherited a farm in southern Scotland from a distant cousin but she suspected that he may have seen military or diplomatic service before that.

Julia mentioned that Hugh had given her a font writer and what fun she experienced in writing cross letters to politicians; he confided that he had always kept a diary. Julia was not sufficiently disciplined to keep a diary; her scribblings were things she needed to get off her chest. Clive suggested she should join a writers' club.

When spring arrived and the worry of a ninety-mile journey for both of them, with the added hazard of fog and snow, had diminished, they met for the occasional evening meal. Hugh, incapable of seeing beyond the practical, suggested that she stay overnight. 'I don't want to be called out at all hours to rescue you if the car breaks down.'

Had it been an encouragement? Julia was unsure whether he was driving them together on purpose or was simply incapable of understanding their relationship.

On that particular evening she felt weary. Over the phone Clive suggested a pub nearer to her, to lessen her driving. He said, 'There used to be an isolated old coaching inn south of Moffat. No idea what it's like now, but we can give it a try. Round about sevenish?'

They arrived in the car park simultaneously. The pub was open but run down, the whitewash peeling from the walls and the curtains, seen from the outside through unclean windows, hanging limp.

Clive said, 'Shall we try somewhere else?' but neither of them could think of anywhere so they went inside.

The landlord was welcoming. On the menu, fish in home-made beer batter with chips and mushy peas. They both enjoyed unpretentious food. A log fire recently lit, its flames hissing at the damp green ash wood. Although it was early summer, they were thankful for the evening was undecided, chilly and muggy at the same time, low black clouds threatening thunder.

Two young lads in gun boots, their waterproofs damp and mud spattered, stood at the bar, their pints still frothy. She presumed they were locals; they doffed their caps to Clive, and Julia thought they knew him and felt guilty, though up to that moment she had nothing to be guilty about.

Whilst waiting for the fish and chips – one portion with two plates, knives and forks, the landlord accommodating – Clive said, 'Just going to pass the time of day with the blokes holding up the bar. They are a couple of keen young lads who act as beaters for one of my friends.'

He moved with a quick animal awareness of his surroundings and greeted them with that certainty which overrides trust. Looking at him, she thought, 'When there is certainty, trust is obsolete, not needed,' and in that instant she knew just how much she loved this slight, insignificant-looking man who avoided deference, so unlike Hugh, who was always in search of it.

Outside, the wind was getting up, interspersed by rain, a sudden noisy gust throwing pebble-hard hailstones against the window. Clive said, 'I don't like the look of the weather. The cloud will be down on the tops and there are no cats' eyes on that stretch of road. I may stay the night...'

He called to the landlord, 'The weather's closing in. Have you a bed for the night?'

'Would that be a double room, sir?' and Julia called out quietly, 'Yes' and Clive gave her a curiously uncertain, boyish look and squeezed her hand.

The landlord was apologetic. 'I'm afraid the room's a bit old-fashioned. We long since gave up offering accommodation but the bed is made up. I'll just pop up and put an electric blanket in.'

They finished their whiskies and stood up.

'First door on the left. Mind your head on the beams. The staircase is a bit uneven. Bathroom across the landing.' In her Liberty bag was the plastic Tesco trifle dish. She would have to explain this to Clive. They were both unsteady; the well-seasoned oak creaked beneath them. Julia led the way and opened the door.

Once it would have been a pretty room but now the rose-covered wallpaper was peeling, the petals dropping, patches of damp fading the background. The matching curtains were lifeless and unlined. Other than the huge brass bedstead (the linen looked newly laundered), the only furniture was an old spindle-backed rocking chair and two side tables, with aged pre-Health and Safety reading lamps, the parchment shades flyblown, scorch marked from over-watted bulbs, shrinking away from the anchor of their metal frames.

Facing the foot of the bed was a Victorian sepia wedding photo in a heavy, brown wooden frame hanging drunkenly at an angle on a piece of string from a rusty nail. Clive felt the need to straighten it. He said, 'Do come and have a look. I think it's rather a sad photo.' A row of stern-faced country folk in alien clothes, the men in high starched collars making their necks look as if they were being stretched, reminding Julia of photos in geography books at school when they had been doing Africa, the caption reading, 'The long-necked, plate-lipped native women of Uganda.' These country folk looked uneasy, the men holding their hats, their large labourers' hands wishing to be busy elsewhere, active on something more worthwhile. The bride, seated, was hard-faced and anxious.

Clive glanced at the bed and then at her, again with that quizzical, uncertain look. 'Well, it's hardly the bridal suite,' and they sat on the rigid edge of the bed, giggling.

She thought of phoning Hugh to say she had decided to stay the night, but thought better of it; he would probably never notice her absence.

How she hated that accepted euphemism for sex: 'making love'. They didn't make love as if it were some manufactured commodity. Love was there already, an integral part of their passion waiting to be exchanged in a different way. They laughed as they examined each other's crinkled and drying-out bodies, revelling in the joy of having each other and that privilege of exploring another person so completely, shy, self-deprecating laughter as they tried to be young again, after so many years of physical denial, uncertain of their ground.

She recalled the words of her children as they witnessed the times when Hugh and she had been at opposite ends of understanding, stagnating in the unawareness and misinterpretation of each other's thoughts. Their anger lashing out at unguarded tender bruises, reopening battered, distressed portfolios of hurt. On the rare occasions when she tried to fight back against his unkind remarks, he would say, 'Oh St Julia, martyr Julia, with a drunk for a father.' Her uncalled for unkind retaliation, 'Well, at least my parents didn't desert me.'

'Don't worry, Mum. One day you'll experience real happiness.'

She hadn't believed them. Her exposure to false hopes had made her resigned. This was a miracle, one of life's bonuses when the future was rapidly disappearing, about to close in, covered by the inevitable shroud of real old age, but Bob Dylan still reminding her, 'It's not dark yet but it's getting there.'

They decided to keep the knowledge of their true relationship from both sets of their adult children. Julia longed to confide in her younger daughter, that carnal love child from so long ago, but wasn't certain what her reaction might be. She didn't want to give anyone, especially those dearest to her the chance to misinterpret; misunderstanding could so quickly cause harm and take over from reality.

She tried to cut down other commitments so she could spend more time with Clive. She no longer accepted invitations to judge cattle. The decision not to restock with sheep after foot and mouth had been a wise one. A few favourites amongst Ferdinand's grandchildren and great-grandchildren remained, essential to her well-being; withdrawal from them might have precipitated cold turkey. Hugh harassed her daily to get rid of them, had long since washed his hands of any involvement in their management. She was not going to let go until infirmity won the day and she was no longer able to walk across the fields to monitor their well-being.

A final trip to Italy was planned. It would be the last. Bill and Jane had already decided to move to the South of France to live with one of their daughters. Bill's future now governed by prostate cancer, he wanted to enjoy one more Italian summer surrounded by an already depleted gathering of friends.

When most of her generation were finding it hard to fill in their remaining days, Julia felt too much going on in hers. She had offloaded her involvement with the WI and was becoming good at saying no to those seeking her help in charitable fundraising activities. She hadn't given everything up, was anxious to maintain her connection with her local favourite charity, and was exploring Clive's suggestion of joining a writers' group.

She noticed the 'For Sale' sign going up on a rundown hill farm two miles away, its tenant occupiers fourth-generation farmers who had wrestled the land from nature to make a living. Victims of foot and mouth and now too weary and disillusioned to make a fresh start, the bureaucratic avalanche of paperwork from Defra overwhelming them like a mental tsunami. The realisation that from then on farming would no longer be a way of life of good animal husbandry and custodianship of the land; it had become big business, a bureaucratic nightmare of form filling. Licences would be required from Brussels or Whitehall to move a cow or sheep from one field to another. Resentment had superseded generations of acceptance and contentment.

Julia remembered Prue's father reading the line: 'That is the land of lost content', from A.E. Housman's *A Shropshire Lad*, and although her thoughts were not what he had in mind at the time, it fitted her present purpose.

Now it was mandatory for farmers to tag, record and have passports for thousands of millions of livestock so that their movements could be traced from farm to supermarket, but the Homo sapiens of Europe and beyond could come and go as they pleased.

Within three weeks the sale boards had disappeared. The landlord of the farm was unable to believe his luck when his tenant obligingly gave notice. The idyllic site commanded a price tag way beyond anything the local young, the true inheritors of that land, could afford.

Rumour had it that a high-powered young family from the south had bought it for a second home. He was something in the City, his bonus for one year more than the tenants of that farm had earned in a lifetime of honest toil.

Passing the farm six weeks later, she saw signs of activity: builders were working and a shiny new four-by-four was parked outside. Julia stopped and decided to approach the new owners. Perhaps she could persuade them to become involved, help with flag days. It was becoming more and more difficult to find volunteers, beginning to feel like a thankless task mustering her team of aged helpers, most of them in their seventies and eighties who found standing for an hour a strain on their legs.

Julia, used to the elements, still enjoyed it. She had no problem standing out in all weathers on street corners trying to catch the downcast, furtive glance of passers-by and, when eye contact had jogged their conscience and they had put their mite in the tin, Julia always tried to engage them in conversation, enjoying the human contact and their concern. 'You must be cold, standing there without gloves.'

As she stood outside the old farmhouse watching workmen tearing the heart out of it, a voice called out, 'D'yer remember me?'

A man with grey hair, halfway up a ladder was smiling down. She thought she recognised him. Was it Fred the stonemason who, as an apprentice, had helped Hugh restore their home four decades ago? He appeared unhappy with what he was being asked to do. A craftsman of the old school, sensitive to the soul of the building and its history which he was now being paid to compromise.

Julia had a quick glimpse of a Gucci handbag on the front seat of the people carrier and felt she had been impulsive in stopping. She was wearing her filthy wellies and a pair of Hugh's old corduroy trousers with a hole in the knee. She was about to give the wrong impression again but it was too late; a slight figure in tight, immaculate jeans, a mass of curly black hair, a sunbed tan, curiously out of place on a January morning came around the corner of the building. Long fingernails painted silvery white embossed with black skulls, her pierced ears sporting a graduated collection of gold hoops. The rumours circulating around the newcomers had been way off the mark.

Julia apologised for intruding, aware that her presence could be interpreted as some old local busybody with nothing better to do. She introduced herself and got straight to the point, 'I'm raising money for a local charity for the disabled and was looking for helpers.'

The response was immediate and friendly. 'Hello, I'm Kylie. Whatever. Cool,' modern forms of affirmation Julia's granddaughter had taught her.

The woman spoke in a mixture of Cockney, Essex and what Hugh called Call Centre-eeze. 'Come in and have coffee. I've got some in a flask.'

She was a modern version of Thelma, a reincarnation of that much-loved parlour maid, the surrogate sister of her youth, all bubbling fun and friendliness. The similarity didn't stop there. Thelma had married her bookmaker from Newcastle and supposedly lived happily ever after. Kylie lived with her much older partner Darren who, it seemed, was making a fortune in the gambling industry based in Manchester. Julia suspected that the whole business was mildly illegal and probably subsidised through the incongruously named Ministry of Culture.

Kylie was like the string of willowy university friends her second eldest grandson, the very good-looking one, brought to their door to be introduced. Julia had difficulty remembering their names and whether they had been before. Confident and glamorous, unfazed when their escort greeted her with an honesty she admired, giving her a big hug, 'Hello, Gran dear, slewed as a newt as usual? This is Charlotte/Kate/Emma/Liz,' until Emma started coming more than the others. They didn't appear to have any restrictions in their lives. Julia needed boundaries, certainties; she wouldn't want to start her life over again, just be allowed an extension.

Kylie and Darren had bought the old farmhouse to renovate, a base for themselves, friends and their speedboats to enjoy on the nearby reservoir. The old cow byres where cattle had once contently chewed their cud were about to be converted into garages.

Better not mention any of this to Hugh. Julia had learned to keep quiet. She knew exactly what his reaction would be to this latest local news. He could never accept that other people found enjoyment in sports and entertainments of which he disapproved, and noisy speedboats in a tranquil area would be one of them. In a way he had only himself to blame; he had been vociferous in his condemnation of powerboats on lakes within national parks. He had won the day and they had been banned, only to land on his own doorstep.

271

For Julia, the most important thing was that she had found an enthusiastic helper. Although Kylie might not quite hit it off with her present, stalwart, tweedy upper-crusty helpers, Julia was pretty certain she would not feel the force of being ignored as some of her more timid collectors did. Kylie would be in charge, coaxing money out of the young males in the town. They would be queuing up to put something in her tin, and those loafing boys from local secondary schools who spent their lunchtime eating take-aways on the street, their strange spiky hairdo's mildly threatening, would take their hands out of their pockets and surrender their loose change.

A day after that encounter, a surprise letter arrived from France, an invitation to Julia from the Salon International de l'Agriculture, Concours General Agricola to be their guest of honour and judge the cattle championship at their national show, held at the Porte de Versailles in March.

The French were not in the habit of asking a woman to take on this task and she considered it a great honour. A lot of Ferdinand's blood was flowing on the other side of the Channel. Hugh's reaction was as expected. Their first choice of judge had probably given backword and they must have been desperate.

In accepting, she would be going against her decision to retire from judging but the temptation was too great.

She suggested Hugh came with her, but he was scathing and declined, saying, 'Get your boyfriend to go with you.' She phoned Clive and he jumped at the chance.

Air tickets and hotel accommodation had been arranged by the French authorities. They were happy to substitute Clive's name for Hugh's; they were practised at that sort of thing.

The evening before the show, there would be a formal official welcoming dinner for overseas visitors. Julia had gone to her wardrobe to look for that little black dress, that ageless standby, a leftover from the heady days. Had she given it to Oxfam years ago? She found it in an unexpected place, hidden under a pile of Hugh's army surplus trousers which he had hoarded when he thought the source was about to dry up. She tried it on in the bathroom away from Hugh's prying eyes and was amazed that she was able to get into it. It didn't look dated and Julia was surprised by her chic appearance. She could get away with it, recalling her long-ago, half-forgotten, half-Italian room-mate with the patched 1930s' couture hand downs from her mother, always elegant whatever she wore. Julia's rarely called upon evening footwear consisted of M&S black velvet bedroom slippers, easy to pack and comfortable, putting no pressure on her bunions which her NHS chiropodist had told her were there to stay.

She wondered whether she could get away without wearing earrings. Her clip-ons hurt and made the lobes of her ears red and swollen. Perhaps thirty years ago yes, but now she wore her abundance of silver hair swept up into a chignon, exposing a scraggy neck which needed something to divert the eye. She would risk the Woolies clip-ons.

They arrived late in Paris due to the incompetence of Air France. It had been obligatory, in order to have

273

their tickets paid for, to fly by the French national airline.

It was a scramble to get ready in time for the dinner that evening. When they were ready to go downstairs and join the official party, Clive said, 'You look marvellous, absolutely stunning.'

Hugh had seldom remarked favourably upon her appearance. It had always been the other way round. She had always said, 'Very distinguished,' when he had asked how he looked.

As they joined the multilingual throng in the foyer she noticed how easily Clive fitted in, speaking effortlessly in the tongue of his hosts. Julia couldn't help feeling relief that Hugh was not with her. There would already have been mumblings about bloody wogs.

The dinner was a formal affair, the eighty guests an assortment of dignitaries from the European Union's agricultural top brass. The three beautiful floral centrepieces on the long dining table were intertwined with the flags of all the participating European nations. Seated on her left was a portly, elderly German, globules of sweat running down his reddened, shining face. They had been formally introduced beforehand. He was the top breeder of Simmentals in his native Bavaria. His fat sausage fingers were now struggling to loosen the shirt collar beneath his black bow tie. Julia felt sorry for him; he was out of his comfort zone just as she was and probably, like her, was beginning to feel unreal and wishing he were back home delivering a calf. As neither of them spoke the other's language their only means of communication was a great deal of smiling, gesticulation and raising their glasses to one another.

On her other side was a suave young Frenchman, immaculately dressed, who spoke perfect English; had she been younger, she would not have trusted him in the back of a taxi. He worked in Brussels, a high-powered influential job creating the rules for the European Common Agricultural Policy, in particular regarding sheep, about which he was honest enough to admit he knew nothing.

Halfway through the evening, Julia became aware of speeches and toasts at the other end of the table. Until that moment she had been enjoying a tender horse steak with a most delicious sauce, the contents of which her taste buds were trying to interpret. Her stomach suddenly churned, went into reverse, realised before her mind did that a toast was about to be drunk to her and in some way she must reply.

Clive was on the other side of the table engrossed in a conversation. She heard the words, '*La marin Britainnique.*' They must have mistaken him for Hugh. To reply in English would be churlish and her mind tried to dredge up a few relevant French nouns which she could string together. Another part of her mind had retreated to the classroom where her efforts at French grammar had been misunderstood and she could see again the red ink on her French prep.

She put down her knife and fork as she burrowed in her memory to unearth the necessary words which would convince her hosts that the British contingency were truly grateful for the hospitality being heaped upon them. Where was the wine waiter? She could do with a top-up. Clive, aware of her struggle, could only give the thumbs up and his reassuring smile. It was sufficient. Out of her surprised mouth emerged long-forgotten words, probably not in the right order, but enough at least to reassure the French that she was making an effort.

'*Merci à vous, amis français, des amoureux élévage du betail, pour votre accueil et votre hospitalité. C'est avec joie que je suis avec vous aujourd'hui et je me réjouis à l'occasion de voir demain vos vaches.*'

People clapped enthusiastically and the ghost of French prep was exorcised.

After the *au revoirs* had been said and a run through of what was expected of her the following day explained, she and Clive retired to their room.

Clive suggested that, as they were already in Paris, they might as well stay for a further two nights so that he could show her the Paris of his youth. He knew a hotel in the heart of St. Germain-des-Prés. It was part of the cloisters of a sixteenth-century abbey, warm and intimate. Julia had rung home to make certain all was well on that front and Hugh said, 'Enjoy yourself,' probably because she had caught him off guard and it would have been his automatic response to others.

The following day's judging was enjoyable. The best beef cattle in Europe came forward for her inspection. The French had always been good at pomp and ceremony; anthems were played, superfluous announcements were made but Julia heard only her father's words: 'When judging livestock, only put up an animal you would be happy to take home with you.'

She was dismayed that so few of that elite band of Europe's best enticed her, confirming what she had always believed: that British livestock was the best in the world. She finally chose a three-year-old bull for the supreme champion. He reminded her of Ferdinand, the same gentle eyes and disposition, perhaps inherited? In the show ring it had been unethical to enquire.

As she left the ring, Clive was applauding, clutching a catalogue. 'You got it absolutely right. He's a great, great-grandson of your old man.'

They were like a couple of young lovers, discovering Paris for the first time. Indeed, for Julia it was the first time. Her only experience of that magical city had been a teenage educational exchange in 1946, when all was drab and austere, the population war-weary, still feeling undercurrents of suspicion and tension. Who had slept with the enemy? The French still retained that aptitude for '*la delation*' spawned by the French Revolution when '*les tricoteuses*' would denounce anyone for sport. *Le corbeau* still causing havoc in small rural communities, revealing imagined skeletons in neighbours' cupboards. It was those 'peace at any price' appeasers who would later go on trial and be found wanting.

She could talk about anything with Clive. They walked around Paris, their arms around each other, one walking stick between two of them, Clive humming Cole Porter's 'I Love Paris' and reminding her of the words.

He suggested visiting Versailles, but their legs advised them against it and Julia felt she couldn't take all that gilding and formal gardens. Instead they decided the Louvre and then the small artists' shops and studios of Montmartre. When they arrived at the foot of the long, long hill leading up to Sacré-Coeur, they looked at the steep incline facing them and wondered whether their knees would make it. Clive started singing the first line of another Cole Porter song, 'There May Be Trouble Ahead' and, hugging each other more tightly, they started the climb.

It wasn't their knees which failed; after fifty steps they were both so breathless that they had to sit down and, as younger calves and ankles sprinted past, they looked up and saw looks of understanding on smiling faces. Clive said, 'If we were in London, we would probably be reported for vagrancy and given an ASBO.'

Whatever failings the French had, they understood the romance of old age.

They spent that evening at Au Lapin Agile on the Rue de Saules, the former Cabaret des Assassins and one of the few nightclubs which managed to retain its original atmosphere. Clive bore testimony to the fact that it had changed little in three-quarters of a century, but was hanging on by the skin of its teeth.

CHAPTER TWENTY-SEVEN

Two months later Julia was at the sink washing up. The dishwasher had gone on the blink yet again; it was usually something lodged in the water inlet pipe from the stream obstructing the flow. Hugh in the snug, reading the obituaries in *The Times* as he did every day, called out, 'I see your boyfriend's dead.'

Her body froze, she felt physically sick. It was the tone of Hugh's voice, he felt pleasure at the telling.

She decided not to go to the funeral or the memorial service in Edinburgh. She had no wish to explain her presence. Instead, she sat in the garden and thought about him, trying to bring his face into her mind, said a thank you for that brief happiness as his face merged into the face of her father.

The obituaries in the media exposed a side of him which he had made efforts to conceal from her. His worldly exploits and successes came to the fore and, as she read them, she knew that she had been privileged to that one per cent of him which he held most dear. That other ninety-nine per cent of him had belonged to other people, that life which had gone on before their meeting and had made him into the person she so loved.

Some weeks later she received a letter. It was from Clive's elder son. It was the most beautiful testimony she had ever received in her life. She could hear Clive's voice in the words.

Going through his father's possessions, his son had come across his most recent diaries and discovered her existence. It was a letter of thanks for the enormous joy and happiness Julia had given his father in the last few years of his life. She wept all day for the kindness of that letter but had no one with whom she could share it...

The devouring pain of bereavement gradually gave way to a dull, persistent ache of gnawing grief. Her mind could still send him messages but they hit a brick wall and bounced back at her. She started talking to him as though he were still there.

Hugh said, 'Talking to yourself again, the first sign of madness.'

She was expecting the return of the black hound, but he didn't come. He was repelled by that letter and the immense waves of joy for what had been, which washed over her bouts of sadness.

Within a few days there was a loss of a different kind. The water supply, fed by the stream, had ceased to run. In a curious way it gave her sadness something to concentrate on, to focus her mind on. In the past Hugh had dealt with these minor inconveniences; now his unpredictable reactions to the most minor of domestic upsets became obsessive. Their lives were, as most households are, full of daily annoyance: the electricity going off, the washing machine breaking down, the car not starting. But now, for Hugh, these inconveniences became personal, aimed at him. Julia accepted that his cursing, shouting and bad temper came from his frustration at no longer being able to do the jobs at which he had been so capable, but she could not forgive his stubbornness in refusing to accept help.

His titanium knee replacements reminded him of their age, the metal alloy under strain, no longer supportive as he tried to lower himself to investigate the plumbing; the depth of old pillows to cushion his emaciated body from the hard flagged floor was cumbersome. And now he would have to submerge his aged body in the cold stream and work against the current. She tried to persuade him to ask Frank for help.

'Can't trust him to keep his mouth shut.'

The deeds to the land Julia had purchased three decades ago stated that, unless specifically excluded, all therein, minerals, rocks, timber, rights of turbary and water belonged to her. There was no exclusion clause for water until Maggie Thatcher created her own and decreed that water would be privatised. Bankers now had access to those pure sources of life to which their boggy highland gave birth, seeping through a moss placenta, finding a narrow passage between tussocks of reed. That first involuntary movement, a tiny flow gaining momentum to become a trickle, sibling tributaries joining in to make a stream, jumping the rocks in the exuberance of freedom to feed the becks. There were protests but the City had won.

When forms arrived to say that the Stock Exchange now owned their stream they ignored them. The official warnings from United Utilities forbidding them to take water from the stream went unheeded. But now they faced a dilemma. They needed to find someone whom they could trust to unblock the pipe without reporting it. Julia suddenly remembered Kevin. He had scribbled his name and telephone number on a piece of paper in the bus on the homeward journey from the Liberty and Livelihood march; it would still be in her Liberty's bag.

Without telling Hugh, Julia rang the number. He remembered her and asked after the Land Rover. She explained the situation. He agreed to come the following morning and at eight thirty she saw an old Morris Traveller nosing its way between the narrow walls. Startling pink letters on its doors proclaimed: 'Kevin – the Cowboy You Can Trust.'

Hugh, standing in the yard, said, 'Who the bloody hell is this?' but before he had time to become obstructive, Kevin had taken command.

'I've met your missus a couple of times and I've to come to unblock the pipe.' He opened the rear doors of the Traveller to display an assortment of rods, hoses, a suction pump, a wetsuit and snorkel.

Perhaps she had misjudged Hugh, for he immediately recognised in Kevin someone who knew their job, one of his Able Seaman whom he could trust under fire.

Julia's suggestion of coffee was declined at first. Stripped to the waist, Kevin entered the water to find the inlet pipe, now silted and hidden by undergrowth. Up to his armpits in water, pushing the rods, he suddenly said, at a time when such a remark could have been interpreted as treasonable, when Bush was shouting victory and all that bloodshed and carnage was still to come, 'Saddam Hussein's right, you know. A warring, divided tribal nation sometimes needs a brutal regime to hold it together.'

Hugh shouted out his agreement above the noise of the cascading water. Hugh knew Baghdad well from the heady days of big business.

Kevin added another length of flexible rod and called, 'I think we're getting there. Confucius got it right, yer know. He said for good governance three things are needed: weapons, food and trust. If a leader can't hold on to all three, he should sacrifice weapons first, then food, but trust must be guarded to the end. One more length and I'll attach the hose and suction pump, it's just got a bit silted up. And here we are two thousand years on still getting things in the wrong order.'

St George and the Dragon glistened on his wet arm, the lance elongated as his arm stretched into the cavernous opening, the dragon's head submerged under water. The suction pump started up and thick mud and weeds spewed back into the water from whence they had come, to be cleansed downstream. Above the noise of the pump Kevin shouted, 'People don't trust each other any more. The earth's food is running out and the world's bloody leaders daily add to their already bursting arsenals of weapons, testing more and more obscene methods to annihilate life on earth.' He switched off the pump. 'I'll have that coffee now.'

He didn't sit down but wandered around the kitchen, holding the mug of coffee for warmth, taking in the old iron range and foundation stones protruding from the walls. Twisting his head, he looked at the family photos which Julia had hastily stuck on the wall. The Blu-tack now dried out, they hung at drunken angles; under one of them she had slipped a sepia postcard. He spotted it. 'I recognise that place. Had a holiday there ... must have been in the sixties. Happy memories. Then Mum discovered Benidorm.'

Kevin's arrival was a turning point. Hugh started finding odd jobs that needed doing and would phone to ask if he could come over. He was beginning to accept that they were getting on a bit, dependent on others.

Jack, no longer able to walk the distance for a kitchen chat, sat at home. Since foot and mouth, his spirit and livestock gone, he gazed into the coal fire, on all year round, reliving his high times, the trophy on the sideboard, the Perpetual Challenge Cup, won outright, three years in succession for the best Swaledale ewe. Childless, his only company was his sullen resentful wife. Julia wondered whether to allow him his whisky and thought of her father. Whenever she could, she popped in to say hello.

Now they looked forward to Kevin's visits. He showed interest in their stewardship of the land and was happy to do any odd jobs, putting poison down in the loft when rats sought the warmth of the house during the winter, their noisy scuffling presence in the loose stony cavities of the three-foot walls disturbing sleep.

Julia and Hugh enjoyed Kevin's company and, if they had ever allowed themselves to be honest with one another, would have admitted to getting on better with Kevin than with their own children.

He had a reassuring honesty and awareness of the

way mankind was heading, an outspoken apolitical incorrectness which buoyed Hugh's spirits. He came once a month to see if they were all right, which was more than their children did; a regular confirmation that whatever politicians and bureaucrats the media threw at them, there were some sane active minds in unexpected quarters out there, sending out different messages. Julia doubted whether Kevin had ever set foot in a church but he retained religious principles long since abandoned by his church-going betters.

With Jack they had discussed the countryside, livestock, farming and neighbours. Kevin's interests were catholic; his mind began to fill the vacuum left by Clive. Married with two sons, he ran karate classes for disadvantaged youngsters in his spare time.

They discussed an Orwellian 'double speak' piece of legislation, the Safeguarding Vulnerable Groups Bill, which had been surreptitiously pushed through parliament, imbuing children with fear and mistrust and parents with paranoia, poisoning that precious relationship between the old and young. It was turning Kevin's altruism into a minefield of form filling.

Julia noticed signs as she waited in the checkout queue at the supermarket. A smiling baby in the trolley in front put out her trusting hand. Julia had smiled and instinctively placed her finger in the tiny hand, to be clutched with assurance. The mother did not smile but plucked the baby away.

She recalled newsreaders, crackling indistinctly from the wireless, Father listening, being told to hush, news interspersed with advertisements for Ovaltine, shrill-voiced children singing, 'We are the Ovalteenies, happy girls and boys,' then the sombre voice of a newsreader reminding people of the real world. The indoctrination of German children by the National Socialist German Workers Party encouraged by neo-Nazi schoolteachers to spy on their parents, to expose Mummy and Daddy if they were kind to Jews.

Kevin's mind sent hers off on a roller coaster; she had tried to rein it in but it had bolted.

Everything was now her concern. Her anxiety levels were at an all-time high. What the nation needed was a prophet who was prepared to shout from the rooftops, 'Stop, you're all going the wrong way,' but one never appeared and Julia began to imagine that she may be the anointed one. She was the vortex through which everything and everyone would be sucked into a spiralling black hole, to emerge, unscathed and triumphant, at the other end to acclamation and blinding light, offering man a new beginning. 'Whoops, whoops, whoops,' a different part of her mind warned. 'Your friends have no wish to change the world.' They moaned a bit but seemed perfectly happy looking after their husbands. Why was she any different? What made her think she could change anything? But time was running out. Something alien had taken hold and was assuring her that she was the only person out there who saw things clearly, and that the whole future of mankind rested upon her shoulders and what was she doing about it?

Well, she tried; the numerous letters to MPs and ministers bore witness. Only that morning before Kevin's arrival, she had been on the phone to the Department for Culture, Media and Sport as they had failed to respond satisfactorily to her latest letter about violence and sex on television before the nine o'clock watershed and had sent her yet another 'round robin'. The buck had been passed, their jobs were secure and the dog of profanity was chasing its own tail more frenetically than ever.

Section 1.7 of the ITC programme code: 'The real world contains violence in many forms. It is reasonable for television to reflect this, but it is clear that the portrayal of violence, whether physical, verbal or psychological can upset, disturb and offend and can be accused of desensitising viewers, of making them unduly fearful or of encouraging imitation. These legitimate public concerns require careful consideration whenever violence, real or simulated is shown. The treatment of violence must always be appropriate to the context, scheduling, channel and audience expectations.'

Chapter 6 Section 8 of the BBC's Producers' Guidelines stated, 'Strong language is a subject of deep concern to many people and is one of the most frequent causes of complaint. Offence is more likely to be caused if audiences are taken by surprise when strong language occurs without warning, is contrary to expectations of the programme's audience or feels gratuitous. In the right context strong language may cause little offence and in some situations it may be wholly justified in the interests of authenticity.'

Of course there were warnings about how things might turn out, those first cracks of suspicion when 'Things could only get better'. Tony holding a party, euphoria at Number Ten.

Julia looked in vain at those quick flashes of newsreel

287

for the nurses, teachers, plumbers, farmers, welders, firemen, academics, doctors and could only see fashion designers, drug-addicted pop stars, film producers and minor celebrities. She acknowledged that this may have been the media being selective; pop stars hit the head-lines, sold newspapers and got a mention on TV, but it had gathered momentum and become the seedcorn of spin, a harlot destined to seduce the electorate and within the blink of an eyelid had moved on to become a new petty God.

Julia wished that the Archbishop of Canterbury had risen to the occasion, made more of an effort to consult his dictionary and look up two words. Homosexuality: 'a sexual feeling for a person of the same sex'; Julia was perfectly happy with that, remembering her crush on the head girl. Sodomy: 'sexual intercourse using the anal orifice, bestiality, any sexual practice unnatural or perverted.' It seemed pretty clear to Julia. No one in Lambeth Palace appeared to have heard of the word 'sodomy' although it was mentioned a few times in the Bible. (She could hear Mother calling, 'Go and look it up,' but knew that Mother, if she had understood its definition, would not have suggested that Julia look it up.)

Julia took her bottle of whisky from its secret place in the kitchen, a little-used corner cupboard, a badly designed unit which nowadays Hugh was unable to reach because of trouble with his back. Her litre of Grouse hidden behind a giant bottle of tomato sauce, well beyond its sell-by date, a culinary concession to Hugh's second childhood.

She decided to phone Lambeth Palace. It took some

time to find the telephone number. Julia realised that advanced technology and globalisation were not going to let her get away with anything as simple as dialling 192, a reassuring number imprinted on her mind.

Now people in foreign tongues were competing to answer her queries and she had mislaid her glasses, which she needed in order to make head or tail of the services on offer. It was only when she had closed the directory in frustration that she saw as large as life, BT Directory Enquiries 118 500 on the cover.

Eventually she got through. The telephone was answered by an extremely polite young man with an impeccable Oxford accent who asked the nature of her call and Julia, sensing that there was no way he was going to connect her to the Archbishop, subjected him to an outburst of her concerns. He received her time-consuming call with such courteous patience that Julia was certain he was in the right job, but she also had a disquieting thought that he may well have gone to his boss and reported that he had just had some batty old bag on the line banging on about homosexuality.

Julia had long since ceased to believe that Good triumphs over Evil. She now knew it was a myth put about by parents to reassure children and keep them out of mischief. Father had been culpable. The concept that Good was finite and would triumph, was flawed. Good was infinite; it could never be achieved, never find a place to rest; it could never be attained, but it would be fought for as long as humanity existed. Even when goodness had been reduced to a dying ember, a spark would be revived, reignited by the bellows of good-will and compassion. So long as that spark remained, however dim, hope existed.

It was the same with Faith. There was something out there that you couldn't put your finger on, an elusive, overwhelming awareness of a greater presence. Call it what you will, God, Allah, Nature, Buddha, like good sex it was impossible to describe. If Julia couldn't explain it to herself, it was a difficult thing to defend against the atheistic rantings of the literary pundits, the clever, clever non-believers, Richard Dawkins, Stephen Jones, A.C. Grayling. If they had never experienced Faith, how could they be against it? To Julia, their money-making books were the outpourings of theatre critics reviewing a play they had never seen.

It would have helped Julia if she could have shared these thoughts with Kevin but felt, in Hugh's presence, she might get in too deep.

On that day when Kevin had gone, after his second cup of coffee, she reached for the diazepam. Julia's kindly GP had been right; her anxiety for the whole world was making her ill, but the older Julia grew in years, the more she felt that she had never grown up. Surely the time must come when she could offload her Sisyphean task? Perhaps Camus had hit the nail on the head when he wrote those essays about the absurdity of life and the futility of man's endeavours.

Julia took another 2mg diazepam, mildly aware that the label on the bottle contained a message from her pharmacist telling her that drowsiness may occur and advising her not to operate machinery and to avoid alcohol. He must have known her better than she imagined.

That New Testament parable, or was it a miracle,

water into wine, could it have another meaning, a hidden agenda? In order to recognise the Kingdom of God you needed to be plastered; wine was not a blotting out but an enlightenment, and all those befuddled and despised alcoholics held the true message of God's love within their often gentle and sensitive natures. Perhaps at the very last minute, resting on the Sabbath after creating the world and knowing that mankind was about to make a mess of it and being a loving God, He had created wine to deaden the torments and sorrow man was about to inflict upon himself, given Homo sapiens a get-out clause. The poppy fields of Afghanistan giving a let-out to tortured thoughts and Julia, when she allowed her mind to return to what others thought as normal, suspected that the Taliban had known this all along, had it up their sleeve as a trump card.

She tried to discuss her relationship with God with the local vicar. It took some time to get an appointment, so absorbed was he with the secular, raising money for church maintenance and attending diocesan meetings. When she finally cornered him with her whim, it was dismissed out of hand. Christ was probably aware that the local water supply was a bit dodgy and didn't want the wedding guests to get E. coli.

Julia never mentioned any of this to Hugh. He really would think she was going gaga. Clive would understand.

CHAPTER TWENTY-EIGHT

Julia noticed that Hugh was losing weight but put it down to old age. He hadn't complained about any-thing, so she had felt justified in leaving for that final week of goodbyes in Italy.

It had been a melancholy gathering; illness and death had depleted their number, sitting in the warm orange glow of those too-hasty Tuscany sunsets, knowing that it would be the last time and wishing they could put it on hold, listening to the muffled tolling of sheep bells... Julia felt a relieved sadness that Hugh had refused to share in that part of her life.

On the evening of her return Sarah, who had been keeping a perfunctory eye on her father from a distance, phoned. 'Has Dad shown you his lump?'

Julia admitted he hadn't. Hugh was always in-clined to confide in others. She hadn't been allowed to examine his body for some years. Now it was separate bedrooms; efforts at civil formality had replaced former intimacies. 'I'm in no hurry, after you,' when they had met outside the bathroom.

She enquired about the lump and suggested a visit to the doctor. Her concern was derided, 'There's nothing wrong with me, I know my own body better than any doctor could.' But by the end of October he felt so unwell that concession was in the air and she was invited into his bedroom to view the growth.

He sat naked on the edge of his bed, a purple tumour the size of a tennis ball protruding from the inside of his upper leg below the groin. She hardly recognised the emaciated scraggy body for which she had nightly yearned in her youth, its torso covered in brown scabs in assorted denominations, like legal tender, the currency of the elderly. And now, against his wishes, some clever alien had invaded his body uninvited and he expected everyone else to put it right.

Julia, having been ill-advisedly joined in holy matrimony for sixty years, was not going to let go when the going got tougher; she was not going to fall at the final fence however much the first hurdles had not been to her liking. It certainly had never been Shakespeare's vision of love which alters not when alteration finds, more a constancy of duty she felt for Hugh born out of habit. Housman summed up Julia's feeling more accurately: '*And the soul that was born to die for you, / And whistle and I'll be there.*'

The county hospital didn't know what that strange growth was and Hugh was referred to the main cancer unit in the north-east, a hundred miles away. The biopsy revealed a malignant, rare, soft-tissue sarcoma. The children remarked, 'Trust Father to have something no one has ever heard of.' They tried hard to see their father as some kind of eccentric; they found it easier to put that label on him in order to deal with his irascibility and constant criticism.

Julia was less forgiving. Time may be a healer but only if you have had the courage to distance yourself, walk away from the cause of the unhappiness. Julia had not had that courage and she knew that she had only herself to blame. She had left it too late and desertion now would be seen by Age Concern and social services as betrayal and downright nastiness.

That Hugh ended up in the care of the finest NHS cancer specialist team in the UK was typical of him, landing on his feet although he would never admit it.

Sarah asked the ward sister, 'Is he driving you mad?' to which the reply was 'No, just the opposite. He's an absolute sweetie, the nurses all love him.' But, of course, the family knew how cleverly he played his cards; Julia knew that her thoughts were unfair, he was as all humans are, a victim of his childhood. Philip Larkin was spot on: all generations are fucked up by their parents.

Only now, when Julia had more time to evaluate Hugh, to think about him because he was away from her, not clogging her mind with his presence, did she begin to understand his emotionally-deprived childhood. He had received none of the hugs to which she had been privileged. Throughout their marriage Julia had longed to experience what she witnessed as a child, Father playfully creeping up behind Mother, putting his arms around her and kissing her on the back of the neck.

She now understood, late in the day, that emotional love was outside Hugh's understanding. His upbringing had conditioned him. Julia doubted whether anyone had actually hugged him as a child. His preoccupation with material things had been drilled into him at an early age, his teaching had been to love his possessions. Abandoned at seven years into the dry, crusty, guardianship of an elderly, aloof, uninterested bachelor uncle, a Prebendary of Wells Cathedral, his home vicarage cold, whilst his parents were abroad in warmer climes serving king and country. He had been left to bring himself up. Strict financial instructions given to the guardian, so much pocket money a week and an account at Gieves when his school uniform wore out or was grown out of. There had been no instructions saying this child must be hugged twice a day.

Hugh had been left to pack his own trunk, ticking off the items on the prep school's clothes list as though his life depended upon it. At seven years old, his life had depended upon it, there was no one to ask; his seven-year-old decisions were the ones he had taken into adulthood. If he got something wrong there had been no one to fight his corner. He had learned the lesson of self-preservation too early. He was responsible for himself and himself alone. Julia saw him lying between clean hospital sheets, a small child still burying his unhappiness, and she had wept. At that age she had also picked up mixed messages but she had been fortunate in having someone on hand to decipher and disentangle them. Hugh now viewed kindness with suspicion and friendship as something to be mistrusted. He had left his prep school to enter public school, a guardian of his possessions and little else.

As he lay there, for the first time in his life totally dependent on others, Julia felt desperately sorry for him, but allowed herself the rare privilege of not

295

feeling guilty. Throughout their long marriage she had accepted that his upbringing had warped his perception. She had tried to explain away his bad temper and unpleasantness at Christmas to the children; until he married he had never had a family Christmas, his rearing in that gloomy vicarage a travesty of faith, a rejection of the true meaning of Christmas. He couldn't understand what all the fuss was about, destroying the children's excitement and pleasure whilst decorating the tree with a terse 'What a waste of money.' She had made excuses for him, but Julia had been fooling herself.

Hugh had emotion but it appeared to be misdirected and enclosed within a time capsule of wartime experience. He wept uncontrollably when veterans marched past the Cenotaph on Remembrance Day, his grief genuine, for he shared another harsh youth with those people whose teenage years had been 'Serving Country', 'Protecting Democracy', 'Defending Freedom.'

Hugh was a survivor, and survive he did against all the odds. Having given him a week to live the surgeon, a delightful man, a native of Madras, had operated immediately and removed the huge growth, an act of immense faith in itself. Julia would have loved to have asked what his faith was but didn't wish to appear nosy and her interest might have been seen as racial intolerance.

During Hugh's five-hour operation Julia went to the hospital chapel to say a little prayer. It was deserted. After ten minutes, a young Asian man came in, the label on his white coat suggesting that he was a doctor or orderly. He was carrying a prayer mat and quietly requested Julia's permission to place it in the aisle, which he explained faced Mecca. His usual place of worship, the mosque across the corridor, was jam-packed, standing room only. In the stillness they prayed silently together to their One God.

Hugh became a semi-permanent fixture in the hospital, christened Lazarus by the ward sister and nurses. Julia was given a camp bed next to his during the first critical days. It had been the National Health Service at its most palliative. All those strangers dedicated to Hugh's well-being; Julia felt humbled. The Filipino and Malaysian male and female auxiliary nurses, trained in Singapore, whose spouses had been granted temporary UK work permits to clean the floors of hospitals and keep health authorities afloat, to the Indian surgeon who had saved Hugh's life.

Surrounded by the erstwhile recipients of his off-the-cuff racism, Hugh mellowed. He descended into a second childhood, regressed into his teens and saw his ex-colonial contemporaries in those around him and was anxious to engage in conversation, to trade memories. When one of the cleaners had asked him, 'When were you last in Singapore?' he replied, 'Recently,' which had been sensibly interpreted as within the last two years. Julia felt it necessary to intercede to prevent further confusion and pointed out that recently meant half a century ago in their grandfathers' day.

The physios had him up and running in no time, remarking on his strength and fitness for a man of his age and, within a month of returning home, he had almost regained his original weight thanks to a bevy of district nurses who came to dress his wound and be flirted with.

Julia had not been allowed into his bedroom during their visits; those good ladies were his personal domain but she was there on hand with cups of coffee and when the radiotherapy sessions started, she drove the hundred-and-forty-mile round trip daily for seven weeks, weekends excepted, to the oncology department of the nearest hospital.

Those journeys had been at the most beautiful time of year, early spring when nature changed its colours daily. At the beginning of March snowdrops carpeted gardens, woods and road verges, bulbs discarded in household fly-tipped rubbish making the most of their new location, pristine amongst the debris, daffodils following and, in the latter weeks of April, the white hawthorn blossomed hedges criss-crossing chocolate ploughed fields.

By mid-May there were carpets of bluebells and banks of gorse. Julia alternated the route whenever possible to make the journeys more interesting for Hugh, approaching the city through the manicured gardens of suburbs with their regimented splashes of purple-hued aubrietia and early tulips.

The therapy sessions took no time at all; there were occasions when they walked straight in but on most days there was a half-hour wait. The anteroom an exclusive club, the same people accompanied by their carers or drivers waiting for radio or chemo; after the initial, tentative, British reserve had been discarded, the location of their various ex-tumours discussed, friendships were established. Julia got on particularly well with an ex-brickie called John from the nearby nuclear power station. His tattooed, muscled, builder's body and hairless, sunburnt scalp gave lie to the turmoil beneath his skin.

He had a grandson of eight, the same age as Harry, Julia's youngest's afterthought. Preliminary exploratory discussions about grandchildren revealed a shared interest in reptiles by their young and Julia mentioned how, as a child, she had loved the feel and beauty of slow-worms but hadn't seen them in the wild for more than sixty years. John's grandson knew where a colony could be found amongst the industrial debris in a rundown area close to his council estate home.

The following day John arrived carrying a moss-filled, plastic, ice-cream container, rough holes punched in the lid, in which were two adolescent slow-worms approximately nine inches long, male and female, the male distinguishable by his faint blue spots and the classier female with a black zigzag symmetric pattern down her back.

It had been a little too much for one or two of the more squeamish patients. John had brought them as a gift for Harry; it would have been churlish to refuse.

And so it was, following that penultimate therapy session, they returned home with Hugh's complaints and a plastic box containing two legless lizards and strict instructions from John on how to keep them alive. A departing aside: 'Just keep them under your hat, they're a protected species, but in my opinion they'll live longer in captivity. Too many predators, dogs, cats, foxes, birds, hedgehogs in the wild.'

Julia felt it unwise to hand the slow-worms, which

she had christened Henri and Henrietta, over to Harry; she had no wish to burden him with a criminal record at eight. So they remained in Julia's guardianship, keeping her company in the so-called dining room during her long spells on the word processor. Harry was allowed to handle them when visiting, witnessing their beauty, their expressive, delicately-lidded eyes and the rapid flick of the barbed tongue sensing for food, experiencing the same thrill Julia had had as a child, an antidote to his ever-increasing addiction to computer games.

Henri and Henrietta's accommodation was up-graded to five-star status by the purchase of a large lizard tank. Julia took childish pleasure in creating a home from home for them, a mini-wilderness, a large, rotten, moss-covered log in the centre under which they could hibernate when the time came, surrounded by leaves and clods of plant-carrying earth.

Finding food for them was no problem. Julia left the larger slugs for the hedgehogs and laid down a couple of rotten planks of wood covered in moss and fungi amongst the dead leaves under trees, creating slug maternity wards where every second or third day she would indulge in slug infanticide, turning the planks over and picking off the newly-born babies. During the summer, flies became a favourite meal; fly sprays and papers were forbidden in the house, every fly a poten-tial slow-worm feast, and when autumn arrived with it crane flies in abundance. Julia competed with the swal-lows gorging themselves on the daddy longlegs before their great migration south. Armed with a lidded jam jar, quickly imprisoning them as they basked in the sun on the whitewashed exterior of the farm buildings, their protesting strength belying the fragility and delicacy of their bodies. By the end of October, Henri and Henrietta had grown three inches and at the end of November they disappeared. Julia resisted the temptation to lift their log to see whether they were still alive.

Like Hugh, they were survivors. They emerged from hibernation in late February having lost their unique colouring and were now a uniform coffee colour. After two days with the vital warmth of the sun, their pigmentation and markings were restored. It had been a parallel rebirth for man and reptile.

CHAPTER TWENTY-NINE

Hugh died at the beginning of December in his nine-ty-first year. The forty-eight hours preceding his death witnessed torrential thunderstorms. Wind-driven rain ceaselessly battered the windows, streams in spate became rivers cannoning down the gills uprooting trees and bushes, the water carrying away everything in its path. The thunderous roar could be heard in the house.

Hugh was fretting that the boundary water rails, which he had cleverly designed and erected decades ago from obsolete wooden telegraph poles, might be carried away, tossed like matchsticks and lodged a mile downstream on the arch of the ancient narrow pack-horse bridge. It had happened once before when Hugh was younger and could deal with such emergencies.

He made a final effort to drag his body up the hill to check, returning to the house wet and exhausted, the icy water captured in deep folds of skin, held prisoner in the crevices of his crumpled, aged face. Julia had long since learnt not to cosset, not to treat him as old, his rebuff of her concern hurtful. But when he placed a weary, white-fingered hand, its circulation struggling for survival, on the table, she placed hers over it, gently rubbing her fingers up and down, massaging between the misshapen tramlines of skeletal bones to restore warmth and feeling. Did she imagine the tiny flicker of appreciation in his watery sunken eyes? Her fingers, the conduit of arousal, reminders of tenderness, caresses once cherished and longed for, but which she had taught herself to do without.

The water rails were still intact, witness to Hugh's practicality and engineering skills. He sat silently at the kitchen table, still accepting her hand, glancing at the build-up of forty-eight hours unopened mail. There had been other priorities the previous day: serious flooding on the lower land, the few remaining livestock to be moved. He slowly detached his hand from hers and, with the silver paper knife given to him by his father on his twenty-first birthday, meticulously slit open the first official brown envelope, stamped it with his date stamp, making certain to place the ink geometrically parallel to the slit he had made and shakily read its contents to Julia. The bureaucrats in Whitehall would no longer allow him to light a bonfire unless he first applied for an exemption.

Lighting bonfires had been one of his latter-day, autumn joys, something he could still do outside, returning to the house all smoke and autumn smells. Disposing of sticks and branches created by pruning, laying and maintaining the miles of hedges lovingly planted half a century before, adding the crisp, russet, tinder-dry leaves of oaks and beeches to ignite damp wood. He had a tried and tested system: crumpled newspapers sprayed with WD40, the swish as a draught caught the ignited paper. He became a small boy again.

Now, unless you got your paperwork right, you were in for a criminal record.

She tried to reassure Hugh that if they read the enclosed Environment Agency's glossy, profligate, twelve-page booklet entitled 'Waste – you can handle it (Registration of agricultural waste exemptions)', they should be able to fill in exemption form WMAW 01. But it was too much. With a shuddering sigh like a vintage car being cranked optimistically for the last time before being written off, Hugh succumbed at the kitchen table.

He wished to be buried in a prearranged field of his choice, wrapped in a jute shroud, covered by the Union flag, the one which flew permanently in defiance of the planning authorities, its indestructibility against all weathers and officialdom assured by the hand-stitched bunting, bespoke from a craftsman flag maker in Consett, County Durham when they had first moved north.

In the end, his resting place was not the actual patch he had chosen. This proved inaccessible in winter. The broad-minded, helpful lady in the office of Births, Marriages and Deaths pointed her in the direction of the green form for home burials, but what Julia needed was practical help so she phoned Kevin.

Explaining Hugh's wishes to his children would only cause argument. Kevin had a friend with a small JCB who was prepared to dig the hole. He did his best but was defeated by the hard, frozen terrain and huge boulders lying beneath the surface. A different site had to be found lower down, one she hoped Hugh would be happy with. She was all too aware that if she fell foul of the Health and Safety Executive, the Environment Agency or Defra she might have to dig him up again. There were strict rules: distance from water courses, three-hundred yards – or was it metres? – from the nearest stream.

Had Hugh still been in a position to do so, he would have fought this bureaucracy tooth and nail. It was one of his joys in later life to take on everyone, his cantankerous attitude towards the whole human race, exaggerated by old age, given full throttle. The local council, Parliament, quangos, the media, the young, neighbours and family had all been on the receiving end of his displeasure. His total deafness hadn't helped, his telephone calls of complaint one-sided; he could never hear what others were saying. Julia had gone to the rescue at times, braving his anger to try and placate irate officials; her efforts torpedoed the peaceful old age she had planned for herself.

Hugh hadn't wanted anyone, particularly the family, at his burial, no prayers said over his grave. Julia tried to respect his wishes but her conscience got the better of her and, as the nice young driver of the JCB sensitively lowered the bucket of the digger cradling the crumbling remnants of boyhood dreams into the ground, she whispered a little something to the effect that she hoped he would now find the peace of God which passeth all understanding, which he hadn't found in life. He had created his own barriers and defences against love, which had been there for the taking. He had failed to see beyond the earring, iPod and tattoos of his eldest grandson. Julia felt guilty about her prayers and hoped he hadn't heard.

She was surprised that officialdom allowed her to bury Hugh at all. Interring a domestic pet on your own land was a grey area. Farm animals were definitely no-go, which she knew to her cost. After completing the correct paperwork you had to wait until a government-licensed wagon arrived to collect 'fallen stock'; the trouble was, it hadn't fallen, it was dead and after three days emitted an unpleasant smell which upset the ramblers.

The plethora of legislation emanating from Brussels and Whitehall on the subject of Farming, Food and the Environment was now running at thirteen a day, four thousand, seven hundred and forty-five unintelligible edicts a year spewing out of Brussels, bombarding the senses and peace of mind. Julia was thankful that she had kept these statistics from Hugh in his last days. It certainly wasn't the custodianship of the land they had envisaged and set out to achieve: a happy harmony with nature at the beginning and end of life, earth to earth, ashes to ashes, dust to dust.

Julia's awareness of her own rapidly diminishing lifespan was brought vividly into focus by Hugh's death. She didn't feel any older than she had in her teens except for the twinges of arthritis in her fingers and unpleasant night-time leg cramps for which she kept a copy of *Country Life* under her bed, its cold glossy cover when pressed against her calf giving instant relief. Her mind, when it wasn't running riot filling itself with unsubstantiated worries, still felt healthy. Sometimes its clarity alarmed her. As her body deteriorated her mind had risen like a phoenix, taken on a new lease of life and, bar the occasional short-term memory loss which

Hugh had suggested may be an early sign of Alzheimer's, Julia convinced herself she had never felt better.

Having recently read an article in the business section of *The Times* warning of the ghastly entanglements, recriminations and family bust-ups which would ensue on her death if everything was not down in black and white, and to give some order to her widow's status, Julia made an appointment to see a solicitor to update her will.

Memory had allowed her mind to harbour an erroneous concept of the legal profession. She expected the gentle, woolly, family friend solicitor of her youth. Of course, Julia appreciated that he would be useless in today's high-thrust, money-driven, litigious society.

She was, however, ill-prepared for the hard-faced, unsmiling, young female solicitor, an expert in inheritance tax, dressed in a dark, pinstripe trouser suit, who cost two hundred pounds an hour, every nuance of government fiscal policy at her fingertips. She mentioned Alzheimer's. 'If you feel you are losing your mind, appoint a power of attorney before it is too late.'

Was it too late? Surely the children would not entrust her to keep half an eye on their homes while they were on holidays abroad if they thought she was going gaga. Was it Irving Berlin, Gershwin or neither who had written those prophetic lines that youth was wasted on the young in a popular song of the thirties? Once upon a time she had been so certain. Now she was being fed doubt. A picture flashed before her: boarding school, the huge, Victorian, sandstone asylum overlooking the lacrosse pitch. Was asylum still an acceptable word for the looney bin?

Having been debarred from seeing their father off and because they felt it was their duty, the family descended upon Julia for Christmas. It was a very jolly affair. Hugh, the source of friction at Christmases past, was at rest, probably enjoying Christmas Day more in his solitude than he ever had when he was alive. He had done at last what he had so many times threatened: gone away for Christmas on his own. They all let their hair down, returning to the type of Christmas Julia remembered and her children and grandchildren had hoped for. Charades, hide and seek, beetle, making a noise without censure. Their shyest, introverted grandson, at last freed from grand-parental ridicule, found his much-practised magic trick fooled everyone, to much applause.

John made a supreme effort to join her, his gaunt face bearing witness to the pain wracking his body, gently carried in his wheelchair by her three grandsons along the uneven, stony track so as not to jar the disintegrating spine and fragile bones as the osteoporosis and spondylitis progressed. Payback time had come earlier than expected.

Everyone left on Boxing Day morning, anxious to be in their own homes before the weather closed in. The forecast was for snow and the surrounding hills were usually the first recipients.

***

Sitting at the table, Julia glanced at the build-up of mail again, late because of the Christmas backlog. She removed the plastic wrappers from the girlie catalogues

308

and put their contents in the paper bin ready for re-cyling, poured herself a second whisky and studied the sepia postcard more closely. Should she keep it? Pin it to the kitchen wall?

She held it in her hand for a few seconds longer, then tore it in half.

***

Two days later Julia, guilt-ridden, felt the need to go and report to Hugh, aware that the difficulties within their marriage, the sixty-two years of niggling dissatisfaction with one another had been as much her fault as his. He hadn't understood her mind and she hadn't understood his. Their marriage had been a bridge, its construction founded on firm foundations but a theoretical miscal-culation prevented it meeting in the middle, like the incomplete wooden toy railway tracks recovered from the attic with which their great-grandchildren played. Too many curved pieces and insufficient straights to complete a workable figure of eight. Julia tried to remember, was it that wise eighteenth-century cleric Sidney Smith who had defined marriage as a pair of shears, so joined that they cannot be separated, often moving in the opposite direction yet punishing anyone who comes between.

She walked slowly and carefully with her stick up to the high land where Hugh lay, carrying a small posy of early snowdrops, Hugh's favourite spring flower, which one of the grandchildren had given her to lay on his resting place. At the same time, Julia needed to be sure that his coffinless body was still intact, hadn't been dug up by foxes and badgers in search of carrion to see them through what might prove to be a harsh winter. Snowflakes were already drifting in the biting wind, blocking access to the gates so that Julia had to climb over them, something she had done a thousand times before but now age had made her balance suspect and her footing uncertain.

The snow fell silently, covering the valley below, familiar landmarks obscured under a thick white shroud of stillness. There appeared to be no sign of disturbance in the area in which Julia thought Hugh was buried, the pristine snow disguising the exact spot. Julia placed the snowdrops where she thought his mind once was and experienced an overwhelming sadness, a sense of loss for what might have been.

She started on the slow, familiar descent, treacherous now, the drifts two-feet deep, difficult to negotiate. The tiny distant dark specks of a party of skiers on Frank and Kerstin's land which were visible during her ascent, were now obliterated. Julia's legs and torso plunged suddenly, disappearing through a small, hidden crevasse. She became wedged, nail-rigid, her armpits resting on the crisp, top layer of frozen snow.

She tried to push herself up with her stick, to lever herself out on her arms and wrists but they had become frail and powerless, unable to support her elderly diminished body. Her Welsh ancestry flashed through her head; she had no wish to 'Go gentle into that good night'. But eventually, exhausted, she lay back, her face to the sky, enjoying the gentle caressing of the snowflakes on her skin, overcome by the stillness and beauty of her surroundings, at peace.

Was there really any need for further struggle, to rail pointlessly against anything? At what age could you be permitted to relinquish the bloody fiasco of life, resign from concern for those you loved? She felt she had begun to resemble one of those matriarchal elephants in a David Attenborough nature programme, her mind a sensitive trunk exploring fallen members of the herd, picking up vibes of distress, unable to help and walking away.

Hugh could no longer call her stupid for venturing out at her age in such weather and, if she made it to the pearly gates, Father might be waiting, his arms outstretched, a warming whisky in his hand. From now on, the world would have to learn to look after itself.

After all those years of walking on the surface of life, had she, in her final moments, cracked it, fallen through?

She received suddenly, from goodness knows where, a picture of Harry, Anna's child, Julia's late-in-the-day last grandchild, spawned by menopausal default two decades after the others. 'Promise me, Granny, not to die before I am grown up.' Clambering into the car, dishevelled and happy when she collected him from primary school after a parental SOS, visibly pleased to see her, unafraid to hug and kiss her in front of peers. 'Of all your grandchildren, Granny, am I your favourite?' Asking the question with the honesty and perception of small children, knowing the answer full well. He also knew that she would find it difficult to answer, to tell the truth, to admit to what he already knew, for she had other loyalties and he had wisdom beyond his years. He had placed her in a sticky position. Before Julia had had time to think of the correct answer he had opened the sunroof of the car, his thoughts already elsewhere, undone his seat belt and was standing on the seat, his head out of the roof, the slipstream of wind flattening the mop of conker-coloured, long loose curls inherited from his father, his small, chiselled, puckish, freckled face looking more elfin than ever. 'How old do you have to be before you can have a gun licence, Granny?' Julia remembered asking why. 'Because I'm going to shoot Mrs Blenkinsop, my teacher.' When Julia had asked why again, 'Because she is unjust.'

If she allowed herself to drift away now, she wouldn't get a chance to tell him that justice comes in many forms and rarely from the barrel of a gun. That heroes are not always those whose names hit the headlines, nor familiar names in history lessons. Courage came in different guises. You could spend half your life in prison and be a hero. If she were no longer there, would he ever hear about Mordechai Vanunu, Aung San Suu Kyi, Liu Xiaobo and old St. Ignatius Loyola of ' To give and not to count the cost' fame. Their messages were often unheard in the current relentless, global twitter of media trivia.

As the cold engulfed her body and she drifted in and out of awareness, Julia was certain she could hear faint, invasive voices becoming more strident, splintering the silence.